To Frank

Best wishes,

Neil DeRosa

Joseph's Seed

Joseph's Seed

By Neil DeRosa

Four Seasons Publishers
Titusville, FL

Joseph's Seed

All rights reserved
Copyright©2002 Neil DeRosa

This is a work of fiction.
All characters and events portrayed in this book are fictional, and any resemblance to real people is purely coincidental.

Reproduction in any manner, in whole or in part, in English or in other languages, or otherwise without written permission of publisher is prohibited.

For information contact: Four Seasons Publishers
P.O.Box 51, Titusville, FL 32781

④

PRINTING HISTORY
First Printing 2002

ISBN 1-891929-86-0

PRINTED IN THE UNITED STATES OF AMERICA
1 2 3 4 5 6 7 8 9 10

Dedication

This novel is dedicated to my friends in Saudi Arabia and to my friends in Israel.

I acknowledge with gratitude the many readers who offered insights while the book was still a work in progress, and who corrected mistakes and gave support. I especially want to thank my brother, Richard DeRosa, for his invaluable assistance in editing, and helping me achieve a finished product.

An Editorial Note

Foreign words, both Arabic and Hebrew, are employed occasionally throughout the novel. This was necessary in order to impart an authentic sense to the characters, and sometimes to convey meanings not easily expressed in English. I have tried to make the definitions clear by explaining their meanings within the context of the story, or by simply giving the English equivalent following the transliteration.

The use of the word *bedouin* bears mentioning in this connection. It means to Arabians simply, "desert dwellers." Accordingly, I have left it uncapitalized throughout the novel. This follows the precedent of Charles M. Doughty's classic travelogue, *Travels in Arabia Deserta*, and Sir John Glubb's *A Short History of the Arab Peoples*.

One

A Traveling Salesman

It was hard keeping his mind clear in the one hundred-twenty degree heat. The air conditioner of the Nissan Pathfinder he was driving wasn't working well, so as the day wore on Frank Costello had to roll down the windows. For the first few seconds while the sweat evaporated, he felt the illusion of a cool breeze on his face. But before he knew it, the coolness was gone and the hot dry reality of the desert began to invade him; to sand blast him, to bake him, to lull him into a kind of complacency. Surprised by the sudden discomfort, he tried to shake it off the best he could and concentrate on the task at hand.

It was almost midday and Frank was beginning to worry. He could not get a sense of direction the way he remembered doing at home. The sun seemed to be always directly overhead here, and there were almost no landmarks.

He had the compass which Rex had given him, only he wasn't sure how to use it. It was the kind you stick to the windshield with a suction cup, where north meant south and vice versa, or did it? He wasn't sure. To make matters worse, every time the car hit a bump, it broke suction and fell off. Finally he left it off. It didn't matter; he had directions.

He had been bouncing down this rocky trail for some time now—maybe two hours. Two hours from the nearest blacktop road. Three hours from the nearest gas station. That wadi should be coming up soon, he hoped. It better or he'd be in trouble. He checked his gas gauge. It read below one quarter.

"Just keep following the fence till you come to a wadi," Rex had told him. "You can't miss it." He had known Rex for a few months now and when he told the old man about his deal with the owners of the company Rex was working for, he had been offered "easy" directions on how to save a couple of hours reaching the project site in the most primitive region of the kingdom several hundred miles from modern Riyadh.

Sure, he thought, easy for someone who's spent half his life in this God forsaken place. Anyway, what was this fence doing in the middle of the dessert? What was inside it? Rex didn't say. He had heard rumors of a city named after some past king, but he couldn't see much beyond the sand dunes.

Let's see, "At the wadi go East," I think he said. Does that mean left, or right? It must be right. Okay, just hang on. You're almost there.

If all goes well, Inshalla, this trip will close a very nice deal and I'll be home with Debbie in a few weeks. Jesus Christ, she'd probably kill me if she heard me say "Inshalla." Probably kill me for the "J.C." too. He shook his head and popped in another Willie Nelson tape.

Presently, he came to the end of the fence and a little further on there was an intersection in the trail with tire tracks going off in eight different directions. Which one was he supposed to take? Oh, well, all roads lead to Rome—I mean, Mecca. This one looks right. He chose the track in the middle and tried to stay on course.

After two more rounds of *Tougher Than Leather,* he came to what looked like the wadi he'd been searching for. The comparatively thick growth of scrub brush

Joseph's Seed

growing around the dry river bed seemed to cling tenaciously to the memory of last year's moisture. He had to slow down considerably to negotiate the winding trail through the small, gnarled trees. Two large camels ambled into his path and stopped to partake of thorny branches on top of the tree in front of him. He blew his horn violently. The camels, after observing him quizzically for some moments, moved on slowly.

Frank tried to move on too, but when he stepped on the gas pedal the car stalled. "Damn!" he said out loud. "I can't be out of gas!" He turned the starter over for five minutes, but it still wouldn't start. Now he had another problem; the battery was dead.

Stay calm, he told himself. The best thing to do is stay in the vehicle. Damn, I should have brought more water. But this looks like a well traveled path. Someone is bound to come by before long.

After an hour, his water was gone. He tried to think positively. I'm alright. It'll be night in a few hours. Then it will be no problem to go without water. By morning someone is bound to come this way. In the meantime, I'll rest. That's the best thing to do–rest. But it's so hot. Slowly his eyelids closed. His mind drifted.

Then he heard something, and opened his eyes. Camels–not just two this time, but many. They passed by slowly and continued toward a clear spot in the wadi where a mass of dark skinned men sat huddled together. After the camels came more men. They were dressed in ragged clothes and wore ragged turbans; some had sandals, some were barefoot. They had their heads bowed and looked weary, as if they had come a long way. They seemed to be prisoners. Soldiers riding on camels–judging by the look of their fatigues, but wearing red checked headdresses instead of hats– herded the men into the clearing with the others. All of the men were now moved down the wadi by the soldiers until they were out of sight. One of the soldiers looked back and shouted something at Frank, but he couldn't understand.

Then Frank squinted to bring into focus something else he saw in the distance. It was a camel caravan, but instead of carrying things, the camels were pulling something. It looked like a tractor trailer, the kind with a flat bed. But there was nothing on the truck. Instead, men were walking behind carrying huge boxes and crates on their shoulders.

He thought of getting out to ask someone what was going on, but it was so hot. He couldn't concentrate. . . he drifted off again.

He felt someone thumping on his car door, and someone was shaking him through the window.

"Wake up!" said a voice. "What you do here? Wake up!" Someone was slapping him. He felt water in his face and it felt good. He was awake.

Two soldiers had gotten out of their army vehicle and had approached him. Frank saw no one else–no camels–no other people. He craned his neck and looked out his window.

"Where are they?" asked Frank, trying to clear his head.

One of the soldiers demanded harshly, "What you do here? Where you work? Give papers, *Yalla!*"

Frank took out his papers. "I'm going to the JADCO project," he explained. "I ran out of gas–you know, benzene–petrol. I need help."

The soldiers conferred among themselves momentarily, and then one of them went to the army vehicle. When he came back he said, "Wait ten minutes. "Come *Sayara,* petrol." Sure enough, in a few moments a fuel truck approached. Its driver filled Frank's tank, and then jump started his engine.

When Frank had the Pathfinder running, one of the soldiers said, "*Yalla,* Go now! No come here again!

Momnuah." Frank shook his head. "Thanks," he said, and he drove off. Then he noticed that someone had placed a bottle of water on the seat beside him. He drank it greedily.

Soon the trail led out of the tiny desert forest and up to a plateau where he could see plowed fields in the distance. That would be the project site. This wasn't so hard, thought Frank, trying to forget his mishap. I'm getting pretty good at finding my way around in the desert, a regular traveling salesman. Frank had been in Arabia selling his wares, farm machinery made by Agriculture International Corporation, for one year now. He was on the verge of his biggest sale.

He found Rex Lawton working with some Filipinos at one of several drill rigs on the project site. He was a tall, red faced man of sixty with long white hair and a beard, neither of which appeared to have been trimmed or combed in years. He was standing bow legged in bentonite mud holding the brim of the green baseball cap he was wearing, considering the job at hand. The cap was monogrammed in gold with the name "Al Tawali." He was preparing to weld in another length of well casing. He exchanged the hat for a welding helmet.

As Frank drove up, Rex got on a knee, flipped the visor down, and struck an arc. Frank had to wait. He got out of the Nissan and almost lost one of his Gucci shoes in the mud. Then he remembered to look away from the blinding arc.

When he was done, the old Texan shouted over the roar of the drill rig's engines. "Yer late, amigo," he said. "Expected you hours ago. You I-talians ain't much better'n A-rabs when it comes to keeping appointments."

"Come off it" said Frank Costello as he reached out to shake his friend's hand. "I'm as American as you are. Where's Mr. Ashamary?"

"He's in his office yonder. " Rex pointed to a cluster of new structures in a landscaped area around a mile away. "Better'n having him out here showing me how to do my job"

"Looks like you could use some lessons," said Frank.

"Reckon you'd know as much about that as he would." The old American grinned and revealed a missing tooth. "Anyway when you finish with him, come on back and we'll go for some chow. There's a little town about ten miles further down the wadi. I'll be waitin'. These fellows here don't need my help."

"Sure, if I have time. I'm supposed to go to a goat pull with some of Mr. Ashamary's associates, but I don't think that will be until tomorrow. Maybe we'll see you later. "

Hijazi ibn Ashamary was sitting at his desk in the pre-fab structure used as the project's headquarters. He was shouting orders in English and in Arabic to two male secretaries from Pakistan who were bowing and scraping to the best of their ability. Their willingness to comply seemed only to anger their boss more. Over in a corner leaning back in a chair half asleep, wearing a red and white checked headdress, jeans and a tee shirt, was a man from Yemen. Mr. Ashamary had on the traditional Arabian garb consisting of white robe, a white headdress more neatly arranged than the Yemeni's, and held in place by a double coiled black silk cord. He was sipping Turkish coffee from a small glass cup.

"Salaam alakum," said Frank, as he strode across the room hand outstretched. Mr. Ashamary remained sitting.

"Good afternoon, Mr. Costello," replied the erudite Arab, taking the American's hand gingerly. "I hope your journey has not been too difficult."

"Not bad at all. Nine hours from Riyadh, and only three of those off the road driving. Rex's directions worked fine. All I had to do was to follow the fence, and there was no way I could get lost." Frank omitted the part about running out of gas–and what he saw, or thought he saw.

"Fence? What fence?" said Ashamary somewhat sur-

Joseph's Seed

prised and agitated. "You mean you did not go by the paved roads?" Frank explained briefly the directions he had followed, wondering what the fuss was about.

"Harrumph," said the Arab. "We have very good roads you know. You did not have to travel that way. It was very foolish to drive through the desert alone just to save some kilometers. I would have gladly provided you with a driver and a guide to take you the correct way. You must only to call our office. I don't understand why Mr. Lawton was involved in this transaction. He is certainly one hell of a technician, but he is supposed to be drilling wells, and not arranging business meetings. He will have difficulty if he does not stay in his own work."

Frank was about to argue the point but thought better of it. "I saw him at the Ag Fair last week, as you know–at your exhibit. That's when he gave me the directions. I'm sorry if I encouraged him to get out of line."

"Never mind," Ashamary waved his hand impatiently as if to brush off any further discussion of the subject. "Tomorrow at eleven sharp my associates will arrive for lunch, at which time we will discuss your proposals. I think you must have a very successful trip. In the meantime, Mr. Muhammad Ali here will show you to your quarters and give you any help you need. Now, with your permission, Mr.Costello, I shall return to my work."

With another quick flick with the back of his hand and a few rapidly spoken words in Arabic, he said something to Muhammad Ali which sounded like an order. But the Yemeni seemed indifferent; he got up lazily and beckoned Frank to follow. "*Ta'al,*" he said. "Come with me."

Following the Yemeni across the neat little complex, Frank noticed the newly sodden lawn, recently planted shrubs and date saplings, and several expensive looking pre-fab structures of different kinds. A reinforced concrete building was under construction.

Frank had been in the kingdom long enough to know that conditions at this camp were much better than average and that meant money was available here. Aside from a few mud huts some distance away, everything here was new. An important personage was probably behind this project, although Frank knew only that his customer was a co-op called JADCO–which stood for the Jabalain Agricultural Development Cooperative, and that Mr. Ashamary was its manager and had full power to write checks. JADCO was in the process of converting thousands of acres of arid desert into farmland, and Frank had the opportunity to provide a sizable piece of the project–and earn himself a big commission. Tomorrow, he knew, could make or break him, and he didn't want to screw it up.

But he wasn't the type to lie on his bed and stew over tomorrow. He was already well prepared; right now he needed some diversion. He decided to go over and throw the bull with Rex for awhile. He had enjoyed bantering with the old redneck on the few occasions he had run into him in Riyadh.

Not finding Rex at the drill rig where he had seen him previously, he asked Muhammad Ali who suggested he go to one of the mud huts where the Filipinos lived. He knocked on the door and was let in to the dirt floored habitat. The workmen were having supper; Rex was with them.

"*Akel* mister, eat?" said a Filipino, holding out a dripping chicken drumstick with bits of rice stuck to it.

"Er, no thanks," replied Frank, feeling a little queasy.

"What's the trouble amigo?" Rex grabbed the drumstick and wolfed it down. "This here's Alex. He's my heavy equipment operator. This here's Frank from New York," he told Alex.

"Pleased to meet you." Frank didn't offer his hand; Alex was eating chicken and rice with his.

"New York number one," said Alex, grinning and making a greasy "thumbs up" sign.

The sun was a large red semicircle resting on a distant sand dune as they drove toward Al Khali, the small village where they would get supper. The temperature had already dropped to a comfortable ninety.

"They got a Turkish restaurant there with pretty good mashwi," Rex was saying as they drove. "You know, shish kabob, and if you pretend the beer is real, why it ain't bad eatin'. Anyway, it's on Ashamary."

"You had better not push him," Frank warned. "I think you're on his shit list for telling me how to get here. He thinks you're interfering."

"He can go to hey-ll. I'm not afraid of that rag head."

"Better not let him hear you say that."

"Guess not." The older man grinned sheepishly. "Leastwise not till my money is safe in some American bank an' I'm back home in Texas."

"Think you'll ever really go home–I mean for good. After all you've been here off and on for what, thirty years? I think it's in your blood."

"I'll go home all right. Soon as this job's done–be retiring with half a million. You can bet I'm finished."

"How's the project going? asked Frank.

"Last fifty pumps and diesels will be in by June. The pvc and hook-ups two months after that. Then good-bye Ass-shamary."

"Will that satisfy him?"

"It better. The bastard's held up four months pay on me. Says I'm behind schedule. Like Hell I am. What's he think I am, one of them 'third worlders'? I'll take him to labor court if he don't pay."

"Do you think it would do any good?"

"Don't know," the Texan scratched his head. "first time for everything."

"Good luck," said Frank.

"Yeah."

Over dinner, Rex started talking about the old days

in the kingdom when he had first come over with the roughnecks to drill for oil. Now, years later, he was still here, but he was drilling for water instead. In such a country, it was hard to say which was the more valuable.

"I knowed this place back when gold was thirty-five an ounce–almost. Practically none of these towns was here," he said. "No roads–nothin'. Only the bedouin and their camels, goats, and black tents. A man was rich if he had a few camels and a few wives."

"Just like in Biblical times," said Frank.

"I reckon. They wasn't bad folks back then. Lived a simple life–now a lot of them's got greedy. But then again, who ain't? Take old Moneef Mulafic," he went on, "you know, the fellow you sold those tractors to last month? When I first knowed him years ago he was a dirty faced boy tending to his father's camels. Now he's a rich sheikh. Goes to Monte Carlo twice a year. Owns a factory in Riyadh and has machine shops in four or five other cities.

"When I ran into him a week ago, he was braggin' how he got a contract to install equipment at the King Waleed Military City construction site. You know, passed it on your way down here–inside that fence you followed."

"Is that what that was? I couldn't see anything. Just some buildings in the distance."

"You mean you didn't know?" Rex turned to look at him–surprised. "No, I suppose you don't. Don't speak the language, do you? Well, couldn't see much from where you was anyway. When it's done it'll be the biggest army base in the country. It's gettin' a lot of new technology I hear. That's what Mulafic was doing there. Has the contract for some kind of underground hydraulic system or something."

"No kidding," said Frank.

"Last week he invited me over to his house for a goat pull–like the one you're havin' tomorrow. After that we split a bottle of whiskey–black market stuff. It goes for two hundred dollars a bottle here—an' he got to talkin' a little too much. Said some things he probably wouldn't have said sober."

"What did he tell you?"

"Missiles," said Rex nonchalantly. "He said maybe he's workin' on the silos for them, only he wasn't sure—you know them A-rabs. Either he didn't know or he wasn't tellin'."

"Why should your friend tell you something like that—even drunk—I mean, he's a Rasheedi, isn't he?"

"Hell he is," said Rex. "You don't know nothin' about this place. Do you? He belongs to the Al Ataibi tribe. They never had no great love for the ruling Rasheedis. Like the other tribes, they're loyal only when it suits them to be. The Rasheedis got the oil, so everyone else acts real cooperative—long as they keep handing out the money."

Frank was getting nervous. He didn't like talking about such things in a public place. Maybe some of the other customers there understood English. Two men at a nearby table seemed to be taking an interest in them. "Let's drop this until we're out of here, okay?" he said.

"Suit yourself." The old timer picked at the space between his teeth with his finger, rearranged his baseball cap, and got up. Then he grabbed two more "near beers" from a cooler, paid the Turk behind the counter, and went out the door. Frank followed.

On the way back to camp Frank seemed disturbed. "I don't get it," he said. "If the Rasheedis are actually installing a missile base, wouldn't our government know about it? I mean, we've got our AWACs patrolling this area don't we? They'd be crazy to do something like that without us knowing."

"Who says our government don't know? Maybe they do. They just ain't tellin us about it is all." Rex threw a beer can out the window. Frank didn't seem to notice. "I can tell you one thing though—they'll be fireworks in Tel Aviv 'fore long."

Frank drove the rest of the way in silence, only half listening to the steady stream of astute observations from the old Texan.

A half a world away in Spring Valley, NY, Debbie Costello was working on a crossword puzzle–and herself into a dither over the Kingdom of Arabia. She had just received a letter from Frank saying that he would be a few weeks longer than expected. He had written that there was a big deal which had to be finalized first. She didn't care. Her husband was there, and she would never feel right about it. Frank had told her over and over that there was no danger, but she didn't believe it.

"They do it all the time," he had said. "Business is business. You can't expect me to give up a chance like this, can you? They're spending money over there like they invented it. If I don't go, my company will just find someone else who will. We'll get left behind. Anyway, our people have always been wanderers, haven't they? Just add one more to the list."

"Bullshit!" She had answered, but she had consented anyway. They needed the money and it would only be temporary. Still, she hated the whole idea. Now, whenever she heard or read about it in the news, she would start to worry again. It never ended. Car bombings, hijackings, kidnappings, murder on cruise ships, airport massacres, suicide missions, blowing up of school busses.

Then the fifteen year old nightmare returned. If she had not stayed home sick that day, she too would have gone on that bus trip to Jerusalem–but her brother wasn't so lucky. During those heady days when Israel seemed invincible, her parents had wanted the family to live there. She was only a child when they immigrated, or made *"Aliyah."* They were settled in Beer

Sheva. It was like an adventure. She was happy–that is, until that terrible day. One hundred fifty children were killed when three buses blew up and tumbled over a cliff in nearby Hebron. She'd never forget, never stop hating the Arabs for that. Now her husband was amongst them.

"Stop worrying," he told her over and over. "It's nothing like that in the kingdom. They're very conservative, pro Western even." "Yeah, sure. They also happen to be shooting each other up every day, and they might just shoot you. You forget what you are. They won't care that you're only half Jewish, if they find out about it."

"They won't," he insisted. But she couldn't stop worrying.

Now Debbie was doing a crossword puzzle. Nine across was, "the number of Jews in the Kingdom of Arabia." She knew that the correct answer was supposed to be "zero," but instead she wrote in, "one," and then tore up the page.

The next day, several venerable sheikhs, two young princes, and Frank sat cross legged in a circle under the awning of the black goat-hair tent which had been set up for the occasion. An expensive Persian carpet had been laid out in the sand for the men to sit on. The Arabs all wore the traditional dress. Frank wore a business suit, but because of the heat, he omitted the jacket. His attaché case lied open at his side. The two elder sheikhs were bearded; the others, including Mr. Ashamary, wore mustaches. The young princes were not much more than youths, but were possibly–or someday would be–the wealthiest of those present. They were clean shaven and wore strong cologne. A campfire blazed nearby. Frank, although having some difficulty sitting "Indian style" for such a prolonged period of time, was determined to make a good impression.

The group was engrossed in the typical festive meal of Arabia, facetiously dubbed by Americans as a "Goat Pull." But if the boiled carcass lying on the large silver platter in the center of the circle, with mounds of brown rice and other delicacies, was really a sheep imported from Australia and not a goat–it wouldn't have made any difference. To eat it, you had to pull pieces of meat off with your hand–right hand only. No utensils were provided. Frank was having trouble. A servant had to continually clean away the mess he was making in front of himself. One of the older sheikhs laughed, and then deftly ripped off a sizable slab of meat and slapped it on the section of the platter facing Frank.

"Thanks," he said, smiling at the sheikh, hoping the guy would not now throw over an eyeball or a gonad and expect him to eat it. He didn't want to insult anyone, especially not today.

"How you like it here?" asked the sheikh in a friendly manner. "*Kway'ess?*" By now the bedouin chief talking to him had skillfully molded several small pieces of meat into a neat little ball of rice with one hand and popped the morsel into his mouth.

"Kwayss," replied Frank seriously, "good." Throughout the course of the meal, Mr. Ashamary had been translating for everyone's benefit. But now and again the other men, as the older sheikh had just done, ventured to communicate with the American on their own.

"Mr. Costello traveled here alone from Riyadh yesterday," said Ashamary amicably patting the American on the back. "He is just like a bedouin."

The sheikh shook his head gravely. "Very dangerous. Your car break down–you *moot*." He made a gesture of sliding his finger across his throat.

Ashamary said, "I was very angry with Mr. Costello for failing to request a guide from us. But thanks to Allah, he arrived safely."

"No matter," the sheikh shrugged. "Now we have

Joseph's Seed

too much sprinkler machines everywhere in desert. You get thirsty, you stop, you drink. No problem." Everyone laughed. Frank began to feel like the scapegoat; the feeling was a familiar one to him.

"I hope I can help you get many more center pivots–sprinkling machines, as you say–and tractors and anything else you need," said Frank, trying to regain control of the situation.

"We hope so also," said Ashamary, "if the price is small enough."

After dinner when the food had been cleared away and everyone had been served several cups of thickly sweet tea, Frank was allowed to make his sales presentation. He talked on for several minutes, when one of the young princes interrupted him by taking a wad of hundred dollar bills out of his pocket, saying, "I want twenty bivots for my farm. How much?"

Before Frank could answer, Ashamary intervened. "If you please, your royal highness," he said. "Mr. Costello's company is negotiating with JADCO at this time. We would like for him to better explain all the technical aspects before we buy. How, for example, does his new design affect the fertilizer injection system and the pre-irrigation cycle?" Now looking directly at the young emir, Ashamary said something in Arabic which was much shorter and to the point than what he had just said in English for Frank's sake. As Frank responded to these last questions, the young prince rose angrily from the cluster of men. He went over to the campfire, squatted down on his haunches, and poked the embers with a stick until the meeting was over.

Frank was saying; "and for only two million dollars more, we can add air conditioning to all the tractors. They will be painted red of course, free of charge." Someone had told him that among the bedouin, red is believed to be a "strong" color.

After the meeting when the party had risen and was preparing to disperse, the young prince, no longer nonplussed, approached Frank. The other young prince had joined his friend, and they were now holding hands. This big project–of prince Bandar," said the first youth, moving his arm in an arc to indicate all the land around them, "no good. Emir Mustapha good."

"*La, la, la,*" said his friend. "Emir Bandar good–good Muslim–very strong." The two young men exchanged some words between themselves, laughed, and then walked away still holding hands. Mr.Ashamary had observed the entire incident but said nothing.

The next morning Rex came around as Frank was preparing to leave. Mr.Ashamary had assured Frank that a sizable purchase would be made by JADCO from Agriculture International Corporation, but had insisted that Muhammad Ali the Yemeni accompany Frank on the return trip to Riyadh.

Frank told his friend about what the two young princes had said and done, and asked what he thought it meant.

"Bandar is a first line prince–they say he wants to be king someday," explained Rex. "He's the one behind this project. Mustapha is his younger brother–governor of Jabalain. They're political rivals, I believe. Them two boys are their sons"

"Mustapha has some big farms too," the Texan added. "You might be able to sell him–might just buy to outdo his brother. Anyway it's worth a try. I know a guy who could be your in. A feller from Wichita named Clement. I'll bring him around sometime."

Two

Arab Metropolis

The Arab metropolis of Riyadh was a city which in a few short years had rapidly expanded into the vast emptiness of the surrounding desert. This new growth was for the most part the result of the Western world's need for Arabia's oil, a sea of which Fate–or Allah–had placed under its sands.

Although Riyadh had existed as an oasis town long before oil was discovered and the period of modern development had begun, that ancient town scarcely resembled today's city of high-rise buildings, luxury hotels, and international trade and finance.

The city was a mixture of the old and the new, but not in the sense one might expect. It was not a case of a modern city being superimposed on an ancient culture, with glass and steel high-rise buildings co-existing with remnants of the city's history, such as is the case in Rome or Jerusalem; although that was the way it seemed.

Here both the new and the old, or more accurately, the modern and the traditional, were being constructed simultaneously. The "new" was being built by Western and Far Eastern firms, following accepted principles of civil engineering and architecture. The structures they built were as good as the honesty and integrity of the entrepreneurs behind them allowed. Which meant that some were of a quality to be matched in any great city, but many were not.

The "old," on the other hand, was constructed according to traditional Arabian principles–directed by Egyptian engineers, seemingly without benefit of plumb line or level. One of the few structural advances employed which could be attributable to modern technology was that cinder block had replaced the erstwhile mud brick. Such modern conveniences as electricity, plumbing, and sewerage were patched on, when they were, as an afterthought. Although the artistic techniques and color schemes of this traditional architecture were sometimes enchanting–there were gold-domed and spired mosques everywhere–such buildings could not long endure, they became ruins before their time.

Old or new however, every structure was equipped with air conditioning. There was a unit in every window capable of heating or cooling, if only the air were able to circulate through the sand clogged filters.

During business hours, the city was a bustling, almost frenzied cacophony of activity: with its many ancient looking–albeit new–souqs, its modern shopping centers, office buildings, and maze-like residential neighborhoods–which viewed from above were endless expanses of crenellated flat roofs–and from below, high-walled enclaves behind which Arabian families lived their private lives, and women could go unveiled.

In other sections of the city there were vast jerry-built industrial areas which employed men from everywhere in the Muslim world except the Kingdom of Arabia. The native inhabitants, besides controlling the many business enterprises, worked, when they did, as administrators; in the countless banks, money-changing establishments, and government complexes of the city.

Tying the whole together was an endless web of city streets noted for their ubiquitous traffic jams and the ever present, sonorous accompaniment of car horns.

The traffic problem was aggravated by the fact that a considerable portion of the vehicles clogging the narrow, unplanned streets were large, late model American cars. But also snared in this city-wide gridlock was an army of green Mercedes trucks of all descriptions, and thousands of red and white Datsun pick-ups laden with sheep, and women cloaked from head to toe in black.

With a population of over a million residents and almost half that number of motor vehicles, no part of the city was immune from traffic jams, except the new pre-stressed concrete "flyover" highway that led to the newly constructed beltway around the city, and from there to the world's largest airport, which as yet, utilized only one tenth of its capacity.

Making the traffic situation worse was the problem of the city's never ending construction program. Fully one quarter of its roads were blocked off at any given time, with maze-like detours running through residential side streets and leading nowhere.

An oft-repeated pattern indicating the type of unplanned chaos which created this state of affairs was the following sequence of events: first, roads were newly constructed, then torn up for water or electrical mains to be installed which someone forgot to include in the original plans. Then they were repaved–then torn up again for the telephone lines to be installed–then repaved–then torn up to be bypassed by a more modern "flyover."

As reminders to drivers confused by the ever changing configuration of the city's map, there were speed bumps to indicate that the road ahead may have given way to a trench. Speed bumps were also used most effectively on highways where traffic signals were not often obeyed. Hapless motorists were thus ensnared by these one-foot high encumbrances, without warning, at any time or place, thereby creating a booming wheel alignment industry for the city.

In spite of–or perhaps because of–the enormous sums of money spent on the development of the city, it remained forever in a state of flux. It was almost as if people moved and acted only to keep from getting scorched by the blazing sun. Characteristic also of that part of the world, advanced technology notwithstanding, was the ubiquitous, if faint, ambiance of human excrement to portent the fact the roads would have to be torn up yet again to install a more modern sewage system.

One thing remained the same, however. Riyadh had been a religiously observant town before the development began and that did not change. Five times daily the faithful, which means all Muslims, heed and obey the call to prayer. This is as it has always been. The difference today is that the Imam's call to prayer is now conveyed by means of electronic public address systems installed in the minarets of the many hundreds of mosques throughout the city. For that reason, during five, half-hour intervals daily, all activity–save the unbreakable gridlock–comes to a halt. On Fridays, Islam's day of rest, even the traffic abates a little.

"Allah hu akbar!" "God is great!" called the electronic witness for the Prophet that Friday morning at five A.M. It was time for the morning prayer. And so they came: The Rasheedis came in their flowing white *thobes* and red and white *gutras* draped nicely, with a double head cord *aghal* to hold it in place, freshly washed and perfumed for the new day. Then came the Yemenis a little shorter, a little darker, wearing identical headdress but with a little less affectation and with brown robes. Then there were the Pakistanis in their colorful, loose fitting pantaloons and wearing turbans. Also present were the cagey Egyptians, many unshaven in

their casual wear which recalled Joseph's striped pajamas, some of whom wore only white skull-caps and others who covered their heads like Arabians.

All of these and more were aroused, solemnly tumbling out of bed and moving in procession like zombies, toward the amplified chant of the neighborhood Imam, "God is great! I certify that there is no God but God, and Muhammad is his Messenger!" He repeated this formula until everyone was present, and then he led the faithful in their supplications. Everyone it seemed, fully accepted this ritual–to be re-enacted every day of their lives–five times a day. Thus began this day also at the Al Tawali apartment complex in Southeastern Riyadh.

Clement Schmidt too lived in the Tawali complex, a wolf among lambs, alone in a sea of true believers. He too sauntered out into the street that morning at the time of the call. But he was not going to prayer.

He had on a pair of Levis boot-cut jeans held up by an embroidered belt with a big brass buckle, a red Western shirt with fancy trim, a large cowboy hat made of straw, and a three hundred dollar pair of boots. He had a handsome face, rough-hewn and sun burnt with a black beard. He was a short muscular man, but he had a long stride. Now he strode out to his red GMC pick-up with a carrying case on a long leather strap slung over his shoulder. The case contained a state of the art camera with an assortment of zoom and wide angle lenses, and a collapsible tripod.

He seemed not to notice the Muslims going to prayer. He was going to where he always went on his days off– to the desert–to explore the immense escarpment fifty miles outside the city, to hike the hills and follow the wadis–to be in the vast openness. He was going, as always, to capture it on film, with its rich variety of wild life and vegetation, so much of it unnoticed by untrained eyes which saw only sand. It was his way of preserving what was, before it was gone.

Clement had been in the Kingdom of Arabia for seven years now. Aside from the one month each year he spent in Wichita with his wife and daughter, and another month spent traveling to parts unknown, he seemed content to let his life drift by just as it was. By mutual consent, he and his family had agreed to maintain the status quo–he loved the freedom and the double life. For two months a year he lived fast and loose; and for the rest of each year he lived a life of stoic solitude. For their part, his wife and daughter had become accustomed to their independence–and the liberal amounts of money he sent home to Wichita.

His job consisted of four-wheeling over rocky camel trails and plowing through sand dunes, visiting both the large farms of rich Arabs and isolated farms of the bedouin in order to repair their combines, generators, tractors, or anything else they could trick him into fixing. It didn't matter; it was all sold and thus had to be serviced by the Al Tawali Company, Heavy Equipment Division, for which he was employed.

Though he had been in Arabia for many years, Clement never spoke more than ten words of Arabic. But his customers never seemed to mind. Their method of soliciting his services was to head him off in their Datsuns as they saw him passing through their part of the desert. They then raved on to him excitedly about their many broken "machines."

Clement invariably said one of two things in their language in reply. He said either "no problem," or "the day after tomorrow." He knew all his bedouin customers by name and where they lived, so when he got to it, and without having necessarily understood what they had said, he simply went to them and fixed everything.

He often worked six days a week in the desert and then returned there on Fridays to engage in his hobby. But today he would stay out only half a day. He had agreed to meet his old buddy, Rex Lawton for late brunch at the Marriott, who had said he was bringing along a salesman friend named Frank. But he still had time. He looked at his watch–six more hours–he scooted down many side streets by-passing the traffic jams, and left the city.

Three

At The Marriott

The luxurious setting of the hotel Marriott stood in sharp contrast to the primitive environment in which men like Clement and Rex spent most of their lives. Out on the job sites Rex often shared the harsh living conditions of expatriate workmen like the Filipinos, at the JADCO job site, subsisting mostly on chicken with rice and often not washing for days. For Clement, living conditions were "no problem." He simply slept under the stars, wrapping himself in a thin blanket. In inclement weather, he slept in his pick up, listening to long playing cassettes of Rachmaninoff, Beethoven, or Arlo Guthrie. He ate whatever his bedouin friends offered him.

When Clement walked into the hotel restaurant late that morning, he saw Rex waiting at a table with a frail looking fellow wearing a light blue suit who was about thirty years of age. The stranger had neatly combed black hair, and a face that would be more appropriate to someone who made a living inventing computer games. He seemed out of place here but then so did a lot of other people. "That must be Frank," he

Joseph's Seed

thought as he approached them.

"Howdy," said Clement, grinning with a straight face and sitting down.

After casual introductions, Rex said, "Frank here wants to meet Prince Mustapha–thinks he can do him a whole lot of good–told him you know him."

"Why sure," said Clement in his Johnny Cash Baritone. "I'll call him from my office tomorrow. Only I don't know if he'll be available for awhile. He's pretty hard to get at these days. No harm in giving it a try though."

"Thanks," said Frank Costello.

The three then went to the buffet table and loaded up on fluffed eggs, hot croissants, beef bacon, beef sausage, Greek olives, an assortment of fresh fruits, and creamed pastries, the preparation of which had been overseen by an expensive French chef. The actual cooking was done by Filipinos. The waiters were suave young Egyptians–all male. The cashier was a Yemeni, and the manager who could be seen occasionally floating by in his white robes, was a Rasheedi. The manager had an assistant, however, who was German, a graduate of the finest hotel school in his country.

"This beats the swill I eat most of the time," said Rex attacking his grossly overflowing plate. "Sometimes I wonder why I keep puttin' up with them inferior workin' conditions Ashamary makes me suffer with for eighty thousand a year. Be gettin' out of here soon enough though."

"You know you love it," said Frank, trying to be one of the boys.

"Those are the occupational hazards which necessarily derive from the contingency of the unique economic phenomena of Rasheed Arabia." Clement said this with a poker face while looking directly at a baffled Rex. Years ago, before breaking loose, Clement was said to have been a sociologist.

"What the hey'll did that mean?" asked Rex, stuffing his mouth with eggs. But you could see he didn't really give a damn. "Fer a Westerner, sometimes you don't talk American any better than Frank here."

"Oh?" said Clement in his melodious voice.

"I think he means," Frank said, "that the Rasheedis were a primitive tribe only a few years ago. But because of the oil money they have now graduated to the middle ages. In other words, you can't expect conditions to be much better here." Clement looked at him with raised eyebrows.

"Don't you thank I know that," said the old timer.

They ate. During which time the two older friends indulged in one of their favorite pastimes whenever they were around other Americans or Brits; they maligned the Arabs. They called them "rag heads," and other names–behind their backs of course. The "men's" section of the restaurant was occupied solely by Western expats, who all did the same, thinking no one cared. Frank wondered if that was so. Every now and then he noticed a silent glance coming from the Arab "family" section of the restaurant.

They ridiculed the Arab religion, his strange logic, the way Arabs said, "Inshalla," constantly, (which meant only, "God willing"). Then they told stories of some of the typical incidents they had seen recently. Clement told of a police car he had seen drive with haste to the scene of an accident only to take part in the crash itself when it arrived, skidding headlong under the previously jackknifed tractor trailer which it had come to investigate, thereby chopping off the top half of the police car. "Speakin' of choppin'," Rex said, "My last visit to Chop Square I seen two Koreans beheaded"

"Gruesome," said Frank grimacing.

"It's the will of Allah," grinned Rex. "Was real interesting the way the chopper pricked the back of the neck to get them boys to raise their heads right up there so's he could get a clean swipe."

They ridiculed the Arabs, but they also felt a healthy respect for them. They were after all in an Arab country–in the most important Arab country, the richest, and in some ways, the most powerful. Though they might make lasting friendships here, they would in a certain sense always be strangers–welcome only because Americans had brought the oil wealth, and because they were good at fixing things.

They knew that at best their welcome was tenuous–that things could change. At any moment–if the political winds changed–they could become "American Satans," members of the country which supported the "Zionist Entity." They could–if circumstances changed–be so accused. At any time, they knew, life could become very difficult here. This was common knowledge among the expats.

As for Frank, certain things made him cautious about this game of Arab baiting. First, he was a salesman, and thus used to being cautious, never saying precisely what he thought. Second, he had a secret, a very safe secret, he believed. He really was Italian–well, half. Third, from what he had already seen, he believed the "time of change" might not be far off. Still he was getting caught up in this game; he felt the thrill of the danger, of tempting fate.

"Tell Clement what you told me about Moneef Mulafic," he said finally to Rex. Rex looked at him strangely, then repeated the story he had told Frank a week ago at the JADCO project site.

"Think it's bullshit?" Frank asked when Rex was done.

"It don't make no never mind if you believe me or not," said Rex.

"Well," said Clement slowly, "there's one way to find out. Let's go have a look."

"You're kidding!" said Frank. "We can't go spying on military installations to see if they're putting in missiles. We'd get our asses put in a sling!"

"Oh?" said Clement. "It's not so dangerous. I've passed that camp a few times going out to Prince Razi's farm, which is about two hundred clicks off the blacktop into the Nafood. King Waleed Military City is about a hundred kilometer square, but there are some good sized buttes a respectable distance away. With a good pair of binoculars and some high-powered lensing, we should be able to get a good survey from atop one of them."

"We'll get shot," said Frank, as if he was sorry he ever brought up the subject. "What do you think, Rex?"

"I'm game." The older man looked at Clement with a grin on his wrinkled face. "When do we go?"

"Would be best on a work day," answered Clement. "I can make it my ostensible purpose to service old Razi's equipment. Frank here can attempt to sell him some more tractors. You can give me some technical back up on his pump work. I seem to remember something he said once about sand in his water."

"All's they got around here is sand," said Rex, "but the rest sounds like fun."

Just then there was a loud crash coming from beyond the waist-high divide in the family section at the other end of the restaurant. A large table had been upended, and food and dinnerware was flying in all directions. Two young Arabs were standing over the table, pushing each other and shouting. There were several other people–men and uncovered Arab women–apparently trying to break up the fight and getting nowhere.

A few moments later, two uniformed, armed soldiers came running into the restaurant with the hotel manager trailing behind. A soldier shouted a harsh command at the youths to which one of the youths replied with a gesture of contempt–an Arabian equivalent of "the finger." Then the soldier shouted another command and this time he slowly but ominously leveled his weapon on the youth. The youth stared silently but fearlessly at the soldier and his gun for a long moment then finally released the wrist of the other which he had grasped earlier, and he stalked past the soldiers and out of the restaurant without looking back. Immediately afterward there was a frenzied effort on

Joseph's Seed

the part of the hotel management to restore everything to its former tranquility. The other youth walked off with the soldiers, joking.

As the first youth had passed nearer to him when stomping out of the restaurant, Frank did a double-take but said nothing until it was all over. Then he asked Rex. "Wasn't that the young prince I talked to at the JADCO project?"

"I reckon," said Rex.

"I'm not surprised, "said Clement. "That's Mustapha's son, his oldest. I've seen him a few times with his pop. He has somewhat of a short fuse from what I understand. The prince has had to rein him in a few times before."

"Wouldn't be surprised if he winds up in big trouble," said Rex.

"What do you suppose that was all about?" asked Frank.

"I dunno," said Clement. "Probably some kind of family squabble."

"All's they got here these days is feuding families and tribes," said Rex who noticed that Frank hadn't seemed to recognize the other youth involved in the fight. "Anyway–none of my business–be gettin' out of here soon enough. The sooner the better."

take as he said, "a decent survey of what might be transpiring within."

The red pickup truck carefully hidden from view behind some big rocks at the foot of the butte, they had begun their ascent. It was six a.m. when they began climbing. Clement intended to complete the climb–the ascent and return–before the heat of the midday sun hit them. There didn't seem to be another soul in sight as they followed Clement's lead to the top.

An experienced mountaineer, it was an easy free-climb for him. But Frank was panting heavily. He marveled over the way Clement skillfully forged ahead, always choosing what seemed to be the most logical path upward. Strapped to his hip in a pack, Clement had his camera paraphernalia, and a collapsible tripod. He also brought a water skin. Rex, who took up the rear, had brought along a pair of high-powered binoculars. For a man of sixty, he was apparently having little trouble with the climb either.

It was Frank, the youngest of the three, who presented the problem. The day before, Clement had persuaded him to shed his Guccis and purchase a good pair of hiking boots at one of Riyadh's many sporting goods stores where innumerable articles were sold for sports which would never be played in that country.

Now, in his new boots, a neatly creased pair of khaki slacks, and a short-sleeve button-down shirt, Frank struggled to keep up with his companions. His unprotected forearms were becoming painfully scratched, and he had a fresh tear on one knee of his pants. He was no quitter, though, and the climb progressed. There would only be another hour's climb, and going back down would be easy, Clement had said. At one point, he could see the small red dot below which was Clement's pickup.

When they reached the top it was, because of the altitude, still a breezy, cool morning. The air was crisp and clean and the sun was low enough on the horizon to be not yet oppressive. Frank looked at the grays and browns of the surrounding countryside and the jagged peaks; it reminded him of pictures he had seen of the Moon.

"Master of all he surveyed," said Clement, as he caught the expression on Frank's face.

Rex was looking through his binoculars. He had already zeroed in on one particular spot.

"What do you see?" asked Frank finally.

"See for yourself." Rex handed him the field glasses.

While Frank looked through them, Clement began setting up his equipment and making adjustments. Frank studied the scene which he had been pointed toward by Rex. It was much larger and clearer than what he could see with unaided eyes, but it moved around a lot. It appeared to him that workmen with heavy equipment were busy with various tasks. He could see several buildings at different levels of completion, but couldn't see anything ominous. In one direction, toward the horizon, he saw what looked like a housing project–innumerable small structures for which he saw no apparent purpose. They were not barracks but very similar to an unoccupied, expansive housing tract he had seen near Riyadh. His thought was that some other salesman like himself had talked the Arabs into buying something useless. Many bedouin, he had heard, preferred the open desert and when they did move into cities, they wanted high walls to protect the privacy of their families–here there were none. No one would ever move into these. Frank shook his head.

But he saw little evidence of military force–no armored cars, no tanks, and no platoons of drilling soldiers. There was what looked like an airstrip in the distance, and he could see some small aircraft, but nothing that looked very threatening. Maybe this was simply to be another ill conceived "planned city" of some rich prince. Rex had said that Bandar was dumping money into JADCO, maybe he was dumping it here also–or the other, Mustapha, whose city, Jabalain, was nearby. Maybe this was his baby. If so thought Frank,

Joseph's Seed

he should be able to sell him lots of tractors.

"It looks like this site is still a long way from being a useful military installation," said Frank authoritatively. "And I sure don't see any missiles." He handed the binoculars back to Rex. "At least we don't have to worry about getting arrested," he added. "Probably no one down there except Filipino workers."

"Don't jump the gun," said Clement. "Maybe we can shed some light on your assessment."

"There's *askari* down there all right," said Rex a moment after getting his glasses back into focus. "National Guard. Just ain't a lot of them. But they're down there. See that jeep over yonder guarding that gate. Notice that hardware they're carrying. Look like Uzis."

"No jeeps in this country–or Uzis," corrected Clement.

"You know what I mean, damn it."

"Right," said Clement, clicking off his first shot. "With this four hundred magnification, high 'f' stop, we should get a good recording. Do you see that concrete casting over there just south of that dome?"

"Yep," the other answered, still peering through the binoculars. "Them's templates for missile silos if I ever been to New Mexico."

"No doubt about it," said Clement, clicking off several more shots. "I've worked on some of those projects myself, years back. That's what they are. And over there are some mobile launchers and gantries going in. Those crates to the right should be missiles; see there one's torn open–and that's Spanish–no Portuguese–writing on them. That stuff is from Brazil in my estimation." Clement then stopped talking and shot several rolls of film.

"I'll be darn," said Rex, scratching his beard.

Frank thought–still, nothing much down there to worry about. But out loud he said, "Jesus Christ," how are you going to get that film developed? You can't just bring it to some camera shop in Riyadh. They'd take it

33

to the police as soon as they see it."

"You're leaving the country soon aren't you, Frank? I kind of thought you would want to take it out with you." Clement was looking at him with his usual deadpan expression, apparently waiting for an answer when Rex burst out laughing.

"Hey, what is this?" said Frank, suddenly suspicious that he was the butt of some kind of a joke.

"Actually it's not all that dangerous," Clement went on. "I'd do it myself, but I'm not going out for another six months. Chances are substantial that they won't even search your luggage on the way through customs. And if they do what will they find, film? There are five hundred camera shops in Riyadh. The Rasheedis are interested in the main only in what's coming in not what's going out. They like sequestering pornography– you can't get any here."

"Yeah, but what if they get suspicious?" said Frank.

"I dunno." said Clement. Rex laughed again. "But I don't think they will."

An hour later, when they had completed their descent, they saw a battered old red and white Datsun pickup parked next to the G. M.C. But no one was in it.

Then, in a flash someone lunged out from behind a rock, pounced on Clement's back and was whacking him over the head with a cane, trying to get his camera. It was a bearded old bedouin in filthy robes which used to be white. The fellow seemed feather light and the only physical problem anyone could have had in handling him was the stench. The desert man seemed to be wearing fifty layers of dried-up perspiration. As soon as Clement had wrestled the apparition off his back, the two men began to engage each other in a nose to nose stare-down contest. The bedouin, seemingly very angry, kept trying to grab at the camera saying over and over, "*Whish hadda*? what is that?" At which, Clement, preventing him with an outstretched arm, responded in his best Arabic with, "*Mafi Mishkila,*

Joseph's Seed

no problem." Thus they continued their battle of wills for some time.

While this was going on, Rex was explaining to the bedouin in Arabic what they were doing there.

"*Ya ustez*," he said. "We are just workman. We are going to serve Prince Razi at his farm. We only stop here for *riyadha*, sport. We do nothing forbidden. Prince Mustapha knows we pass this way. You should ask him."

The old Arab replied sternly: "It is forbidden to be here this close to the project, and it is also forbidden to take pictures."

"*La, la, la,*" the Texan insisted. "We are not taking pictures. We bring only food and water. *Taffadel.*" Rex offered the man a big juicy looking Washington State apple which the other refused. Rex took a bite out of the apple.

Gradually, the bedouin calmed down and began to sink, as it were, into lethargy. Finally he shrugged and quit the stare down contest with Clement. He was backing down. When they knew it was over they got into Clement's truck.

"Whew," Frank said, as they closed the door. "That was close."

"Nah!" Rex laughed, and slapped Frank on the back. "I knowed that mad as this tribesman looked, if I talked nice to him he'd be okay. He was probably a Mutawah— you know, religious police—just tryin' to feel important. Didn't hurt to mention Mustapha's name, even though I never met the man. That carries a lot of weight in these parts. The bedouin ain't likely to bother 'Americees' who know him. Didn't hurt for Clem to stand up to him either; they respect strength."

"*Salam alakum*," said Rex as they were leaving.

"*Inshalla,*" said the old *bedu* without expression.

Frank wiped his brow with his forearm. "I still say that was close."

"You're too paranoid for this country," said Clement. "That was nothing more than an everyday happenstance." Then they drove to sheikh Razi's farm to help him make the desert bloom.

When they arrived at their destination two hours later an American farm manager greeted them and informed them that prince Razi was not there.

"But he instructed me to purchase a combine from you," smiled the farmer.

"Great," replied Frank. It was the best thing that had happened to him all day.

Five

A fold-out Map

The DC-10, Al Jazira Air Lines, flight from Riyadh to Rome which Frank had taken, was less than half full. He watched from his window seat as the big jet flew over the Red Sea into the cloudless blue. It was still early morning–a beautiful day–and Frank was in a great mood. The air conditioning in the jet worked and he felt a cool breeze which he imagined was coming in from the desert sky.

He was leaving the good old Kingdom of Arabia and everything had gone well. A few more trips like this one and he would be in a position to decide his own future. His next challenge, when he returned, would be prince Mustapha's farms. When he had called the prince's business office following up on Clement's lead, he was told that the emir could not grant him an interview for at least one month, but to please call back when he returned to the kingdom. But that was next; for now he would enjoy what had already been accomplished.

He had closed a large order for Agriculture International. JADCO, through Mr. Ashamary, had purchased one hundred heavy duty farm tractors with eight-wheel drive and air conditioning–painted red for extra strength. They had also purchased two hundred center pivot irrigation systems to water the vast acreage for which Rex was now busy providing the wells and pumping systems over a dubious underground reservoir. The letters of credit were signed and sealed, thus payment was guaranteed. More would be purchased later, Mr. Ashamary had assured Frank–Inshalla–if this phase of the deal went properly.

The commission Frank could expect was more than he and Debbie had hoped for–and he would be seeing her soon. Everything was great, yet something nagged at the back of his mind.

He had tried not to think about the film. Just throw it in the suitcase with the rest of your junk–tourist photos–and don't think about it. It had worked. They didn't even look in his suitcase. If only he wasn't so paranoid, like Clement had said. He didn't know what he would do with the film when he got home. Clement said to have it developed and send it to an address he had given him in Wichita. But he, Frank, had got it out hadn't he? Maybe he should decide for himself what to do with it.

The jet was flying over Egypt now. The world below was brown and blue. He could see tiny sand dunes–or were they pyramids? Soon, according to the map he had just looked at, he would be over the Mediterranean Sea. Then northward on to Rome.

The flight had skirted nicely around Israel–the "Zionist Entity" as the Arabs called it. On the map, a large glossy fold-out in the in-flight magazine he had looked at, there was no Israel, no Tel Aviv, no Jerusalem–only Palestine and its capital city of *Al Kuds*, in the upper left hand corner of the Arab world. The slick magazine was made by an American conglomerate which had agreed not to deal with Israel in exchange for the kingdom's lucrative concession.

Frank shook his head. Maybe it was none of his business. What he wanted to do was to make money.

Why should he care? The jet was approaching for a landing at Rome. Barring another hijacking or airport massacre, he'd soon be on an American flight en-route to New York.

He was now unconsciously leafing through the English language newspaper regularly supplied on that flight; the Riyadh News. He stopped to scan one of many recent articles about the exploits of the Arabian folk hero, Baal Bazz, who had just executed another successful airline hijacking of an India Air flight from New Delhi. The ordeal had gone on for ten days during which the jet had landed and refueled at several Middle Eastern airports–and four hostages–two Americans and two East Indians, were killed and dumped onto the Tarmac.

At the end of the ordeal, Baal Bazz had traded the lives of his nine fellow "freedom fighters" for the lives of the remaining ten hostages on board. The freedom fighters were then spirited away by the South Yemen authorities who had negotiated the release of the remaining hostages.

Frank shook his head again. What could he say about a world where people couldn't tell the difference between freedom fighters and terrorists? There was no answer. Selling massive irrigation projects in a land with virtually no water was much easier. Frank wasn't much of a drinker, but when he got on his next flight, he would order a real beer.

Six

The Reunion

Prince Bandar Jibreen Ibn Abdul Lateef, soon to be Governor of Riyadh, had long since decided that if he were ever to have a chance of making headway among his thirty seven surviving brothers, he needed a cause that would set him apart from the rest. At age forty-five, he was one of the youngest of the first-line princes, still far removed in the fraternal order of succession—still a long way to go to become king. Only his brothers Saud and Mustapha were younger.

Although most of his elder brothers, for various reasons, had little interest in standing in the royal queue, there were still seven aspirants—more or less—ahead of him in line. Under normal circumstances, he would never make it. But circumstances were no longer normal. Unlikely as it may have once seemed, he believed in his heart that Allah would let him have what he coveted. His day would come, for Bandar was the champion of a cause that moved men's hearts.

He was proud of who he was; proud to be the son of the great Abdul Lateef, founder of the modern day Kingdom of Arabia, the greatest and the wealthiest of the Muslim nations, guardian of the Holy Places. He was

Joseph's Seed

proud to be, in his own right, a leader of men–in prayer and in war, though his war experience was limited to the days when he had served as a captain in the National Guard and had helped put down some minor bedouin rebellions by machine gunning a few dozen recalcitrant tribesmen. Mostly, he was proud of his recognition as an Islamic scholar and proud also to have been Western educated. He had attended a California University where his father had sent him and his younger brother Mustapha. He later acquired his PhD. at Oxford.

He had given up the position of Dean of the University of Riyadh which he had held for many years in order to accept the even more coveted position of Emir of that city and province–a great and noble duty which he would begin in one month. Only his great father Abdul Lateef, when he had first conquered the city many years ago, had ever been Emir of Riyadh at a younger age. Yet that was what he would soon be. His prestige and fame had increased many fold on the day he had been promised control of the kingdom's largest city. And this was only the beginning.

Prince Bandar was indeed proud of all he had been and all he would be. But he was also afraid. He had always secretly acknowledged the shadow within–lurking in the recesses of his mind–the nagging dread that he would in the end fail.

Years ago, in California, when he had first taken up the cause of Palestine, his younger brother had advised caution. But he had scoffed at that advice, giving money and support wherever he could–even lending his prestigious name. Now he was being rewarded. His star was finally rising while his arrogant brother had been relegated to a mere governorship of a minor desert province. Yes he was governor of Riyadh now and this was just the beginning.

What he wanted to do had never been done before, though many had tried. Now, history commanded that he too must try; thus he was committed to a course he could not reverse no matter what his fears. In truth he knew only Allah could help him. Perhaps God would be there when the time came–Inshalla, he thought, as God wills.

All in all, it was a fine morning when Bandar arrived in his gold Rolls Royce at the campus where he had not long ago been dean. He had driven in alone, inconspicuously, from his palace on the outskirts of the city to see a dear friend and colleague he had not seen in many months, who had just arrived from London. He had not wanted his princely entourage with him for this occasion.

He came today as a scholar, not as the governor designate. He would hear his friend lecture before the assemblage of students, faculty, and dignitaries which would be gathering in his friend's honor. He would grant him that honor today by being himself humble. But first the two would talk. They had much to talk about for the man he had come to see today was intricately linked to the cause which had catapulted Bandar to power.

The man he had come to see today was the famous Dowi Al Harbi; renowned Palestinian and Islamic scholar, author of many books on Palestinian History and culture, professor at the University of London–and Prince Bandar's protégé and loyal servant.

Al Harbi's most recent work was the result of new research by a Lebanese archaeologist which was causing quite a stir, even in certain Western academic circles. In conjunction with the other scientist, the professor had formulated the theory that the lauded Holy Land of the Zionists was in reality situated in the Hijaz which is in the western sector of the Arabian Peninsula–far to the south of Palestine. Hence he had demonstrated that Israel and Palestine were two separate places–two distinct entities.

His colleagues at the University of London scoffed at his new theory as they had scoffed at many of his theories; but he had proof–and also many friends. He would be among those friends today. He was going to lecture, among other things, on his new book.

🐫 🐫 🐫

Bandar fumed when he came to the parking spot reserved for the dean and found it occupied. Then he remembered he was no longer dean. Doggedly, he maneuvered his big car through the crowded lot, which like most parking lots in that city was much too small for the number and size of the cars it was intended to accommodate. Finally he located a small spot and squeezed the Rolls into it, only slightly grazing the car next to his and twice bumping the one in front. "*Al hamdilila*, thank God," he muttered, as he left his car without locking it.

Then he walked up the path to the Islamic Sciences building. He was a tall and majestic looking man in his traditional bedouin attire. He was the type of man who could be quite imposing if he were to be taken seriously. He knew that now finally he was beginning to be.

The sun glistened white on the modernistic, pre-stressed concrete buildings of Riyadh University. It was in the new part of the city, the part built by men like Frank Costello–Western businessmen–but used in ways they were only beginning to comprehend. Filipino workers were planting date-palm saplings in the gardens. Nearby, ten thousand honking red and white Datsuns laden with sheep could be heard on the city streets. Around him, white robed young men with red checked or white headdresses traversed the many flower lined paths of the campus carrying notebooks; many were holding hands.

It was good to be back to such a wonderful place of learning, thought Prince Bandar as he entered the building.

Professor Dowi Al Harbi was waiting for him in an office that had been given over for his use. He was sitting in a leather swivel chair with his feet on the glass top of a large mahogany desk, leafing through some notes and eating dates. "Asalamu alekum, your royal highness," said Al Harbi barely looking up when the prince entered the room. "How are you? Congratulations on your new appointment"

"*Al hamdilila*," answered Bandar. "Now get your feet off that desk, and come over here to greet me properly. You have grown accustomed to the ways of the Europeans with whom you associate."

"They are put to good service for our cause." The Palestinian rose, taking both of the prince's hands in his. They embraced, and then began the ritual of kissing each other alternately on the right and then the left cheek, all the while smiling and muttering blessings and words of endearment to each other. It was an act long prescribed by the traditions of their culture but these men added much feeling to the ritual. They really seemed to mean it.

"Allah grant peace on your house," said Bandar, kissing his friend on the cheek.

"And on all your houses." Dowi Al Harbi returned the affection.

"May you live and prosper many years," continued the prince, kissing his friend again.

"And you, many thousands," his friend replied, kissing him.

"May your wife and children share in Allah's bounty," –another kiss.

"And all your wives and all your children," –kiss.

"May your great land be restored and your people returned to their rightful homes,"–still another kiss.

"And death to the Zionists," –and a final kiss, moving away still lingering, holding both hands, smiling gently.

"And death to Zion," –kiss.

"How goes the Jihad?" asked the prince then, releasing the other's hands.

"My people are long patient, your highness. But in the end we must prevail."

"*Inshalla.*"

"*Inshalla.*"

"And now sit, habeebi, my dear friend, and let me hear the news." An Indian coffee-boy had just entered the room carrying a tray on which were a silver urn, two finjans, and a plate of dates. Silently, he poured the coffee into the small cups and served the two men of eminence. Dowi Al Harbi took a sip of the bitter, green liquid, considered for a moment while chewing a sweet date and removing the stone from his mouth, then began his report.

"They search for Baal Bazz where he is not. They know not even for whom they search. This month he was believed to be in Tripoli, last month in Beirut, before that Baghdad. But all the while he is in London, a peace loving teacher of Arabian history, imparting wisdom to pompous British Arabists. It is true that I am peace loving. I only want what is mine by right, *Bismallah.*"

"Allah will save you," consoled the prince.

"You know of course of our operation at Zurich Airport, 85 Zionist sympathizers captured, the jet re-routed to Beirut; and you no-doubt have read of our most recent victory on the flight from New Delhi, in which our brothers the Yemenis assisted us in our struggle. You know of the execution of CIA spies in Bangkok, in Rome; and we have as you know, plans for New York. All this and much more is the result of our efforts. But I will fill you in on the details later. Now I will discuss actions which the West does not even suspect yet. They give us little credit, and that is to our great advantage.

"Our efforts to install people sympathetic to our cause in positions of power and influence–that is the most important work. That is how our enemy has always defeated us and how we shall now defeat him. They will wonder why suddenly the news and public opinion in many countries begins to favor us. But it is the result of years of your effort, your highness. Even this month one of our people has been elected to the Congress of America. . ."

"You have done well, *habeebi*," said Bandar.

"*Takht amrak,* your highness, at your service. But it takes much money."

"You know I am doing everything in my power, but even my resources are not unlimited. Many of my brothers do not see eye to eye with me and refuse to give all the money we need. True they have consented to contribute to the rearmament. The King Waleed Military City and others like it are progressing nicely.

"But they fall silent when asked to finance our jihad against the Zionists. However it is they who will be silenced one by one. With each of your victories, our brother Arabs are rallying to us. My own brothers will not long be able to resist. Soon the traitor Mustapha will be finished."

"Until then Yusuf Al Tawali will pay your bills." said Al Harbi. "It is good that our friend Doudeen has been able to convince the great sheikh to contribute so freely."

"*Insha'allah,*" lamented the prince, shaking his head in sorrow and disgust at the thought of his hated rival–not even hearing the last sentence spoken by Al Harbi. "But until then you must continue with your great work. The time is not yet when you may remain here in Riyadh. But when that time comes, you will be greatly rewarded. For my part, I will persist with such puny efforts as I am able."

"Your efforts are not puny, *ya emir.*"

"Halas," said the prince rising. "Enough of this for now. I came to hear your lecture. Are you prepared?"

"Yes, your highness."

The two men then went together to the lecture hall in the Islamic Sciences building. They walked hand in hand and talked of lighter matters.

Seven

The Warrior

Dowi Al Harbi the Palestinian stood behind the lectern on a podium in the acoustically sound lecture hall of the Islamic Sciences Building. The large room was walled on one side with curved sheets of glass facing a newly planted desert garden, but the glass was concealed by heavy, red, ceiling-to-floor drapes. Two other walls were dominated by larger than life portraits of past Rasheedi kings–beginning on the right with the founder of the kingdom, the great Abdul Lateef, and ending with the fifth of his many sons to be king after him–the current king, the benign and gentle old King Waleed. All were arrayed simply but majestically in the traditional bedouin attire.

A huge flag loomed on the wall behind the podium. It was white with a rendition, in gold, of the Dome of The Rock, where the Prophet Muhammad had ascended into heaven. On it, in red, were the words written in classical Arabic script: "There is no god but Allah and Muhammad is his Messenger." It was the national flag of the Kingdom of Arabia.

As a boy in his homeland, he had gone many times to pray at that great mosque–a thrill few men in the

Arab world now had the privilege of experiencing. Once, while there, he had listened to a great man speak. It was then that he learned to love his homeland. From that day he became dedicated to his cause–the cause he had never since forsaken. . .

Now it was he who stood before an assembly to speak. A figure of a man, powerfully impressive to the young Arabian students who listened raptly to his words, but also impressive to the older faculty members, *Ulema*, and dignitaries who had come to hear him speak. They all were moved–some by blind devotion, for his reputation as a scholar had preceded him–but others were moved by caution, for something about the man inspired a feeling of foreboding. Some had the feeling that he might open fire on them at any moment. A few knew that this was a man who must be stopped. All however applauded him enthusiastically now, as he prepared to speak.

In the audience among the others were two familiar personages. One was the influential businessman and general manager of the JADCO project, Hijazi Ibn Ashamary; and the other was the young prince Mugrin Ibn Mustapha who was a student at the University of Riyadh.

The speaker exuded strength and vitality, even beneath his loosely fitting thobe. Framed by his headdress, his handsome face was hard. He had an aquiline nose, chiseled jaw, and dark eyes illuminating passion. It was the face of a holy man–or a maniac.

He wore his gutra in the manner of the men of Syria, Jordan, and Palestine–the corner flaps crossing loosely in front of the neck and then draped in a masculine way over the shoulders. He was clean shaven even to the point of being without the standard mustache which many Arab men wear.

Although he was known widely in the Arab world as a scholar and writer, there were also rumors, in certain circles, of other exploits; but nothing was clear. He was a mystery man, and the mystery added to his charisma, at thirty-three years of age, this was a man to be watched.

Prince Bandar also watched his young protégé and the effect he was having on the audience. He sat toward the rear of the lecture hall fingering the frayed corner flap of his gutra, wondering. He remembered the first time he had seen the man now standing in front of them. It was fifteen years ago while he was taking his doctorate at Oxford.

At that time, the younger Prince Bandar was already known for his many well intentioned political, and public relations efforts in support of the Palestinian cause, yet he was having little effect. The pro-Arab politicians he had nurtured in Britain and America seemed to do nothing to jeopardize their positions–nothing but take his money, that is. The few who did take a stand to his satisfaction usually spent the next several months apologizing for it to Zionist special interest groups who were found to have more power than he at first suspected.

One benefit however, derived from his efforts. He was beginning to become known as an unabashed friend of Palestine. Many came to him to support activities ranging from letters to the editor, to research efforts, to more clandestine activities.

He had been at Oxford for over a year when he heard about the triple bus bombing in Hebron. He knew the extreme difficulties involved in executing successful operations against an enemy so obsessed with security, especially within their own borders. He appreciated the significance of the event, but wrongly judged its source.

He wondered how Yassar Ararat's boys had accomplished this one. He dispatched his aids to inquire behind the scenes to see if they could discover anything that the newspapers weren't printing. Their findings amazed him. It was clearly not the work of the

Palestine Restoration Society, or of any PRS splinter group. The Iraqis weren't taking credit, nor were the Iranians. No, something or someone completely new was involved here. But no one had any idea as to who it was.

Bandar brooded over this for some time. He read every piece of news he could find on the subject. He discovered that someone named Muhammad Daweesh had been convicted by the Zionist authorities, but was believed to have been only an accomplice to the operation. The mastermind was never found.

Muhammad was known to have a brother named Ahmad, who was a studious boy and not a suspect. Ahmad had gone to the University of London to study one week before the incident.

A certain student was located at that University some months later by Bandar's men. The student had achieved a kind of notoriety. It was soon discovered that he was Ahmad with a new name. He had changed it to *Al Harbi*, "the warrior."

Among the coterie of Arab students at the university, Dowi Al Harbi soon became known as the brother of the famous Muhammad Daweesh of the Hebron Holocaust. But the thing that occasioned the most curiosity among his fellows, and the mystique that was to soon grow around him, was the fact that he did not brag about his brother, and this was most unusual behavior.

Any other young man even remotely associated with a successful action against the Zionists would inevitably brag–if only to his friends–about the number of Jews he had personally killed, how they had squirmed in shameful fear just before being executed, how cold and calculating an executioner he was. The usual meaning behind this bravado, which everyone knew but no one admitted, was that it had not really happened like that at all. The truth was that there was rarely ever a successful strike which didn't involve the *majaneen*, or "crazies," the men and women, and sometimes, the

Joseph's Seed

children, who formed the suicide squads.

Al Harbi stirred up curiosity because he did not do any of this. When questioned about his brother he would reply only that if they wanted to know more they should ask Muhammad.

When Prince Bandar heard of this unusual Palestinian, he decided to see for himself. He invited Dowi Al Harbi to visit him at his luxury suite in London. He knew that even one such as this could not consider refusing his invitation, for Bandar was a first line prince in the most honored house in the Arab World.

Now, sitting in the lecture hall listening to his protégé speak, he recalled that first meeting.

"I understand you were born and raised in occupied Palestine?" he had asked the boy.

The arrogant boy had replied rudely: "I am an Israeli Arab, if that is what you mean. We live with that reality because no one can change it."

"But you mean to try." queried the prince.

"What can a teen age Israeli Arab do?" The impudence in his voice was a challenge to Bandar. Their eyes locked in a battle of wills. Finally, the prince broke the stare with a shrug of indifference.

"*Ma'alaish*," he said, "It is of no matter. Let us eat."

A week later Bandar had bid the boy again to come to his suite. When he arrived, the prince came right to the point.

"Was it you?" he had asked.

"I don't understand," replied the boy, his face blank.

"No you don't," said the prince. "So I will tell you.

I have studied all that is available–all that is known about this bombing in Hebron. None of the organizations are involved. It was an independent operation for certain. Your brother was not capable of it–at least not the part that matters." He put his finger on the boy's temple.

"You departed from occupied Palestine quite suddenly? Did you not?"

Al Harbi had been looking out a window but with the

last question he turned sharply to face the prince.

"What does that mean?" he challenged. "I came to England because I am enrolled at London University. I am an honor student and my family are not paupers. We have been merchants in Beer Sheva for many generations. I have been planning to come here for some time."

"Yes, yes. I have no doubt. But please," the prince continued, "hear me out. You have no need to be alarmed. I now know what you did. You are a very intelligent young man–sly like the Jews you live among. But you are inexperienced. You made mistakes.

"However, do not be concerned. I have connections in the Arab world which the enemy knows nothing about. Your bedouin relatives may manage to cross borders freely, though I fear that will soon end. But they had to purchase explosives and false documents on our side–that I could discover."

"False documents?" asked Dowi Al Harbi, visibly shaken.

"Yes. I tell you, there is no need for fear. The few men who know the truth have the greatest respect for your accomplishment. We know, for example, that you did not leave occupied Palestine one week before the operation as is believed, but exactly one day after. There was an exchange of identities and with your perfect Hebrew, you were able to escape from their midst–unnoticed–as an Israeli Jew."

Al Harbi said nothing.

"You admit it then?"

"Is it necessary?"

"No," said the prince. He put his hands on the boy's shoulders and gazed at him with compassion. Tears were in his eyes. Then they embraced and their souls met. The older man kissed the boy on the cheeks several times.

At that moment was created between them a bond which would not easily be broken. Bandar needed this boy, and Dowi Al Harbi needed power, the kind of power

Joseph's Seed

only a Rasheedi prince could give him.

Thus began a relationship which continued till the present day. Since the day they had made their pact, they would never veer from the course they had set. They continued their normal lives as students, and later scholars, but at the same time they pursued a relentless and calculated course. To these men and others like them there existed an undying hope combined with a religious sense of destiny, a sense that their mission was guided by the hand of Allah.

Their portentous meeting, the apparent uncanny success of Al Harbi's first operation, his prodigal abilities, the prince's unique access to resources and seats of power in the Arab World, and the burning hate which consumed both of them; all now combined to create a potential to achieve the thing for which they both prayed.

Over time, Bandar provided the funds for the creation of a new organization. The most capable young men in the Arab World were selected and sent to training camps in several Arab and Islamic nations for training by world renown terrorists, or as he preferred to think of them–freedom fighters, and the best Western soldiers of fortune that money could buy. They were trained in all the arts of war. They learned also the secrets of covert operation. A high powered Palestinian businessman organized the whole and made it professional.

All of the key operatives of the organization were taught to lead double lives; as students, professors, diplomats, businessmen; but each would be assigned at various times to carry out a mission.

After each success, a communiqué would surface claiming credit for the "Terrorist act." The communiqué would be signed, "Baal Bazz." or The Lord of the Hawks.

Thus began the legend of Baal Bazz. Prince Bandar had no doubt as to the identity of this great freedom fighter for he felt that he himself had created him. This was the impression he gave to his brothers and other men of influence in the Kingdom of Arabia. With each spectacular success of Baal Bazz came an upsurge in Arab pride, and Bandar took the credit. His prestige grew steadily until finally just a few days ago, he was given the coveted governorship of Riyadh.

🐪 🐪 🐪

Now he sat listening to the man who had helped him make it possible.

"Allah is merciful," said the man at the podium. "Even as I stand here before you, our loving brother Arabs—yes also the black and yellow fellow Muslims whom we welcome to our lands with open arms—are rallying to our call. We are many and the enemy are few.

"Oh, my people Palestine! My forlorn ones! When will we be able to walk tall in the sight of Allah once again? When will our Diaspora be over?"

The effect this was having on the students was electric. They were standing and waiving their fists. "Death to *Al Yehudi!*" they shouted. "Spill their blood in the streets of *Al Kuds!*" "Al Kuds," means, "The Holy" in the Arabic, it is their name for the city of Jerusalem.

Dowi Al Harbi was now raising his hands for quiet. A smile played on his lips. "We are not anti-Semites," he cautioned now in a soothing voice. "We do not wish to kill the Jews. You know as well as I that they are our cousins; fellow children of our grandfather Ibrahim. No, we do not seek their destruction, only to redeem them, and retrieve what is ours.

"How many of them are there after all? A mere few million? We are many more. We will welcome them into our Nation. They will become part of us. They will speak Arabic in the end. But what is ours will be ours again!"

He pronounced his last sentence with such force, such anger, such lightning change of mood, that he startled the audience. His face had turned a deep

Joseph's Seed

purple; his body was trembling. He was shaking his fist at God. Then, as suddenly as it had begun, it ended. He bowed his head in weary exhaustion and said nothing for some moments. This time the audience made no sound.

From his seat, Bandar watched all of this with great interest. Although he had known and supported Dowi Al Harbi–and Baal Bazz–for several years, he had not, until now, understood the man's strength. This man burned with a much deeper hatred then he, Bandar could feel. Whereas the prince wanted power, the other it seemed to him now, wanted something quite different. "He can do me much good," thought Bandar, "above what he has already done; He has taken the name of master of the birds of prey, but I will have to watch him as the hunter watches the falcon which does his bidding. He must be tied to the block lest He scratch out the eyes of his master."

Two hours later, Professor Dowi Al Harbi was completing the lecture which although interspersed with such breathless emotionalism, as had just been related, had also touched on many other subjects. The speaker had raised his listeners' ire–and their Islamic consciousness. He had instilled them with pride–and determination. He had quoted the Koran, Karl Marx, and Malcom X. It was clear that he had the makings of a great orator. The fthought that his reasoning was at times erratic and disconnected and that his facts raised some eyebrows, did not escape some of those present and did not matter. No Arab speaker like him had been seen or heard since many years earlier when the Egyptian dictator and early advocate of pan-Arabism, Muhammad Diab, who was also quoted, had died of a stroke.

Now Dowi Al Harbi was concluding his lecture with a brief exposé on his most recent book which he had coauthored with the eminent Lebanese archaeologist, Dr Wahan Al Mukhless.

"*Ustez* Mukhless has proven by his excavations that

the so-called 'holy land' of the Christians and Jews never existed in Palestine at all, but far to the South. Look at the names of the cities and towns of the *Hijaz* and the *Asir*. You will see in them the names of the Old Testament towns with sometimes only one letter altered here and there from their original spellings.

"There you will find the fabled 'Eden,' now called Aden; there you will find the 'Jordan' which in the Hebrew language means 'going down. ' This can not mean that small stream which trickles from the lake of Tiberius, which now uses that name. No, it must refer to the great ridge which forms the *Hijaz* from North to the South where one 'goes down' from the desert plateau above. In the Bible it is never called a 'river,' but only 'Jordan.'

"To the East is 'Sinai,' the great Arabian desert, which means in the ancient tongue, 'Eastern Desert,' one hundred times larger than the desert which today bears that name. How could any tribe get lost in the puny modern Sinai for forty years?

"Why else would our ancient city in the West be called '*Jeddah*,' which means 'grandmother,' if not that 'Eve,' the grandmother of all men lies buried there. Why else would grandfather Ibrahim have promised to sacrifice his son Ismael, and have built a house to Allah in Maccah, in the *Hijaz*, if that city were not at the center of all holy places? How else would the name for the holy city of Medina be the self same word for the Hebrew word for 'nation,' if not that *Al Medina*, which means 'the state,' in the Hebrew language, is the city-state of the Al Nebi–The Prophet? "How else could the prophet *Musa* escape from Firon in Egypt by crossing the Red Sea if not by going from Egypt to Arabia. Look at any map! And of course, *Jabal Musa*, the mountain of Moses, is right here in Arabia and not in the so-called Sinai Dessert. What lands border on the Red Sea? Palestine has no Red sea, *wallah*; it has only the Mediterranean on its shores.

"It is one of the tragedies of history," concluded the

eminent professor, "that the Zionists have robbed the Palestinians not only of our land, but also of our historical legacy. Jews did not come into our land until after their Babylonian Captivity. It was then that they first usurped our heritage. They called us Canaanites; the Greeks called us Phoenicians. We call ourselves, as we have always done; *"Philistine,"* the people who love their homeland.

"I tell you, *Bismallah*, both will be redeemed, the history, and the land."

With those closing remarks he bowed his head and left the room. There was silence for several moments and then pandemonium broke loose.

"Please, no more Arab bullshit," said Debbie Costello as she lay naked on top of Frank at that very moment very far away. They were making love for the third time that night.

She was a beautiful woman if "beauty" was the right word, because there was a look of inscrutable wrath in her face. But it was only a hint; it was a face which promised unimaginable pleasure–or the destruction of the seeker.

She had classical features with blue eyes perhaps a little larger, and a little more slanted, than they should have been. Her mouth was hard and soft at the same time. Her body was exquisite, but perhaps a little smaller than the average.

Her left elbow now rested in the hollow between her husband's ribs–actually right on his solar plexus. She was contorted in that awkward position because her right hand was busy elsewhere. She was holding up her chin with the palm of her left hand. Her long blond hair cascaded over his boney shoulders. They were having a discussion during sex-play as they often did and Debbie was getting fed up.

"Owww!" yelled Frank when her elbow dug deeper into the hollow below his ribs with the sudden pouting motion she had made, a temper tantrum almost, as she reacted to what he had just said. He had broken the news to her that he wanted to go back to the Kingdom of Arabia.

Eight

The Spy

Before the events now transpiring, Frank Costello had been a somewhat different person. Now he was undergoing a subtle if imperceptible change; but to what and from what he was not quite sure. Nor did he think about the fact that the change implied a commitment to something that he had never felt before.

Frank didn't think in these terms however–that is to say–about himself. What he could and did do, however, was to observe the world around him. He paid attention to the details, and he knew how to solve problems. Until recently, he had chanelled this ability into computers. Then he had become adept at thinking about personal gain. But computers were his first love, and for many years it had been his great escape. Now he felt like a computer which was being slowly but inexorably reprogrammed.

Growing up an only child, he had been sheltered by a domineering and protective mother. Had she prevailed in molding his personality and planning his life, he might have become nothing more controversial than a doctor or a lawyer. But she hadn't prevailed. The course of Frank's progress had been diverted by a cynical, slightly warped father who couldn't leave well enough alone, who forever flitted from one scheme to another and could never be quite satisfied with life as it presented itself at any given juncture.

His father was Italian and his mother Jewish–a combination not unlikely in New York's Melting Pot, where many a divergent boy and girl meet, and due to the superficial resemblance of their cultures, and mutual attraction, are drawn together only to thenceforth live out stormy lives, which often though not always, end in tragedy.

Frank's parents stayed together but there was no such thing as "domestic tranquility" in his home. To escape from the ongoing battle of wits between his parents he took refuge in solitary hobbies. First it was Ham Radio, then later computers.

Perhaps it was a reaction to the turmoil of home life, or it may have been because he knew he could never win an argument with either of his parents; he discovered early that he might as well try a different tactic. Thus he became agreeable, easily led or cajoled, seemingly naive, compliant–though under all that there remained a more determined core–it was a determination not to let his parents wreck his life.

It couldn't be said that he developed a "feminine" personality although that sometimes seemed to be the case to others. Actually all of his physical and mental urges remained functional. What probably happened was much simpler. He decided at some point in his childhood that it was just easier to accept things, and life, as he found them–than to fight it. But to compensate, he needed to create his own private little world. If everybody else pretended–he would pretend. If everybody else lied–he would lie. In short, he developed all of the traits of a natural salesman.

He had met Debbie in college and after a few years he married her because it seemed like the natural thing to do. Besides being a knock-out, she was interested in everything; politics, religion, ideas–all of the things that his parent's petty rivalries had led him to avoid. He was attracted to her, aside from purely physical reasons, because she provided the spark he needed to become real. Her reasons for choosing him were a mystery which he never sought to discover.

He had no doubt that he loved her–except that he wasn't sure what love was, or where their life together would lead, or why. He believed that people were supposed to live life the best they could, and he knew that life after marriage went on. He had to earn a living, and that settled things. Debbie, for her part married Frank because he threatened her in no way and he was "Jewish enough," as she had told her troubled parents. She wanted to become a writer, but that comes later.

A year before the events now taking place, Frank had gone to the Kingdom of Arabia to get rich. He had no other motive. With the waxing and waning of the economy, he left the computer programming field for which he was trained to try his hand at selling them. He did well at first and they were able to buy a house; but when inexpensive PC's flooded the market, bigger systems became hard to sell and big commissions became difficult to come by. Frank had to find a job.

Then he heard about the obscene profits being made selling–selling anything–to the Arabs. So, on an impulse, he took a job with Agricultural International with the understanding that he would go to Arabia for a year at most, and afterward be given a position in a home market, maybe move out West with Debbie. He knew nothing about agriculture but thought he could sell for them anyway.

He had been in Arabia for a year now aside from trips home every few months. But due to the very large commission he had just earned from the JADCO deal, he had decided to take an extended vacation and then go back while the opportunity still existed. He wanted to strike while the iron was hot, so–he told

Debbie–they would be set for life. Lately he had begun thinking the time was near.

🐪 🐪 🐪

When Frank had arrived home with the negatives, he declined at first to talk to his wife about their contents. As with the other times they had been reunited after being apart for months, they spent most of the time during the first few days together in their water bed. When they weren't doing that, and when Frank wasn't at his PC, they practiced their mutual hobby which was cooking and then eating gourmet delights in the nude. If it is a cliché that absence makes the heart grow fonder, it was true for them.

As for the photos, he was afraid to broach the subject with her so he simply avoided it. Thinking he would probably send them to Clement's address, he had them developed. Then one day, while he was busy watching baseball, she went through them slowly and carefully on her own initiative. Then, as her mood completed its metamorphosis from the light-hearted happiness in which she had reveled for the past few days, to a cold anger; as her beautiful continence mirrored the change, she confronted him.

"What the Hell is this?" she demanded.

"They're photos a guy named Clement took of some construction site. Uh–actually it's called King Waleed Military city. He wants me to send them along to his home in Wichita," he told her, trying to avoid her glare.

"Are you crazy?! She asked in incredulous disbelief.

"Why?" he said sheepishly.

Debbie was far too intelligent not to realize that the mere fact that Frank had these photos in his possession implied that he was an ass-hole of the first order. It meant that he had endangered himself taking them out of that barbaric country. It meant that he probably had been involved in some hair-brained escapade which had entailed the taking of the pictures under illegal circumstances. It meant that her man–her jerk–had been duped by others and had haplessly risked everything for them. She made him tell her the whole story. When he finished, she knew that her suspicions were absolutely true.

After she digested this latest idiocy of his, and because he was after all safe in spite of it, she calmed down enough to begin to plan out what to do with about the photos.

"I have to send them to Wichita, as I promised," he said.

"That plan is history–null and void–you're under no obligation to this guy, after being used by him the way you were. You're not sending them anywhere, at least not till we find out what this is all about." Frank knew there was no arguing with her "I know a guy in the Jewish Defense Force," suggested Debbie then. "He lives in Brooklyn. Maybe he can tell us something."

"That's out," insisted Frank, adamantly. "I'm not getting involved with radicals. I know how you feel, but that's out."

"Well, what then?"

"What about Lloyd Olsen?" suggested Frank stupidly. Lloyd was a neighbor. The Costellos socialized occasionally with Lloyd and Cindy Olsen. "He's an engineer. Maybe he can give us a technical opinion of what we have." Although Frank's intuition told him that the photos didn't amount to much, he wasn't sure. Neither did Debbie know despite her strong feelings on the matter.

"Nah," said Debbie, shaking her head. "Lloyd's a jerk too–earns a living measuring nuts and bolts. He won't know. Besides, the Olsens are bores; I don't want them involved in this."

"Well, what then?" asked Frank. Thus they mulled over the problem for the next few days. They went back to their previous pastimes and tried to avoid thinking about the subject as much as possible.

During that period, something strange occurred.

Whenever they went out, there were always one or two men in suits hanging around the neighborhood. They discussed this with each other and decided that they must be real estate prospectors scoping out the area. But once while they were eating in a nearby restaurant, someone was staring at her over the top of his newspaper. She couldn't get a good look at him but he had a huge salad on his table which he wasn't touching. Debbie gave him a dirty look once and he raised the newspaper up. She figured he was just ogling her; it made her sick.

Finally they arrived at a tentative course of action. They would send a letter to the CIA discussing the subject in general terms, and play it by ear after that. They couldn't just ignore what they had; it might be important, Debbie insisted. Israel might be in danger. To be sure, they didn't know that to be the case, but even if it was a long shot, they couldn't just do nothing.

So they sent off a letter, and in the meantime, while they waited for an answer, they placed the photos and negatives in their plastic home-safe, tried to forget about them, and got back to their hobby of gourmet cooking.

A few days later they received an answer. The letter requested that they come to an address in Trenton. Then they got a phone call in which someone asked questions and gave them more specific instructions. They had an appointment to see someone named Mr. Snead, and they were to bring the photos.

A well filled out man of indeterminate age, wearing a grey business suit came out into the waiting room where Frank and Debbie had been sitting. "I'm Jim Snead," he said to them in a pleasant voice. "Thank you for coming down. Listen! I thought we might get a bite to eat and talk at the same time. I know a place that makes fantastic Roquefort dressing. I'm starved!"

They agreed, they were hungry also, having been too nervous to eat anything that day. They left the seventh floor suite of the modern office building through a door which bore no identifying marks save the number "75." Mr. Snead guided Debbie's elbow toward the elevator with the palm of his hand. Frank followed.

They took the elevator down to the parking lot in the building's basement and located Snead's car, which was parked in a spot marked "reserved." As soon as they were seated with Debbie in the front seat and Frank in the back, Snead turned and asked in hushed tones. "Did you bring the photos?"

Frank produced an envelope from his coat pocket. "Is this all?" inquired Mr. Snead.

"No, there's more but not here," replied Frank cautiously. The CIA man then thumbed through the thirty or so photos Frank had given him, stopping occasionally, apparently to study one in greater detail. "Where did you get these?" he asked when he was finished.

They had divulged very little information in the letter Debbie had composed, other than to say that they had some photos brought home from abroad which might have some bearing on the "national security," (of which country they didn't say), and that they would like to show them to someone who could tell them if they were important or not. Now that the nervousness had left them they felt a little ridiculous at the idea.

"We told you in the letter," said Debbie, "My husband Frank brought them home with him from a business trip–a friend gave them to him to be developed–and we thought they might be important."

"What you haven't told me," Snead began harshly, but then just as quickly returned to his friendly-fatherly tone, "was that Frank brought them home from Rasheedi Arabia where he's been working. Listen! You came to us with something, now you have to tell me what it's all about. Did you take these?"

Frank's natural inclination was to clam up, to become recalcitrant, when pressured. Still, he and Debbie had decided to do this, hadn't they? Now they had to go through with it. Reluctantly though cautiously, Frank started to talk; but he was no match for Snead. Soon

Snead knew all that he wanted to know.

"Okay," said Snead smiling, when Frank had finished. "That's better. Now let's go get that Roquefort salad–and don't worry, you're doing the right thing."

Just before Frank and Debbie departed from Trenton to return home, Snead turned and said, "I'll need to keep these photos for the time being. Eventually we may want to see the others also. We will be in touch with you.

"I want you to know Mr. Costello," he gave Frank an earnestly concerned look, "that what you did was quite foolhardy and could have in fact been very dangerous. I wouldn't advise you to attempt anything like it again. Matters are less stable in that region than one might expect."

"But it's not like that there, really," said Frank. "You get the impression that the Arabs are not aware of what's going on–like they're half asleep. Believe me, I've been there for a year."

"You are wrong," said Snead. "They can be very dangerous."

Frank and Debbie waited patiently for a few more days. They didn't know how one went about the business of espionage but they wanted to learn, so long as they could practice it from the safety of their own home–along with gourmet cooking.

The day after returning from Trenton Mr. Snead had called to thank them again for coming down. He said that he was going to discuss the matter with his superiors and would like to see them again soon–as soon as a decision had been reached. He may have, he told them, important information for them, and this might after all be a security matter of considerably more significance than he had thought previously, so would they please not talk to any one about the matter, or show the photos to anyone until he got back to them.

It all sounded more mysterious than they had ex-

Joseph's Seed

pected, but really they hadn't known what to expect. Now they were curious. What could he possibly want to talk to them about?

Then finally, Snead called. Would they mind if he came to Spring Valley? He would like to pick up the remainder of the photos, and also to talk to them concerning the Agency's position on this matter. They agreed to his coming the following day. The next morning at nine, Mr. Snead was at the door.

"I hope I'm not too early, Mrs. Costello," he said, removing his homburg, and revealing neatly groomed hair that was graying but only around the edges. He was wearing his usual grey business suit, but with a striking red tie and no clip. He held a cashmere overcoat on his arm. It was an autumn morning, a bit brisk, but not cold enough for the coat.

"Well a little," said Debbie. "But we're up. Come in." She led him into the den, took his coat and hat. "Coffee's on. Like a cup?"

"Sounds great," he smiled cheerfully, sitting down.

"Fine. I'll get some and call Frank. Just be a minute."

"Sounds great," repeated Snead.

Ten minutes later Frank, Debbie and Snead were sitting on stuffed chairs around a low, glass topped table eating plump, whole wheat bagels with crème cheese and cherry jelly. The coffee, which was kept hot in a white ceramic pot, had been freshly ground and smelled delicious. There was a brown envelope on the table also, which Frank had just placed there.

Snead took a sip of coffee and said. "Are these the remaining photos? May I?"

"Go ahead," said Frank. Snead took out the five individual packets and studied them for some time between sips of coffee and bites of bagel.

When he was finished, he began in measured tones. "I want you both to know that the government appreciates the fact that you have informed us about this matter. You can rest assured, Mrs. Costello, that your husband did the right thing in taking the film home with him—although we don't advise him to repeat it—there was in fact some slight risk involved..."

"Slight, now?" interrupted Debbie, looking up dubiously from the brim of her cup. "Last time it was 'very dangerous'."

"Well, let's say that we didn't ask him to do it but since he took it upon himself, it probably turned out to be the right thing."

"Probably?"

"Be that as it may," Snead went on, after clearing his throat. "What I'd like to talk about now is where we should go from here." He went on quickly, sensing that Debbie was about to ask another rhetorical question. "I say 'we,' because you may be able to help us—err, to serve your country—in other ways. Though we wouldn't ask you to take any risks, of course. You're not trained for it.

"But first, before we go into that, I'd like to clear the air about a matter which should have been obvious to you, but apparently wasn't. You must understand that what you think you've 'discovered,' is in fact a matter of the most routine nature in intelligence surveillance. Even if our government had no diplomatic relations with the Rasheedi Regime—which we most certainly do. But let's say, for the sake of argument, that we didn't. Even in that case, we would have already known every detail of what you have shown us. Surely you have heard about advanced warning radar and satellite photography?

"What you have told us is of much more interest to us, and much more significant, than what you have shown us—and the fact that you have surprising access to people and situations which might be potentially interesting to us. Actually we've been quite weak in this particular area because that society is so closed to us—more closed than the former Soviet Union was. We've got very few men on the ground there...."

"Just what are you getting at," said Debbie who was

Joseph's Seed

beginning to suspect the worst. "Are you saying that you want Frank to spy for you? Because if you do, I think you're out of your mind. Those people have sworn to destroy Israel. I'm not going to allow you to put my husband into that kind of danger. He's not equipped for it. And if he were, I still wouldn't allow it. What he's done already was stupid enough."

Snead paused for a moment, took a sip of cold coffee, wasn't offered a refill, and then went on. "I appreciate your concern, Mrs. Costello. But you must remember; this is America. Our interests and those of the State of Israel are not always identical." Then seeing the look on her face, he continued. "Even if our interests were identical, perhaps you weren't aware that some Arab countries, and also some leaders in potentially hostile countries are relatively moderate–even friendly to us."

"Bull."

"Be that as it may," continued Snead. "You have become involved in this matter, perhaps unwittingly–a little naively? Nevertheless, you would do a great service if you would consider cooperating with us now, in some small, extremely low risk ways–considering the fact that you're already working in that country, Frank, and have considerable mobility there."

"Of course we'll cooperate," said Frank who had been for the most part quiet till then. "I'd never do anything purposefully to cause my country any trouble. Neither would my wife."

"I know you wouldn't. That's why my superiors thought it necessary that I speak to both of you together–so there wouldn't be any misunderstanding."

"What do you want me to do then?" asked Frank. "I don't know anything about espionage."

"Err, that won't be a problem," said Snead. Actually, we don't want you to do anything different from what you have already done. Less in fact–no more photography–no microfilm–nothing like that. Just keep your eyes and ears open, and when you come home you'll talk to us–that's all. I understand that you've been returning every few months. We can arrange for that to be more frequent–say once a month for a week? I'm sure Mrs. Costello would appreciate that change."

"I don't like this at all," said Debbie. My husband may be a little naive, as you put it, but I don't like the idea of you using him. If he started snooping around, it could be dangerous as hell for him. You don't know Frank, he's liable to blurt something out at the wrong time and get himself killed."

"I can't force you to do anything," said Snead. "This is a free country. But we wouldn't want Frank to do any 'snooping' as you put it, just his normal job, and to talk to us only when he's safely home."

"I'll do it," said Frank, looking at Debbie with determination. "I want to. I agree with Mr. Snead that it won't be dangerous, and I like my job–I want to keep doing it for awhile.

"Honey, try to understand. I've known for a long time that people tend to laugh at me under their breaths–you even do it a little. It's not your fault. I'm just that kind of person. Now I have a chance to do something important–I know it could turn out to be nothing. But it could be–to us as Jews. I know I've never shown much interest in that–it's the way I was brought up–but I do care."

"I know you do," said Debbie looking at Frank now with a look of tenderness–or was it sympathy? Then to Snead: "But I still don't like it. Will you be paying us for this?"

"That would be difficult at present ma'am, since your husband won't really be doing anything. Our budget is severely constrained these days, however, I'll see what I can do."

"Sure, sure," said Debbie.

Within days Frank had completed arrangements with Agricultural International, obtained the necessary visa, and was ready for another round of sales in the

Joseph's Seed

Kingdom of Arabia. His company had arranged an appointment by fax with his royal highness Prince Mustapha Bin Abdul Lateef. Destiny was calling Frank, and he relished the prospect. He would miss his wife and the fun they had together, but the missing-pain only went down to a certain point. He couldn't think about that now.

Not long after Frank had gone, Mr. Snead again telephoned to the home of the Costellos. He had something urgent to say to Mrs. Costello. No, it was not about Frank. Could he please come as soon as possible to discuss the matter?

Again Mr. Snead sat munching a bagel in Debbie's den, but this time Frank was not there.

"The subject I wanted to discuss with you, Mrs. Costello, is rather sensitive," he said. "May I call you Debbie?" He waited a moment, and receiving no response, continued.

"You realize, of course, that when you and your husband first came to my attention, we conducted a thorough and extensive background check on both of you. It soon became clear to me that the significant person in this case was not your husband, but you.

"We discovered that several years ago you were more or less associated with a certain incident–a terrorist attack in Israel–in Hebron to be exact–in which three school buses were blown up? I understand that your brother, Samuel, was killed in that tragedy?

"The event was dubbed the 'Hebron Holocaust.' I believe that was the name the media used. In retrospect, we know that the mastermind of that operation was in fact, never captured; although certain accomplices were convicted and imprisoned, including one Muhammad Daweesh."

Snead paused for a moment then said, "By the way, does your husband know about this tragic event in your past?"

"Of course," said Debbie. "But we don't talk about

it."

"Now it also has come to my attention," Snead went on, "that there was a certain young Arab who left Israel to study in Briton around that time–an Israeli Arab to be exact–whom you knew from the high school you attended while living in that country. A strikingly good looking boy, and very intelligent. His name was Ahmad I believe, Ahmad Daweesh, Muhammad's brother. You created quite a stir when you..."

"Just exactly where are you going with this Mr. Snead. I don't know if I want to...."

"Please bear with me, Debbie–the name's Jim, please–better yet, I'll bet we can easily find a place that serves a good Roquefort salad in your neck of the woods. Got to watch the weight you know. It seems that this young Daweesh soon surfaced under a different name or names, and you may be quite interested in what he has been doing. But let's talk about it over that salad."

They went to a local restaurant, one she and Frank had often frequented. When she saw him sitting across from her, something struck her.

"Have you ever eaten here before?" she asked.

"Why no." he said. "How could I? I'm not from these parts."

Nine

An Old Kibbutznick

Snead devoured Debbie with his eyes as he forked the last tomato from his Roquefort salad. "A very beautiful woman," he thought, "and available–at least for the moment." His pragmatic mind raced ahead.

"What do you think then?" he asked after he finished his meal. "Could you break away long enough to spend a few days with me in Washington? There is someone I would like you to meet."

"Who?" inquired Debbie without interest. She knew what he was thinking; she had seen that look before. It made her tired.

"Just a certain Israeli functionary you may want to know, an elderly fellow. For someone in my profession, he's not very useful anymore, from what I understand. Getting a bit senile. But still you might find him interesting; he's had a long standing interest in your friend Ahmad."

"He's not my friend–the bastard. If what you've been telling me is true, then bastard is too good a word for him." She sat quietly for a moment then went on. "Thinking back though, I can see how it could be true. He was two years older than me. I was only sixteen and kind of heavy."

"I don't believe that," said Snead.

"Nevertheless, it's true. I don't think he even knew who I was; he did know Sam though—my brother.

"I considered him kind of a rogue—you know, different—but very attractive. I was a rebellious kid. Believe me it was scandalous to think that way about one of them—especially where I was. I mean, we were at war after all. But he was sort of alright, I thought, because he was an Israeli Arab. They were supposed to be loyal—boy was I naive. When I wrote that story, I had no idea that he."

"I know." Snead put a hand consolingly on her arm, then waited for her to continue.

"All right," she said finally. "I'll go with you. I want to meet this Mr.—what did you say his name was—Bar Kama? But you can forget any other ideas you may have; it's not like that. I'll tell you that right from the start."

Snead smiled wistfully. "You can't blame an old boy for trying." Then he straightened out his red tie, jutted out his chin somewhat, and cleared his throat. "Be that as it may," he said. "You really are a remarkable woman. You'll be able to accomplish more than you realize."

Two days later, Debbie stood looking out her hotel window at the Washington monument; but she wasn't noticing it. What Mr. Snead had told her had affected her severely, and she could think of little else. There was a madman loose in the world—a madman who had killed her brother and many of her friends. She shook with revulsion. How could she have had a crush on someone like that?

He was pure evil. As a child she couldn't have known. She had written a passionate story about him only weeks before the bombing. How could she have known?

But now she knew. She resolved to do whatever she could to stop him. She would do it even if it killed her.

She had no idea of how the world of power and intrigue worked, but she was smart; she could learn. She decided to use Snead to learn what she needed to know–even if she had to give him what he wanted. She didn't care anymore.

He was picking her up soon to take her to another one of his "great restaurants." There they would meet Sadya Bar Kama, Israeli agent without portfolio, and persona non grata, according to Snead, in diplomatic circles of many countries. She waited, still looking blankly out the window, wondering how one went about killing a man.

The Israeli was sitting at a corner table. He was a bent old man of perhaps eighty. But he still had a full head of hair; it looked like white sheep's wool cropped close. He had a glass eye. He looked like a man who, though he had always been small, was now a shriveled up version of his former self. He was dreaming of other things when they walked up to his table.

"Mr. Bar Kama?" Snead prodded the old man gently.

"–Yes?–Oh, hello, Mr. Snead. I must have dozed off as you say."

"I have brought the young lady I told you about," said Snead. "May I present Mrs. Costello?–Mr. Bar Kama."

The old man stood up slowly, smiling. "Sadya, please." He extended his hand to Debbie. "We kibutzniks are very informal, you know. I am very pleased to meet you Madam."

"Call me Debbie," she said.

"Ah, yes, Dvora. Please–sit down. You will eat?"

After ordering Snead began: "I have told Mrs. Costello of your theory. She is inclined to believe you. But she would like to hear it from you."

"I would be most happy to do so," said Sadya. "I have read the little story which you published in Israel many years ago. It was very interesting, and not very far from the truth as I see it. Your psychological insight into the man was quite clear for the child you were at the time. In fact, I have re-read your story many times over the years.

"I will tell you how I came to my present belief about Ahmad, but first understand how such an evil seed could be sown–the 'roots of our problem,' so to speak. Do you care to hear of these things?"

"Yes," said Debbie. "It's what I came for."

The old man's face became animated as he began to speak of things which had been pre-eminent in his mind for many years.

"He was a singularly striking boy," began the old man. "First in his class, already beginning to discover his charismatic personality, Ahmad had, at eighteen years of age, his whole life to look forward to. He was a child prodigy who might one day do great things– except that he had one problem. He was an Arab child in a Jewish State. He had just graduated high school. At home he had the 'Honors Certificate' he had received from the *menahelit bet-sefer* of the Beer Sheva High School as reward for his outstanding scholastic achievement. On the certificate she had written: '*Coll Ha Cavode Ahmad, Ubihatzlakha.*' 'Congratulations Ahmad, and Good Luck.'

"Viewed in a dispassionate way, objectively, if such were possible, one might observe that our Jewish State had little to do with Ahmad Daweesh's dilemma. It had treated him well. Had he been born in an Arab country, he may conceivably have been able to look forward to a future in politics or business. But he seemed far too intelligent for either of those paths. Perhaps, had he lived in his own culture, he would have become a religious leader, immersed in the complexities of the Koran and Sharia, bound to its rigid traditions. Most likely, he simply would have been one of the *fellaheen*, a peasant destined to live out a short and brutish life. In such a world, therefore, he could have done little or nothing to improve the lot of his people.

"But intelligent as he was, Ahmad could not know that what he dreamt of could not be achieved. What he knew was his only reality. With his great potentiality, he discovered that although he had been successful and almost assimilated as a child Arab in a Jewish land, if he stayed in Israel, he would always remain a second class citizen. He knew that he needed freedom to thrive and seeing no possibility for that in his homeland, he made plans to leave it. He was going to college in England. After that anything might be possible.

"I first met Ahmad while the lad was working on a summer job at my kibbutz for a contracting firm which employed Arab construction workers. It was the last summer before Ahmad would leave the land of his birth to make his way in the world.

"I was the kibbutz gardener and my flower beds would be disrupted by the excavations which the new housing required. Ahmad came as a general laborer to work on the multi-family unit which the kibbutz had contracted to be started that summer. Since I had frequent interactions with the Arab crew, as they proceeded with their work, thereby threatening my flowers and shrubs, I soon came to know the unusual young man who was Ahmad Daweesh.

"I had been a kibbutz member since coming to Israel–over sixty years ago. I am of Iraqi Jewish extraction. My family had immigrated to Palestine during the second "Aliya." Though I had gone back to Baghdad on several "missions" in my early years, Israel was my home, the center of my universe.

"I was among those who had helped to found the country. Through our own blood and sweat, we turned deserts and swampland into flowering gardens. I loved the land and fought for it in many wars. You can see that I lost an eye in the effort. For me, Israel was an indisputable fact of life, but so was the Arab culture in which it was immersed–for better or worse. I had grown up with Arabs, shared their land, traded with them and exchanged ideas. We used the same slang, told the same jokes, and shared the same sun and sand. The *souqs*, (*shouqs*, in Hebrew), where daily needs were bought and sold in open-air markets, the cities and towns where goats, sheep and camels mingled with motor vehicles. The sounds, the sights, the smells–all were the same. *Nu*, why should the Arabs be our enemy?

"What separated us was only religion and history. To my mind–though mine was an unpopular opinion of late–the two people coexisted as a matter of course. I spoke Hebrew and Arabic fluently and also a little English, for those were the languages of the part of the world in which we lived. There was no other way for us."

"Your English is great," said Debbie with a smile.

"You are very kind *motek*," said the old man and returned to his tale.

"That was one of the reasons why, since the founding of Kibbutz Bet Davidka in the Negev many years ago–of which I had been a founding *haver*, or 'member,' as you say–I had always welcomed Arab cultural and economic exchange and participation whenever possible, and had argued for their continuation at the kibbutz planning sessions which I attended. In fact, it was through my insistence that an Arab work crew was permitted on the kibbutz at all–though the construction company they worked for was a Jewish one–Weiss and Volvovitz, if I recall. In any event, my stubborn proclivity was tolerated by the more conservative members only because of my life long contributions.

"But I was getting old. What I wanted most, more and more was just to tend my gardens and enjoy my first love–reading. I read Torah–not for the religion, but for the history and culture. But I also read many other things. Our religion has always had almost a secular meaning to me; that was because the dream–the return to Zion–had come true during my lifetime.

"I loved the Hebrew culture, and history, the *Tanach, Mishnah, Kabbala*, the Jewish seers and philosophers, especially *Rambam*, known also as Moses Maimonides. But I also read the modern works, and whatever Arabian literature and history I could find. Many of our people considered the Arabs and especially the bedouin as savages, but they were certainly not that. They have had high culture for many centuries.

"But I was becoming tired. I could not fight them all. Still I tried. I believed the prophet who said: 'If I am not for me, who then is for me? When I am for myself, I am myself. If not now, when?' –And the words of the modern poet Haim Nahman Bealik: '*Koomo to'ay medbar–od ha derrech rav, od rabba ha milkhamah...*' Arise desert wanderers–still the road ahead is hard, still harder is the struggle. Sometimes I was reluctant to return to the real world. The boy Ahmad Daweesh forced me to do just that."

Then the world-weary yet hopeful old man told Debbie the story of what happened many years ago.

Ten

The Hebron Holocaust

A younger Sadya appraised the construction crew which had just arrived at the kibbutz and quickly set to work. With his one good eye, he took in the whole scene: Five Arab workers led by their leather skinned foreman; their "tender," which was the old battered pick-up truck with a canvas covered back, which provided them with both passenger space and room for their supplies; the disapproving glances of *"havereem"* walking by going to their jobs. Most of all he noticed the boy.

"*Marhaba*," he said in Arabic to the youth when his stare met that of the boy.

"*Shalom, Ma neshma?*" said the Arab boy in Hebrew, looking at the old man quizzically. At sixty-five, he looked old even then, but stouter, strong yet wiry, perhaps dangerous. He had close cropped, tightly curled, salt and pepper hair, a dark complexion from many hours in the sun and his Sephardic genes, and a patch over his right eye.

"You look like a happy bulldog," said the boy, "but not dumb. You speak my language?"

Joseph's Seed

"A little," said Sadya. "You speak mine?"

"Perfectly." said the boy. "I was born and raised in Beer Sheva, as was my father. He has a hotel in the Old City. I went to school with Jewish children. My brother goes to the University of Ben Gurion. Do you have a problem with that?"

"I? No." He said sadly. Then he changed the subject to the matter at hand. "That is my flower bed you are digging up. I only came to request of you that are careful to take out no more of it than what is absolutely necessary." The boy was already digging in them with a shovel with little concern, to stake out the boundaries of the foundation.

"We will be sure to stay within the specifications, exactly," he said as he slid the shovel under some chrysanthemums.

"*Shukron.*" Sadya winced, but thanked the boy anyway, again using the other's language.

" '*Al lo devar*' " said the boy. "Think nothing of it." He spoke not just Hebrew but the vernacular, as if to challenge the old man; but Sadya merely shrugged.

As the work progressed that summer he had occasional contact with the workers who commuted daily to and from their homes in Beer Sheva. He was anxious to protect his horticultural domain but he also interacted with them if for no other reason than his sense of civility. Very few of the other kibbutz members would do the same–they or their families. They felt they had simply been hurt too often by Arabs, but was there prejudice involved also? Sadya had always wondered. So they couldn't–or wouldn't see the other side. The Arab workers therefore were treated–except when communication was absolutely necessary–as nonpersons.

But Sadya had always done things in his own way. He continued to do so now. He would bring the construction workers tea at break time. Sometimes he would even take them into the hadar-ohel, the communal dining room, lead them through the serving line for breakfast or lunch, and then to an isolated corner table where he joined them either alone or with his daughter Shulamit, who was a nursery school teacher and her husband Buxie, the plumber. This raised eyebrows, but no one said anything.

One evening the Arab crew had worked late because they had to unload a late arriving truck with building materials on it. They worked past sunset and were now sitting by their equipment tent drinking tea before beginning their long trip home. Sadya came over with Shulamit and Buxie. Shulamit was carrying a pan with some freshly made *halvah*, a taffy-like sweet common in the Middle East.

The Arab foreman, Da'ud, a man of thirty-two who looked much older, smiled showing his missing incisors, and took the offering. "Thank you vedy much," he said in strained English. "Please sit down–drink *shiy*."

"We want to apologize for the way some of the havereem are treating you," said Shulamit. "It was very kind of you to work extra time today. We only want you to know that it is appreciated."

"It is nothing," said Da'ud. "We are accustomed to it. Our work is good? No? You like the house?"

The reinforced concrete foundation and other structural work were complete. Cinder block walls were now being laid. "The building looks fine," said Sadya. "It's not that. . ."

Then the boy Ahmad spoke. It was as if he had read the old man's thoughts.

"We live in your country." he said. "We do your work. Is that not so? We follow your laws because we must, but they are not our laws. Is that not all that can be said?"

"We only want to live in peace," said Buxie, who had already fought in two wars, and had seen several of his friends killed.

"We also want peace," said Ahmad, a smile came to his lips, but only his lips.

Joseph's Seed

Amidst the strain of politeness felt by some, they finished the tea and halvah. The Arab foreman was talking to Buxie about the access lines to the water and sewer mains of the kibbutz to which they would have to connect. Shulamit was discussing some of the latest rock groups with the younger workers. Ahmad said nothing. Sadya too sat quietly sipping his tea, but he was worried.

One morning soon after that he noticed that Ahmad was not among the group of workers climbing out of the arriving construction crew's tender. When he asked Da'ud where his young friend was he was informed, "He is not coming. He go to England–out side–to study at University. He is very smart waled." Although he said nothing, Sadya was surprised. From what he had gleaned, he had not expected the boy to leave for some time.

The next day he read an article in the Evening News. The test scores, of honor students form the various high schools around the country had been examined by a national review board for the purpose of determining a winner from each school of a Meritorious Academic Achievement medal-an award given each year along with a modest scholarship grant. Ahmad, the son of Mo'amar Daweesh, a local Arab merchant, was the winner from his school. The school principal, a woman who was widely respected in her field, had nothing but praise for the youth. The article mentioned also that Ahmad was the first "Israeli Arab" to win the award.

Sadya wondered.

Then one week later the news broke. All over the world people witnessed the horror vicariously. It was front page news in the "Times" of many cities. Denny Rasner of the famous Tonight's News program devoted the entire half hour to its coverage–hoping it would up his ratings. It did, for the next few days. The world was shocked–The Arab world cheered.

A computer simulated version of the event was

shown over and over, as were filmed scenes of the wreckage. Three tour buses exploded in quick succession while rounding the winding mountain pass on the Beer Sheva-Jerusalem road in Hebron, which in those days was open to travel to Israelis. Then they crashed through the flimsy barrier-railing bordering the precipice, and flew over the edge into the rocky canyon far below. Over and over it was shown–the children inside screaming, hopelessly trapped–doomed.

Then the outrage came, the inquiries, the investigations, the crackdowns. How could such a thing happen? Denny Rasner and others asked again and again. But no answer was forthcoming. Just endless speculation and in the end, business as usual.

It was a summer recreation trip to Jerusalem organized by the Beer Sheva high school, and it ended in tragedy. One hundred fifty children killed, plus ten adult chaperones and three drivers. High explosives were soon discovered to have been hidden among the picnic supplies.

Subsequent investigations revealed the exact type, and the locations in which the explosives had been concealed. Plastic explosives had been hidden inside loaves of sliced bread which had been prepared at a bakery in Beer Sheva where Ahmad's brother Muhammad worked part time. The bread had been packed along with the other supplies by a food preparation committee of youths organized for the three day outing. There were two Israeli Arab youths on the committee. They had packed the crates in which the bread was included. They had taken care to insure that each bus contained crates with explosives hidden in them. The two boys were also killed in the explosions.

Muhammad was arrested as soon as the evidence pointed to him. It never became clear where he had gotten the explosives, but their availability made abundantly clear that the Israeli Arab community could no longer be counted on for their loyalty to Jewish Israel.

After a speedy trial, Muhammad was convicted and

received a life sentence without possibility of parole for his part in the crime. Many of the details of the crime never came to light, including exactly by whom and in what manner the explosives were detonated at precisely the right time to create the type of spectacular crime they did.

Neither could any connection be made concerning Ahmad, the brother of the accused, although his name was considered and his sympathies were under suspicion. He had however, many fervent supporters in liberal and academic circles because of his outstanding scholastic achievement. He had long been considered by many to be "more Jewish than Arab." Due to the fact that he was at Kibbutz Bet Davidka during the entire planning stages of the crime, and had left the country before the explosions took place to study at the University of London; and due to the fact that no prima facie evidence of any kind was available against him, no extradition was sought.

Sadya, to be sure, had many doubts as soon as the evidence became known to him. Since he had often worked 'under cover' in Arab countries in his younger days, he believed he had some experience in Arab psychology and treachery. He argued with the authorities for Ahmad's extradition but they were not impressed by his arguments which they interpreted as nothing more than an old, slightly eccentric man's psychological speculations. They brushed him off.

"It could be true," the chief investigator told Sadya with a wink, after hearing him out, "but this is not a paperback murder mystery–this is real life. We have been unable to establish any link. We are a civilized people. We cannot condemn a man simply because he is related to the accused. We believe that either Muhammad acted on his own, or as an agent of the Palestinian Restoration Society. Ahmad is too studious–not the type to commit murder. You talk of motive, but they all have a motive. Besides, we already have our man. So go home old friend–rest."

So the old man shrugged and went home to his flowers and Rambam. But he could not rest. He could not forget. "You will probably never hear of this Ahmad again," the chief investigator had said. "He will likely go to America to live the good life." Sadya had hoped the chief was right, but he didn't believe it.

🐪 🐪 🐪

Years later he felt more than ever that his suspicions had been correct. Ahmad the boy was now a man of boundless hate. He was known to the world as the professor of Islamic History and author, Dowi Al Harbi–and secretly, it was rumored in some circles, as the arch terrorist, Baal Bazz. Still no one would listen to Sadya–except Jim Snead. But Sadya had never found a way to convince the world–not until now. Now he had a way; he intended to capture the great Baal Bazz in the act."

🐪 🐪 🐪

What Sadya didn't know at the time was that months before the news of the Hebron Holocaust broke; sixteen year old Debbie Rosenbaum lay on the couch on her stomach in the family dira on *Derrich Hamishahrarim* in Beer Sheva. A glass of iced coffee with a large scoop of vanilla ice cream in it was on the table beside her. She had just returned from summer ulpon, remedial Hebrew class which she so sorely needed. Because of the stultifying heat, and since there was no air conditioning, as soon as she got home she had undressed down to her panties and bra. She was composing a short story which she had thought up during ulpon. Now she was concentrating and the sweat was pouring off her.

"Damn," she said to herself, "I had it an hour ago–

Joseph's Seed

let's see; 'Ahmad caressed her tender thighs. He couldn't bear the thought that she would soon be leaving him forever–' No. I better not call him Ahmad. Better change the name. . . let's see, Suleiman caressed. . .

"When Sarah first met him at the *Zanav Ha Suess* ice cream parlor," Debbie wrote, "how was she to know he was an Arab? His English accent was so adorable. And he was sooo cute. She had seen him around school. Then later when her friends had found out, she became rebellious. 'So what!' she told them. 'It's just for fun. Girls back home even go out with shvatzas. And he's sooo adorable.' They said he was a genius, but Sarah was soon to discover that he was more than that.

"So it went on for most of the summer. He would pick her up in his father's car. They would drive down to the beach in Ashkalon and Eilat. They would go swimming on the hot summer nights–skinny dipping. She already knew about birth control. There was no problem.

"Then Sarah's parents had found out and the shit hit the fan. She had to stop seeing him immediately or the family would leave Israel at once. She knew they meant it, so, stubborn as she was, she relented–besides he was starting to become a little too possessive; she was a little afraid of him. She knew she would have to end it sooner or later anyway. She broke the news to him.

"He was furious. She hadn't expected that. After all they were just kids. He wanted her to go to England with him. They could get married there. That was when she really got scared and just stopped seeing him."

This–with a little added to flesh it out–was her story, her first attempt at writing for publication.

She had a friend translate the story into Hebrew and sent it out to several publications. To her surprise, it was soon accepted and appeared in a glossy

Tell Aviv "True Life" magazine. It gained her a certain curious notoriety for she had written about a taboo subject. She was invited to speak on a controversial talk show. She went, but she did more stammering than speaking. Her Hebrew was terrible. It was an embarrassment for her and she tried to forget it. But many people had seen it, including Sadya's daughter Shulamit, and Da'ud, the Arab foreman.

Her parents, who had not given their consent to this escapade, also saw the program. Ahmad, who watched very little television, did not see it.

Then, one month later Debbie and her parents were preparing to leave Israel. But they would be leaving without her brother Sam. He was dead. Debbie was in a state of shock over her brother and over her aborted dream of Israel but she made no connection, had no thought, at that time that Ahmad might be involved. She had forgotten all about her stupid little story.

Not long after Debbie left Israel with her parents, Shulamit found a copy of Debbie's story and gave it to Sadya. After reading it he told his daughter: "I must meet this American girl some day."

"*Nu hamooda*," said Sadya, when he had finished telling her his tale. "What do you think of my idea–my theory as you would say?"

"But I still don't understand," said Debbie. "I can see where Ahmad was filled with hate. But why are you so sure it was him? I mean, you don't have any real proof. I'm sure the Israeli authorities would have gone after him if they bought your story. You are very nice, but–I don't know how else to say this–why should I buy it?"

"It is the psychology, *hamoodi*, just as I said. Ahmad is just the type who could commit cold blooded acts.

Joseph's Seed

But what is more important—and I have studied much on the subject—I know of no one else capable of the type of crime he committed.

"Still, I have always known that I had not much to go on. That was why I followed the career of Dowi Al Harbi, whom I know for a fact to be one in the same person as Ahmad Daweesh. He is now the protégé of a well known Rasheedi prince who is believed by some to be a supporter of terrorism. I have also kept a record of the exploits of the famed Baal Bazz. I am now convinced that the method of operation in many of his acts of terror matches that of the Hebron Holocaust.

"Notice that Ahmad masterminded the Hebron bombing without himself taking part in the actual work. He left loyal "stooges," including his own brother Muhammad, to be captured in his place—sacrificed for the cause. So now Baal Bazz is the elusive mystery man; never seen, he uses many proxies. Instead of being an honor student he is now a professor of Islamic History, but the terror continues.

"I have watched the career of Al Harbi for many years now and have recorded many facts. Much of it the authorities still believe to be circumstantial. Only Mr. Snead is convinced. If you wish, I will give you my files to study. If you agree we will talk further."

"I'd like that," said Debbie.

"After that you may agree to help us. I understand you are married. Will that be a problem?"

"Frank doesn't have to know a thing about it," said Debbie as she got up to leave.

Eleven

A Royal Succession

Prince Bandar, governor of Riyadh, arrived in Tunis the night before the World Islamic Convention. There had been some last minute decision making and consternation in the royal family's inner sanctum as to whether or not he should be allowed to attend. The House of Rasheed, through the figure-head of the benign King Waleed, preferred to present a unified front of moderation, stability, economic conservatism and respectability in the face of the extremist, left-wing fanaticism they knew they could expect to encounter from the leadership of many Arab states.

Although the fact was not widely known, within the family it was no secret that Bandar had long supported the most militant, or depending on one's point of view, the most patriotic of the Arab causes. He was staunchly, though discreetly anti-West. He was a long time supporter of the Palestinian Restoration Society. And most significantly, it was known in the highest circles that his was the money behind Baal Bazz, the world famous Palestinian Freedom Fighter—or terrorist—again, depending on how one looked at it.

Joseph's Seed

Thus, by the conservative standards of the faction of the house of Rasheed now in power, Bandar was potentially dangerous. He threatened stability and friendly relations with the West. But mostly, it was felt that prosperity, and the vast process of modernization which had been made possible by the oil wealth would be jeopardized if The Kingdom of Arabia took an extremist turn.

The ruling faction–led by the old and frail King Waleed, who would have much preferred spending his time out in the desert hunting with his falcons, or sitting in informal majlis and drinking tea with old and trusted friends and telling tales of "the old days"–was rapidly losing ground to the extremists. But recently the moderates had acquired a dynamic new spokesman.

This voice was Mustapha, the second youngest of the forty-three sons of the great Abdul Lateef Ibn Rasheed, founder of the kingdom. He was a sentimental favorite of old King Waleed his elder brother, who could easily have been, in terms of years, his father. The young Mustapha, still in his thirties, was a capable leader in his own right who had in the past five years as its governor, gained respect of his peers by turning the ancient town of Jabalain into a model city. Of late, this rising star, also Western educated like his brother Bandar, was the clearest voice in stemming the tide of extremism. But it could also come to pass that this voice would be drowned by the rising tide of fanaticism. For the future is never certain.

For this event, Mustapha had been told by his brother the king, to stay at home. He had not been invited to attend the World Islamic Conference. He obeyed.

Bandar, however, could not be made to yield. His party was strong and increasing in influence. The Crown Prince, Muhammad, Bandar's chief supporter, had prevailed upon the king to allow him to attend. Muhammad's argument was that Arabia would be seen as the "stooge" of the West if Bandar were silenced. In the end the old king relented.

Now he had arrived, and accordingly he was received with great honor and fanfare by the contingents from the more fanatical of the Arab and Muslim states present—which meant, by over fifty percent of the states represented. Tomorrow he would have his opportunity to speak to the assembled leaders of the Islamic world, to state his case in a forum where it really mattered. Tonight, he sat in his hotel suite and planned his speech.

In another part of Tunis someone else also made plans. He was Baal Bazz, the Lord of the Hawks. His plans, he knew, would be a great leap forward in his years long quest of setting his people free.

Emotions ran high the next day in the large banquet hall of the Ambassador Hotel in Tunis. The Rasheedi Prince Bandar was speaking now and the leaders of the Arab world sensed a new direction in the foreign policy of the Rasheedi regime. Finally the fabulous resources of that country would be made available to them. There was a feeling of optimism in the air, a new hope that the hated Zionists could one day be defeated. Perhaps one day soon.

At tables laden with the most exquisite delicacies—laid out in silver and crystal—were the dignitaries of many Arab nations. There was a table for the Kuwaiti contingent, one for each of the two Yemens, North and South, one for Pakistan and another for Bangladesh, one each for Iran and Iraq, several for the Egyptian entourage in order to accommodate the innumerable bureaucrats who had accompanied the president of that country; and many others. The Rasheedi contingent was seated at two large tables at which members of both political factions were intermingled—eating together in peaceful coexistence. Between the two

Joseph's Seed

Rasheedi tables sat Yassar Ararat and his contingent from the Palestinian Restoration Society.

Farthest from the dais were tables set aside for prominent Arabian businessmen and intellectuals who had been invited to attend. Two tables to the rear were occupied by the top executives of Al Tawali enterprises. Ustez Doudeen, who had led the delegation on the previous day, had been called out of town on urgent business. Professor Dowi Al Harbi was also seated at one of them looking good in his dark blue business suit. This time it was he who sat wondering while he watched his master speak.

"...everywhere," Bandar went on, "our people are rising up."Allah has provided well for us so that we may use his bounty for His glory–not for our own personal and selfish needs." He spoke of the great construction of Riyadh and about the massive irrigation project which he himself had sponsored with the aim of feeding millions of poor Muslims.

"The poor, the oppressed of the Islamic world on three continents cry for our help. And we Bismallah must help. It is not our choice. We must submit to the will of Allah. This is the meaning of our religion.

"More than any other of our people, our Palestinian brothers cry out for our assistance. Against enormous odds they have for two generations carried out their crusade. But the Satan of the West is too powerful. The Palestinian people can not prevail against him without our help–our full commitment to their cause. Their cause is our cause."

Bandar went on and on. He had much to say. At the Rasheedi tables the old King Waleed yawned. He had heard all of this before. "*Ma'alaish*, he said to one of his brothers, "did I not give the persistent Yassar Ararat another check this morning to pay his bills. He is not so bad. They tell me that the Americees treat him like an old friend–so why should I not? My young brother worries too much."

At that moment the maitre d'hotel diffidently approached Crown Prince Muhammad and whispered in his ear. The king noticed; an important message from home most likely, a financial matter perhaps. The king yawned. But Muhammad got up quietly and left the hall.

Then it happened. The explosion shook the twenty storey building but its structure held. Inside the banquet hall however, it was another matter. The blast had originated from the Palestinian table. It was clearly an assassination plot, but against whom was less sure.

The gentle King Waleed perished. With him went three of the seven princes in line for the crown ahead of Bandar. The others had not attended the conference. Fifty-four other Islamic dignitaries also perished in the rubble. Scores of others were hospitalized.

Miraculously, the inimitable Yassar Ararat emerged unscathed. Those seated at tables far removed from the Rasheedi contingent suffered the least amount of injury. Prince Bandar had thrown himself behind the dais, thus shielding himself from the flying debris. Professor Dowi Al Harbi suffered only minor cuts and scratches and was released from the hospital within a day.

Denny Rasner of Tonight's News and other famous journalists put forward theories that an extremist wing of the Palestinian Restoration Society was responsible for the massacre, although no one had taken credit. It was an act of revenge, they postulated, against the sycophant and moderate Yassar Ararat, and against the Rasheedi regime for supporting him. That wing of the Palestinian Restoration Society had not sent a representative to the convention, complaining that it was too pro-Western. For that organization then, it was business as usual.

The Kingdom of Arabia went into turmoil. But the family had suffered and survived other setbacks. It would survive this one also. Within a week, Crown Prince Muhammad was proclaimed the new king. But selection of the next crown prince took longer.

Elsewhere Sadya Bar Kama sat reading about the incident in the Evening News. "Of course," he said to himself. "But what will come next? Perhaps our Dvora will be convinced now." He picked up the phone.

– Twelve –

Jabalain

Frank passed between the two jagged peaks marking the gateway to Jabalain not long before sundown. The trip from Riyadh had taken just over ten hours, at speeds which would have earned him a revoked license back in the States.

He was tired but suddenly he began to feel exhilarated. This was a beautiful place. It seemed almost make believe. Everything was orderly and neat, but picturesque. The two small mountains he had passed upon entering the city, and the ridge of jagged peaks with their unlikely shapes which formed a back-drop to the buildings lining the main boulevard, all looked more like a painted theater set or the jacket of a science fiction novel than the real thing.

The boulevard was landscaped with large, carefully pruned date palms in a neat row down the center island. They weren't even dusty. But it wasn't just the trees–every town in the kingdom had its palms. It was the rest. Everywhere: around the palms, in the continuous roadside gardens, next to buildings, on rooftops–were green, large leafed, manicured tropical plants of all shapes and sizes. Frank didn't know their names. He had never seen anything like them before, but they struck him as remarkable nevertheless–almost enchanting.

Interspersed with the foliage were–for lack of a better word–sculptures. There were bronze and silver urns thirty feet high and other gleaming metal objects. Some of them he recognized as cups, goblets, saucers, and various other shapes. He imagined them to be a type of modern art, only they didn't look modern. Except for one which he decided must be a rendition of a telephone, most looked more like they belonged in "The Arabian Nights," or "Alice in Wonderland."

But the thing that impressed him most–though he was conscious of it more as an absence than a presence–was the city's cleanliness. There were no flattened out Pepsi and Near Beer cans strewn layers deep on the ground as was the case in many other towns throughout that country. There were no plastic shopping bags, or water bottles littering the gutters or windblown against shrubbery or buildings. There were no half-finished buildings. There were no open trenches.

Indeed, everything looked as if it had been specially prepared for Frank Costello's coming, but of course that couldn't be so. He was a nobody and he knew it. The only person who even knew he was coming was someone named Mr. Fahad, Prince Mustapha's manager with whom Frank's company, Agricultural International, had made a previous appointment and Frank had called to confirm. Mr. Fahad had postponed the interview for several weeks but finally one was granted.

Now, following the directions he had been given over the phone, he found the hotel where he had a reservation. It was not a modern place, but like everything else here, it seemed efficient, clean and well run. Frank checked in and then prepared for another day; a day which he hoped would be very profitable.

After a shower and a change of clothes, he took

dinner in the hotel's restaurant. Aside from a few European-looking businessmen eating at nearby tables, the place was empty. Frank ordered a steak, salad, "battata," which he knew would come out as French fries, and a Pepsi. He couldn't decide which country the waiter was from–India possibly. Whatever he was, he was extremely polite and he produced Frank's order within minutes. Indeed, many things here were different.

After eating, Frank retired to the TV lounge where the News-in-English, broadcast from Riyadh, was just coming on. To the tune of "What's New Pussycat," but without the words, Frank watched an array of Arabian dignitaries parading across the screen, disembarking from jets, kissing other dignitaries on cheeks, welcoming Yassar Ararat on another of his many visits.

Then the announcer, who sounded like a British professor, announced the beheading of two unnamed Filipino workers for certain undisclosed crimes. The execution was carried out, he said in his most upper crust accent, "according to the will of Allah."

After that, the announcer went on to another laudatory commentary on the latest exploits of the great freedom fighter Baal Bazz. And finally, almost as an afterthought, he announced the recent decision of King Muhammad, and approved by the royal Council of Princes, to select as his new Crown Prince the Governor of Riyadh–His Royal Highness Prince Bandar Bin Abdul Lateef.

Frank shook his head. He hoped this latest change wouldn't affect things here, especially his business prospects, though he made a mental note to tell Snead everything he had seen. The next day he was received by Mr. Fahad in a small, modern office building on the outskirts of Jabalain.

"*Shlonik*," said Fahad. "How do you do, Mr. Frank Costello?" Fahad took both his hands and smiled. He struck Frank as a Richard Pryor in Arab dress, but of course Frank didn't show it.

"Your friend, Clement, was here just yesterday. It's too bad that you missed him. He told me that you and he and some other guy had quite an adventure with an old bedouin while you were taking pictures. You should really be more careful. They are very angry with tourists now, very afraid of cameras."

Mr. Fahad's immediate intimacy took Frank by surprise, but he felt that he did an adequate job of masking it. Fahad seemed to know a lot about him. This raised many questions in Frank's mind, but he pushed them back and instead tried to be matter-of-fact and pretend as if nothing out of the ordinary were happening.

"Yeah, it was really something," said Frank. "We were just doing a little mountain climbing and that old fellow got quite upset. I couldn't understand it, but then I don't speak Arabic."

"Only a little climbing, aye," said Fahad who was smiling broadly. Then he gave Frank a slap on the back and said, "Come with me. I want to show you something."

Fahad then led Frank by the hand into another room which had an elaborate computer against a wall, and a table on which was mounted a scale model of a small modernistic town with surrounding, developed farm land. The scene looked familiar to Frank.

"That's the JADCO project," he said. "Isn't it?"

"Not exactly," said Fahad. "It is similar, but it will be much smaller than JADCO. We think it will be much better." With a stick he then pointed to some of the tiny structures which depicted buildings and other things.

"This will be a completely automated egg producing facility," he said pointing to one. "And this will be a dairy facility. Here is a research laboratory. Here, the computerized greenhouses. Prince Mustapha is interested in the kind of development which will improve the lives of the people. It isn't always true that bigger is better, although I am sure that is what you like best. Anyway, we will be big enough for you to make lots of money." Fahad gave Frank another friendly pat.

"This looks very interesting," said Frank. "But what do you have in mind? Your faxes to Agricultural International have not been very specific. We still don't know how we can help you."

"We prefer to do business in person," said Fahad. "What we would like from you for now is five large corrugated metal grain bins with augurs, elevators, climate control–everything. We have examined your product and find it acceptable so long as your bid will be reasonable. You can talk about the specifications with our engineer on the project site if you like. We can go there tomorrow."

"Okay," said Frank, shaking the Arab's hand. He hadn't expected it to be so easy. But he never argued with money. They made arrangements to meet the next day and drive together the fifty kilometers to the "prince's farm," as Fahad called it.

Frank then went back to his hotel to call AIC and Debbie and tell them the good news. He looked forward to hearing her voice, but he would talk to Debbie about little of importance over the phone for he had heard that they were bugged. When he tried to call her however, there was no answer and it was six in the morning in Spring Valley. Funny, he thought, she's been out an awful lot lately.

The first thing that José Veracruz from California, who was the farm manager and agricultural engineer of the prince's farm, said to Frank the next day when he went into his sales pitch was: "Don't Bullshit me pal. I know everything about this business and you probably don't know shit. So I'll tell you what I want, and you write it down. I got enough problems with that Cockney incompetent Flint. He's the guy putting in the irrigation and fucking it up. He's supposed to be an engineer–sheeyit. If he's one, so are you. We can't

Joseph's Seed

plant a thing till he's done. I don't need no more problems."

So Frank, who always knew how to bend with pressure. Took orders and let everybody else feel important.

Later in the day, while Fahad was giving Frank a tour of the site, a white Mercedes pulled up and a man got out. He was dressed in the usual white robe which all Arab businessmen wore, but he had nothing on his head. He was a handsome light-skinned man with a neatly trimmed mustache and luxurious black curls. He impressed Frank as having a sense of his own importance, although he spoke and acted in a casual manner.

The man and Fahad had been speaking for some time in Arabic when finally Fahad turned to Frank and said, "This is Ustez Doudeen, uh, Mr.Doudeen. He is the General Manager to the Sheikh Yusuf Al Tawali. You know, the owner of Clement's company. Mr. Doudeen would like to speak to you on a business matter. He asked me first if I would object, and of course I do not."

"It's very nice to meet you," said Mr.Doudeen in a high pitched, sing-song voice. Frank thought that his voice sounded very different in English.

"I would very much like to speak to you about a little project I have in mind. Perhaps you would care to come to my office, let's say in two or three days from now in Riyadh? We are interested in bins also but perhaps a few more than five. I will leave my telephone number and you can call me. If I am not in, you may leave a message with my secretary where you can be reached. Fine?" When he said "fine" he nearly sang it.

"Great," said Frank. "We're always willing to help in any way we can."

Frank realized that this might be something big, maybe bigger than JADCO. He had once done research on Tawali, and knew that he was the wealthiest non-

Royal personage in the kingdom–perhaps the wealthiest, period. Although there were no exact figures to be had, he knew that Al Tawali was a banking magnate with several international corporations and extensive interests in the Arab world, Europe, Brazil and New York. He had never expected that Tawali would buy from him since he had his own agricultural supply company, the one for which Clement worked. It was a conglomerate, with factories all over the world. In his new enthusiasm Frank nearly forgot about Mr. Snead and their agreement.

Who cares what their reasons are, thought Frank as he daydreamed about this new prospect, long as the green keeps rolling in.

Later, back in Jabalain, Frank and Mr. Fahad finalized the details of the new grain bin sale to Prince Mustapha's farm, including a schedule for delivery, construction, and "turn key" start up–all to be complete in four months, in time for the wheat harvest. Frank remembered what José Veracruz said, and he doubted that there would even be a planting on that farm this season, let alone a harvest, but he agreed to everything anyway.

After making tentative plans to maintain telephone contact with Fahad and to meet with him in a few weeks in order to monitor progress, Frank intended to go to the hotel to rest and prepare for the long trip back to Riyadh which he would commence at five in the morning. As he was leaving, Fahad said something strange.

"Doudeen's boss is very rich and he will promise you the world. Be careful."

That evening in the TV lounge, Frank caught the tail end of the Arabic language version of the news from Riyadh. Although he couldn't understand it, it looked essentially like the English version except that they didn't play "What's New Pussycat."

Joseph's Seed

Frank saw Arab dignitaries sitting in a majlis, drinking tea. He recognized the face of Prince Bandar, the new crown prince, who he had seen the night before. He also found that he recognized two other people in the majlis; they were the young prince Mugrin Ibn Mustapha, who Frank had encountered now twice, once at the JADCO site and once during the brouhaha at the Marriott–and Mr. Doudeen, who was wearing a headdress for this occasion and looking more somber. The scene was on film so Frank assumed that it could have been shot at any time, since Mr. Doudeen would scarcely have had time to return to Riyadh so fast, even by jet.

Frank thought again about his lovely wife and felt a pang. He would try to call her once more. He dialed the phone.

"Hello," came the familiar voice at the other end of the line. Frank breathed a sigh of relief.

"I've had trouble reaching you lately. Is anything wrong, honey? Where have you been?"

There was silence on the other end of the line for a moment, and then Debbie said," I've been busy. Look! I don't want to talk about it now. But I've decided that the next trip you make, I'm coming with you."

"Gee, I don't know if that's possible. I mean it's very hard to get visas for non-Muslim women."

"Well, all I can say is you had better try hard if you know what's good for you. That's not a threat, just a fact of life. I'm not staying alone anymore. Do you understand?"

Frank understood that he'd better not argue the point any further. "I'll try, honey," he said.

Frank was puzzled about the sudden change that had come over his wife. But there was one thing he knew. He didn't want to lose her. He intended to try to get her a visa, and if that couldn't be arranged, then he would quit his job in the kingdom and go back to selling computers.

That night, all kinds thoughts raced through Frank's

mind as he calculated every possible scenario he could think of; another guy, something he might have done wrong, his own sexual inadequacy, women's lib. . . But it was all just guesswork. He'd have to try to find out next time he saw her.

There was one thing, however, that he hadn't even imagined. He had no way of knowing that had Debbie been with him tonight watching the scene Frank had watched on TV, she would have recognized someone also. It was someone she had once known and now wanted to kill.

While Frank was preoccupied with his new worries, and had already put being a sleuth on the back burner when Mr. Doudeen presented him with the prospect of making more money than he had ever imagined, there were others who were getting or had already gotten, much closer to the heart of matters.

For one there was his wife Debbie. With the help of Sadya and Mr. Snead and information they had given her, she was preparing to come to the kingdom to begin to act out the part they had planned for her. Whether or not she had the ability to succeed was unknown but she was strongly motivated and highly intelligent, and in Sadya's opinion she had an advantage: she knew the man they were after. She knew his "psychology" as Sadya put it. She did not expect, to be sure, to kill or apprehend Ahmad personally– although the thought had crossed her mind. What she expected to do first was get information, and she had a plan to do just that.

Another person who knew more than Frank was Rex Lawton, although hitherto he had little interest in doing anything with his knowledge. Over the years, Rex had been everywhere in the kingdom, had worked for many important sheikhs and had an understanding, after his own fashion, of how the Arab mind worked. He had another advantage which could come in to play eventually. He was too numb to feel fear. And he had no real hope for life except in that dim distant gleam that somehow he would achieve happiness when he was finally home and retired in Texas.

Then there was Clement Schmidt. Besides the steadfast surety he had in his own personal worth, Clement had one advantage. He had long been a friend and confidant of Prince Mustapha, who liked the American Westerner because he never cowered or fawned. That was a refreshing change for Mustapha. Clement would thus be in a position to exert great influence when the time came. Whether he would use that influence for good or ill, however, remained unknown.

As for Mr. Snead; except for the interest he had shown in Sadya Bar Kama's manhunt, who else and what else he knew remained a mystery.

For his part, Frank was only beginning to see glimmerings of these things.

Thirteen

Man in Fatigues

At the same time that Frank was flying at ground level, traversing the seven hundred mile span of highway between Riyadh and Jabalain, listening incessantly to Willie Nelson's reveries on the subject of reincarnation and love that never dies, and trying to no avail to figure out what had suddenly gone wrong with his marriage; back in Riyadh, Rex Lawton was having troubles of his own. Clement had accompanied Rex "for moral support" to the American consulate in Riyadh. Rex was now sitting across from the consul trying to lodge a complaint against his employer, Mr. Ashamary, who had not paid Rex in six months and, apparently had no intention of doing so.

"A'll shoot the son-of-a-bitch," said Rex Lawton.

"Now calm down," said the consul. "Your best alternative, and the approach which I am obligated to advise you to take, is to try first to settle your dispute with your employer personally. If you want to take the case to labor court on the other hand, I'm not saying you won't win. What I'm saying is that you will then be subject to the laws of this country. You'll be challeng-

Joseph's Seed

ing them in effect to enforce their own laws. It could go hard on you."

"But the son-of-a-bitch robbed me of forty thousand dollars. I have a contract. I'm American for Christ sake. This is supposed to be an American Embassy."

"Please calm yourself Mr. Lawton. Firstly, this is a consulate not an embassy. Secondly, this Mr. Ashamary claims that you haven't fulfilled your side of the contract. I have a letter from him in response to my request for information on this matter. He states among other things that you have been insubordinate and have frequently been absent from the job site."

"The work was finished on schedule," insisted Rex. "I arranged everything and supervised everything. That's how I always worked since I first started with him six years ago. It's always been fine with him before. He knowed what I was like, and I knowed he was a two faced son-of-a-bitch . Only difference now is he ain't got the money. His boss Bandar has other uses for it. So he's in debt up to his ears. I'm not the only one he owes, but that don't do me no good."

"You may be right, Mr. Lawton," said the consul nervously. "Still I must advise you as I've done. I will give you an official statement from this office to that effect. To my knowledge, Mr. Ashamary has not yet lodged a complaint against you concerning your refusal to work. Should he do so the authorities may caution you or even arrest you. In such an eventuality, you should show them this letter and attempt to contact us. We would do what we could but I assure you it won't be much."

"If I get arrested, I won't be allowed no phone calls and they won't look at your letter. Thanks fer your trouble. Maybe I should be glad to get out with my skin and forget about the money."

"Well," said the consul, rising, "if there is anything else we can do, please feel free to call us. Now if you'll just wait in the lobby for a few moments, your letter will be brought out to you."

"Thanks," said Rex, "fer nothin'."

Clement was waiting in the anteroom of the consulate where Rex had left him. Sitting beside him now was a remarkable looking man–an Arab–whom Rex did not know. He and Clement were engrossed in a conversation. His face was animated with expressiveness and he seemed to be absorbed in what Clement was saying.

Now that's what they should be like, thought Rex as he approached the two men. Then he wondered why he should have such a thought. The man was dark skinned. Elsewhere he might have passed for black, but he was most definitely of bedouin stock. There was something about him though. Rex, who usually never lacked for an opinion, couldn't find the words. "He looks..." thought Rex."Hell," he shook his head, "I been in this damn place too long."

Clement looked up from under the brim of his cowboy hat and saw Rex standing there gaping. "Want you to meet Prince Mustapha–Rex Lawton," he said.

"Nice to meet you," said the Arab in an easy California accent. "But please, just Mustapha, not 'Prince' or 'Your Highness. ' You Americans don't buy that British Monarchy crap, and anyway, I hate it. So why say it?"

"First time I ever heard one of you say that," said Rex, "and I met a lot of princes during the years I been in this country."

"I'll bet you have," said Mustapha.

"Clement told me he knew you," said Rex, "did some work on your farms?"

"Only when the stuff was under warrantee. Those guys are too expensive."

"You know I don't set the prices," said Clement.

"Yeah, I know," said the prince. "It's that tightwad Tawali." They laughed. Then Mustapha turned to Rex, his smile turning to an expression of concern. "Clement tells me that you're having trouble with your sponsor. I know the man. Is there anything I can do to

Joseph's Seed

help?"

"Don't reckon I know," said Rex.

"Listen!" said Mustapha, eying four big Arabs who were standing by the doors and windows. "I've got an appointment here. Clement has the address of my villa in Riyadh. I'll be here for a week on business. Why don't you come over on Friday for lunch–say at one? We'll talk then, okay?"

At that point someone handed Rex the letter which had been prepared for him. The Americans agreed to come Friday, and took their leave. The prince then walked down the hall of the consulate. Two of the big Arabs walked ahead of him, two followed.

Mustapha's Riyadh residence was modest by the standards of Rasheedi royalty. Every top ranking prince of the royal family had a palace in Riyadh–this in addition to his normal place of residence. To be sure, Mustapha had a luxurious palace in his domain of Jabalain; in fact he had two: a newer, up to date facility had just recently been completed, and there was the ancient palace of the Rasheedi dynasty which still served many functions. But in Riyadh, although he spent much time on business there, he kept only a villa, and only one of his wives–his favorite–Rina.

The house was a white stucco structure with the usual Arabic motifs: it was surrounded by eight foot high walls the same color and style as the house. It was garish architecture, with red crenelated parapets, turrets and rounded cornices. There was a portico at the front entrance. Rex noticed that there was no one around; no workers, no guards, no princely entourage. There had been however, a few Arabs in traditional dress chatting on the walk outside the walls–including one rather large fellow.

There was nothing one could do about the house, It was a victim of circumstance–Arabian architecture implemented by Egyptian engineers–the kind of thing which Mustapha was not inclined to contest. What struck one—in this instance Rex—about this particular house was the landscaping; the courtyard with its fountains, date palms and many various tropical plants and flowers. Aside from that, everything was clean, neat and in perfect repair—a state of affairs virtually unknown in that country. Rex immediately noticed the difference and was amazed by it, but he shouldn't have been, for he had seen Jabalain since Mustapha had become its governor.

The prince answered the door himself.
"Howdy," said Clement.
"Salaam Alakum," said Rex, tipping his green "Al Tawali" cap. "Come on in," said Mustapha. He had on army fatigues with no markings. He wore no headdress. "Excuse the duds, I was doing some gardening and these are most comfortable. I have to wear traditional dress in public. Even my supporters would be shocked if I didn't. But in my private life—I allow myself. You don't mind, do you?"
"Yer kiddin'." said Rex.
A tall, beautiful woman approached them. She had long, lustrous brown hair and was dressed in a conservative, but attractive outfit. She held out her hand. "I'm Rina," she said. Now to understand the significance of the moment, one would have had to live in that country for many years as Clement and Rex had, and to have been invited into Muslim homes many times without ever having seen the woman of the house. Rina apparently was having none of that.

That being the case, and despite the fact that Clement had not seen his own wife in almost a year, and Rex hadn't had one for ten, they remembered that they were all civilized people and that no astonishment was necessary in what had just happened—except the astonishment of knowing that this wasn't done here.

Neither were they taken to the majlis, the cushion-lined room with no other furnishings, where men gathered in Arabian homes. They were led instead to a modern, comfortable den where they sat in cushioned chairs and were served drinks–non-alcoholic–by the prince.

"Sorry I can't offer you anything stronger," he said. "But that is one of my country's laws which I think is right on target. Can you imagine what our highways would be like if our people were drinking also?"

"Not a happy sight," said Clement who drove extensively every week and saw endless pileups of dead and maimed, who insisted on ignoring every rule of the road ever devised to save lives. "I guess the fact that I was once a race driver is all that has kept me alive so far. We don't need another handicap."

"No we don't," said the prince. "Our people never fail to amaze me. They are so submissive in many ways, so easily cowed and unquestioning, but get them behind the wheel and they are the bravest people I've ever seen."

"Maybe it's not a question of bravery," said Clement.

"Yes, yes, but let's mull that over later, okay? I want to talk to your friend here about a job. What do you say Rex, interested?"

"I might," said the Texan, "seein' I might be in jail soon if I don't do somethin'."

"You won't go to jail," said the prince. "I can still handle men like Hijazi Ashamary. What I propose is this. I'll have your sponsorship transferred over to my office. You'll get a new exit re-entry visa. Your sponsor will be my business manager Fahad. You can quit whenever you like, of course, I hope you won't. But if you do, I would appreciate a month's notice.

"I need you to bail me out of the mess I'm in at my new experimental farm. I have only two months to complete the irrigation project and the fellow I have just can't handle it. I'll pay you what you were making with Ashamary–when he paid you, and if the project is completed in time there will be a bonus in it for you as well. Will you do it?"

"Well," said Rex. "I reckon I ain't had enough of this

country yet. I'll do it. Besides, since I haven't got paid in so long I might not have enough for a ticket home."

"Good, come to my Riyadh office tomorrow and we'll start the ball rolling. Now let's eat. You're in for a treat today. The servants are off and Rina's cooking. If you didn't think there was such a thing as Arabic cuisine, she's going to change your minds."

No sitting on the floor here. The attractively arrayed teakwood table was laden with unfamiliar but delicious dishes identified by Rina as: *moutable, fattoush, bamya, freekeh,* and several other things. They had thick, medium-rare steaks which they learned–after they were consumed–had been camel steaks.

The after dinner conversation was casual and all four took part. Rex, as he always did, told anecdotes of the early days in the kingdom. They all agreed on how much progress had been made.

"For women, the progress has not yet come," said Rina.

"It will," consoled her husband. "But first we must have a Renaissance, a Reformation, Enlightenment, and an Industrial Revolution. Then it will be time for a women's movement. You know I'm joking dear, but seriously you know it is not time for that yet."

"Nevertheless, it would be welcome," she said. "The sooner the better."

"How serious a threat is your brother?" asked Clement then, as if he were not at all speaking out of context. "Can he succeed?"

"I have faith in our people," said the prince, frowning. "But I would not like to spoil this enjoyable day by worrying about such matters. Things as you say, have a way of working themselves out."

Later, when they had left Rex said. "I knowed you had guts Clement, but wasn't you taking a big chance back there. You know how thick that family is–no matter what it looks like to the outside."

"Just testing the waters," said Clement. "Anyway, I

don't think that's true anymore. No. I think we are in for many more significant changes. You know, if you and I weren't crazy, we'd be thinking very seriously about getting the hell out of here."

"Yeah, but we're crazy," said Rex.

Fourteen

Joseph the Tall

Yusuf Al Tawali looked like a cross between Yassar Ararat and Buddha. He dressed like a Rasheedi Arab and was obviously of Arabian stock, but he had the demeanor of a guru–of a man who was totally beyond material concerns. It was rumored that he was worth many billions of dollars, but no one, not his four eldest sons who managed the various tentacles of his far reaching empire, not his many Egyptian accountants, no one–with the possible exception of his personal and business manager Ustez Doudeen, knew for sure.

He had many sons, grandsons, and great-grand sons. He had business interests all over the world. He owned European and American conglomerates. He owned mines in South America, plantations in the Philippines and Africa, an export company in Hong Kong, and a Korean Construction Company. He had a chain of banks and another chain of chicken restaurants throughout the Arab world. He lent money to governments–and was paid back.

Coming from a long line of merchants, slave traders, and money lenders, he was already a millionaire

Joseph's Seed

sixty years earlier, with business networks and connections throughout the Arab world. During the great Abdul Lateef's rise to power, he had been a major financial backer of the latter when Abdul Lateef was a penniless adventurer, and thus helped to make possible the unification of Arabia. Later when King Abdul Lateef had tried to conquer Yemen, Kuwait, Iraq; Al Tawali became a major impediment to the King's ambitions by lending money to his adversaries. He had not wanted the king to become too powerful.

But the king was satisfied with what help he did receive and accordingly bestowed due honors on Al Tawali. In later years, when the Rasheedi oil wealth began to amass, Tawali was granted concessions, monopolies, land, and other favors; first by King Abdul Lateef himself and then, after his death, by his sons. Thus Yusuf Al Tawali's growth had paralleled that of the Kingdom of Arabia.

During his ninety-three years he had acquired perhaps as much as any man living. It would seem, then that there could be nothing more to want. But it is said that the human spirit is unquenchable. As much as a soul may acquire, there is always more to desire. At age ninety-two he had purchased a beautiful Rasheedi princess for a wife for the sum of five million dollars. She was fifteen years of age.

Beside this latest carnal interest, he turned also to the sublime. He began to think of religion with a renewed fervor–and in a new light.

If it is possible for a Muslim to be an atheist, Al Tawali was. Although he went through the outward motions of the prayer ritual whenever he was in the public eye, he was by nature a thorough going materialist–that is, until recently.

Of late, a change had come over him. Instead of his old sole preoccupations with business and pleasure, he was lately referring more and more to what he called his "Islamic duty." He began to speak to the endless stream of people who made the "pilgrimage" to visit him in his isolated desert palace seeking favors and handouts, of the need to turn the world once more to the ways of Allah. He spoke abstractly of things which many who knew him thought were uncharacteristic–of the coming unification of the world's religions according to the true path set forth by the Prophet Muhammad– and of the one who would come after him.

This last struck people as very odd since the idea of messianism, though it exists, is not important in Islam; and most unusual to be coming from the mouth of Yusuf Al Tawali. People who knew him began to suspect that age had eroded the great man's mind. In his increasingly rare excursions away from his desert retreat, his General Manager Ustez Doudeen was almost always seen in his presence, apparently to protect the old man from himself. Recently, the great sheikh had had a massive stroke. Miraculously, he emerged from it physically as active as ever– still desirous of his now sixteen year old wife. One thing had changed however; his faculty of speech had become grossly impaired, his former command of language having been reduced to a few words and phrases. Everyone knew that the end was near. Of late, Ustez Doudeen had assumed the role of the sheikh's spokesman, especially when they ventured away from Tawali's desert retreat.

Today was one of those occasions. Al Tawali and Ustez Doudeen sat comfortably in the back seat of a white, custom built Mercedes. The Sheikh's new personal chauffeur, Muhammad Ali the Yemeni, was taking them to Riyadh to meet with a salesman from a company that could supply them with grain bins.

"We should, ya sheikh, begin with a purchase of five hundred of these corn storage machines," said Ustez Doudeen as they were driven over the unpaved desert trail in air conditioned comfort. "This would suit our needs at present, but we will surely need more next year. Fine?"

"*Al hamdillilah,*" said the old sheikh.

Fifteen

In the Empire State Building

When Frank called his supervisor at Agricultural International to tell him of Debbie's request, the latter frowned upon the idea of Frank attempting to bring his wife with him on his next trip to the kingdom, and tried to talk him out of it.

"Why spoil a good thing?" The supervisor complained. "Your sales potential–and commissions–are fantastic for the near future. Why jeopardize that? With this new Al Tawali connection the sky's the limit. Frankly, I can't understand your attitude. Your wife should be willing to make a small sacrifice. Of course, if you're not happy with us, there are plenty of other people willing to earn the kind of commissions you've been earning lately. It must be fairly easy since you're doing it. I might go there myself."

"Nevertheless," Frank insisted. "I would appreciate it if you would submit my request. I'll be coming home next week. You can give me your answer then. If it's no, then I guess you can take my place because I won't be going back. It wouldn't be worth it."

"I'll see what I can do," said the supervisor gruffly.

"In the meantime, don't botch the Al Tawali deal. It could increase the value of AIC stock by two dollars a share."

A week later Frank and Debbie were going up the elevator to the eighty-fourth floor in the Empire State Building where the international sales offices of AIC were located. Apparently there had been a change of heart on the part of the supervisor. The visa had been processed and was already waiting in his office to be picked up.

"Good morning Frank, Debbie," said the supervisor cheerfully when they entered his office. "Great job on the Al Tawali deal. Everything is preceding full speed ahead. No problem with credit on that one, heh, heh, heh. He owns the bank.

"Here's the visa, Mrs. Costello. Don't know how your husband did it. Day after I put in the request–which I did incidentally immediately after he called–phones started ringing off the hook. Vice president in charge of sales, Chairman of the Board, even the Old Man called and I never hear from him. 'Get that man what he wants,' he tells me. So who am I to argue?

"Apparently they all think you're doing a fantastic job out there. So I guess I do too. Incidentally, I was instructed to give you this little check–an early bonus–in appreciation for the extra effort you've been making. You have a real team spirit, Frank. Keep up the good work."

"Thanks," said Frank.

The day before was Frank's first day home in a month. One of the first things he did was to call Mr. Snead in Trenton. He was told that Mr. Snead was not in but that he would return the call as soon as possible. He never did.

Frank noticed immediately that something was bothering his wife. When he asked her what it was, she avoided the subject. He knew better than to push her. Before they went to bed, Frank again tried to get Debbie

Joseph's Seed

to talk about it, but she couldn't be pinned down.

"Nothing's the matter," she insisted. "I just wanted to come with you this time. That's all. I knew that unless I acted determined about it you wouldn't take me seriously."

"You know I always take you seriously, honey," he said. "I just didn't think it could be done so easily. That part really surprised me."

"Be that as it may," said Debbie. "I'm going. I have to do some shopping tomorrow. I'll need different clothes–conservative things. Want to come?"

"Sure," said Frank.

When they made love the worry pain returned to Frank. This was the first time that Frank could remember that he actually had to initiate things. Usually she was all over him. This was different–but still– not bad.

"Is anything wrong, honey?" he asked her once.

"No. Do you think there is?"

"Well, not exactly."

"Then shut up and come here," she said.

"Things could be worse," thought Frank. Then the worry pain disappeared.

Sixteen

A Short Fuse

The *Majlis*, besides being a cushioned lined room devoid of all other furnishings in Arabian homes, was also an institution. It was the time honored tradition in which kings, princes, and tribal leaders would sit down as equals with the lowliest bedouin to share coffee and dates, and to hear their complaints and petitions. It was the democratic forum of the desert where almost anyone who wished could attend, even ones enemy's son. It was therefore a setting which more than once in the history of Arabia had provided ample opportunity for assassinations.

So it had at one such majlis held by the newly appointed Crown Prince Bandar, next in line for the kingship of Arabia.

Several men of prominence were in attendance at this session in addition to the many common bedouin who came and went. The businessman Hijazi Ashamary was there, as was the high powered executive Ustez Doudeen with his chauffeur Muhammad Ali the Yemeni. The young Prince Mugrin Bin Mustapha was also in attendance. He seemed to be brooding because the new Crown Prince had refused to hear his petition to order the break up of the JADCO project into smaller,

Joseph's Seed

more manageable units.

At the end of the majlis when the men were standing to offer homage and farewells to their prince, the young prince Mugrin struck. Swiftly he lunged out at Bandar with his dagger. The crown prince tried to move from the knife's path but still it entered deeply into his shoulder. Just as Mugrin pulled out his knife and tried to lunge again, someone clubbed him over the head with a cane. It was Doudeen's chauffeur, Muhammad Ali the Yemeni. When the unconscious Mugrin was dragged away, the bleeding crown prince, having regained his composure somewhat, turned to the Yemeni and said: "You will be greatly rewarded."

Denny Rasner had even less luck figuring out the latest imbroglio emanating from the Kingdom of Arabia then he had in previous attempts. No one in fact could make much sense of it. Finally they concluded that it had been nothing more than the act of a disgruntled youth spoiled by extravagant wealth, indulged all his life, allowed to act out his every whim, seeped in the hopeless political turmoil of the region, overly protected by his father.

This time his father, though he might a powerful man, could not help him. The young Prince Mugrin, son of Prince Mustapha, emir of the province of Jabalain would be executed by beheading. It was announced first in the Riyadh News and then relayed to the syndicates of the West.

At a time when stability had only briefly been restored to the kingdom following the assassination of the late King Waleed one month earlier, there was no choice. The boy would have to pay. Failure to condemn this act of the young hothead Mugrin would set brother against brother, tribe against tribe–it would mean civil war.

The crown prince had not been seriously hurt, but it was announced nevertheless that after a planned investigation to determine if the would-be assassin was part of a wider political plot to destabilize the kingdom, possibly led by his father, the assailant was to be executed according to the will of Allah. It was desert justice. It was barbaric. Mustapha could do nothing to stop it, in fact he publicly agreed with the verdict. It was a hot news story. Denny Rasner ran it for three days.

When Frank saw it on the News-in-English on Riyadh TV, he shook his head as he always did when he encountered things which seemed too dumb to be comprehensible.

"I met that fellow twice," he told his wife. "He tried to pay for pivots on the spot with a fist full of hundred dollar bills. What a stupid way to throw away your life."

Debbie was lying on the bed next to his in their room at the Hotel Marriott in Riyadh. They had arrived in the kingdom together two days earlier.

"His father is one of my customers–though I haven't actually met him yet. I bet he's upset–but maybe not. I guess they don't value life the way we do."

She was sipping a Perrier, wearing shorts and a monogrammed tee shirt with a picture of a beagle on it which she had just put on. The heat was oppressive to her even though it was already late autumn. She felt horrible. Maybe it was jet lag, she thought. They had just returned to their room from an exhaustingly frustrating day in Riyadh's traffic. She longed to go swimming in the hotel's luxurious pool but knew she couldn't–no women allowed, especially not in bathing suits–so she had settled for a shower.

Oh well, she sighed to herself. She had been warned about what to expect here; ankle length black dresses, no skin showing except the face and hands. The kingdom was modernizing; they allowed her that much.

She was advised to cover her hair though. With her looks, although it was technically not required of non-Muslim women to do so, it would be a good idea. She refused.

"Where did you meet him?" asked Debbie, suddenly interested in what her husband was saying. "Tell me all about it."

"Not much to tell," said Frank. She got up, went over to his bed and cuddled up against him.

"Be that as it may," she said. "I want to know. Tell me." She tickled his ribs.

The kingdom was never like this before, he thought to himself. He was beginning to like the idea of bringing her on this trip. He told her. While doing so, he had a thought; this country could be on the brink. But he didn't say it.

🐪 🐪 🐪

In another part of that country a few days later, was a father who very much valued the life of his son.

"What do you expect me to do," he said to his friend Clement, not caring very much about protocol at the moment. It was more a statement than a question for he knew the answer. He felt, or wanted to feel, he could be truthful with this American and that what he said would not go beyond them. He needed someone to talk to who wasn't directly involved in all this. But sometimes he believed that he was making a mistake to trust this particular man. Right now he didn't care.

"What should I do? Go out for revenge? Start a war? No, my brother did what the people expect him to do. Nothing more. He is more clever than I have given him credit for being. My son, Mugrin was a fool to try what he did. It could accomplish nothing."

"He could have succeeded."

"That is possible." The prince smiled almost proudly. "But the truth is he failed. My son has not enough ability to suffer and bide his time."

"A short fuse," said Clement.

"What did you say?"

"Oh," said the American. "Just a figure of speech–I said your boy has a short fuse."

Mustapha then released the falcon which had been fettered to his padded wrist. It flew rapidly in a large arc and then began its descent on the lame bustard which had been set in position for that purpose. The crippled creature, which even in a healthy state could run very rapidly but could not fly, tried in vain to escape and would have been an easy kill were it not for the electronic sounding device fastened to the falcon's neck and activated by one of Mustapha's men who now called the bird back to its master's wrist in the nick of time. The bird obeyed. This was training time for Mustapha's birds of prey, and they were doing well.

Mustapha then took the bird to its block–a stake hammered into the sand, which resembled a large golf tee–and carefully shackled the bird to it. The falcon fluttered its wings in indignant protest. He gave the bird a chunk of raw meat while one of his men retrieved the bustard and carried it back to its cage to work another day. The man was a huge bedouin named Abdullah, who Clement had seen many times with the prince, including the day he had met Rex at the Consulate, and when they had visited Mustapha's Riyadh villa.

Clement had arrived not long ago at the prince's farm knowing that his friend would be there that day. He knew this was where Mustapha went to relax–and to think. His getting away time was more important now than ever; for his burdens were heavy. But Clement knew the prince would not stay long. When he left, Clement would check up on his old buddy Rex.

"What will you do about it then?" asked the American. "I don't believe it'll be nothing."

Mustapha stared for a long moment at the other and then said, "First, my brother must do his worst.

Until then I can not act. When that time comes, I will need allies. My people will be too caught up in their own emotions to be of much help in saving themselves. They will be then like my crippled bustards–easily used, easily killed, unable even to run. Some will have courage, but many will not. No, I will need stronger creatures for my battle. If my son dies before that time, then it is God's will. Are you surprised to hear me say that? But I believe it completely. Do not forget that I am a bedouin."

Clement found Rex in a trench two hours later. He was arguing with the foreman of the pipe-laying crew, a man named Ranji.

"God dammit, Ranji," yelled the old Texan. "I don't care what Flint told you. That's not the way you lay pipe. It would take a week for this line alone."

"But Mr.Rex," said Ranji. "We not like you. You big. We small. We can not do what you say. You send us home, okay? Maybe that better." The Sri Lankan then gave some polite sounding instructions to his crewmen and they proceeded slowly to fasten an elaborate clamp contraption attached by a hand winch to two adjacent sections of the heavy, ten inch PVC mainline they were laying. Each clamp had four industrial sized flange bolts to be tightened, which, as they became exposed to the sand, took progressively longer to do each time. Then the winch had to be adjusted and the pipe aligned. Down trench, a Filipino back-hoe operator was gingerly lowering sections of pipe into the trench he had dug one month earlier. The whole process of joining one section of pipe to another took an hour.

"Bee Jesus," said Rex, throwing up his hands in frustration. "You guys are just like the union boys back in the states. You can't do it like that–we'll never get done in time."

"Then we will finish next year," said Ranji rolling his head in a circular motion. "We will still be here. We have two year contract. Two hundred dollar a month–

all money we send home. We stay here long time—unless you send us home boss, but maybe prince not like that. Nobody to work after that."

"All right, all right," said Rex. "Boy I wish I had Alex here right now. He's a Filipino—your size, but he'd work circles around you.

"Ranji, tell your boys to take a break. Drink tea, alright?

Clement, give me a hand fer a few seconds, will ya?"

After the six crewmen and the back-hoe operator had gotten clear of the trench, Rex and Clement moved down the length of the trench carefully but quickly dropping ten lengths of pipe into the trench by hand. Then they went back to the point where the Sri Lankans had left off and jumped into the five foot deep trench. Rex removed the red checked gutra he had wrapped around his neck like a bandanna, pulled the hard rubber gasket out of the belled "female" end of the pipe, wiped it clean and replaced it. Then he took some soapy looking lubricant from a can which had been left in the sand by the joint, and smeared it on the gasket and the "male" end of the adjacent pipe with his fingers. After that, Clement changed places with him and picked up the pipe while Rex moved to the other end of the joint to be inserted. Clement carefully placed the lubricated pipe into the "female" end with the hard gasket in it and held it up a few inches to align it while Rex took the other end in his hands. He straddled the pipe with his back facing Clement. Then with one lunge backwards and a snap of the wrist, he popped the length of pipe six inches into the other. They repeated the process ten times and were done before the men had finished their tea.

"It's all a matter of finding the hole and not letting the rubber slip," said Rex. "Almost thought I forgot how." Clement chuckled, hopped out of the trench, shook the sand out of his straw cowboy hat and put it back on.

Joseph's Seed

"Now you boys try it," said Rex to the crew.

"We cannot do," said Ranji, his head moving in a circular motion. "We not strong enough."

Rex went over to an old Nissan Patrol and took out a long steel bar with a pointed end. "You don't have to do it by hand like I done. You use this to push the pipe. If it takes three men to do it, then use three, or four. It don't make no never mind. But that's the idea–like we just showed you. I'll work with you. This line will be done today, I reckon."

That evening while Rex and Clement were eating some cinnamon flavored mutton stew, Rex muttered," I can take a lot of things, but one thing I'll never be able to stand is Indian cooking. I tell Abu Baker, the cook, I want something different, an' you know what he says? 'I Indian cook,' he says. 'I cook Indian food.' Bee Jesus, this job is harder than I thought it would be."

"Tastes good to me," said Clement, chewing a mouthful.

"When I try to get any cooperation from that Mexican farm manager of his," continued Rex," all he ever says to me is, 'I ain't got no time now man–come back later.' I don't know if I can get done in time like I promised the prince. This is pretty bad."

"You'll do it," said Clement.

"I know," said the old Texan.

"How's he been acting lately?" asked Clement then. They both knew who they were talking about, and why the subject had changed.

"You can tell he ain't happy about it. Though he don't say much. He comes down to the farm a couple of times a week, does some disking or runs the crane to unload materials–anything to keep his mind off his problems, I guess.

"Day after they caught his boy, he came over to where we was flushing out a new well–couldn't get the sand to clear out for days and he asks me how I'm doin'. He thanks me for how much I'm helpin' him. I ain't done nothin'. I never seen one like him before and that's a fact."

"How long do you think they'll wait before they chop him?" asked Clement.

"From what I seen other times, at least a month, probably more. They'll be up front about this one. I mean, they won't keep it a secret. I think they're trying to goad him into doin' something stupid, so's they can finish him. It's the father they're after, not the son."

"Obviously."

"If I were him," said the old timer, "I'd go for it. That Bandar is a bastard. He'll ruin this country if he gets the chance. He's got to be stopped and there's no one else to do it."

"It's too early," said Clement. "He'd lose. What he needs to do will take years, not months. Even then, I don't know if it can be done. This part of the world is radicalizing at a rapid pace. The numbers are working against him. In any event, if he tried to rescue his son now, he'd never succeed. There's too much to lose."

Rex ate quietly for a few moments chewing slowly, and then he looked up and said, "I don't agree with you, amigo. I think it can be done. If a body knowed Riyadh like the back of his hand; if he had a little help in the right places; if he had some hardware; if he didn't rightly care if he lived or not.

"I know someone who's got nothin' to lose old buddy."

Seventeen

Shareef

"What a knock out."

"I beg your pardon," said Frank to the receptionist.

"Ahh, nothing, sir. It was just something I heard in an old Bogie movie I saw back in Egypt. I meant no disrespect, ma'am. It just slipped out."

"It's okay," Debbie smiled at the young man. He had the kind of face that's hard to get mad at. Funny—only it didn't seem as if he were actually trying to be. He was wearing a reasonable facsimile of Western clothing, but they were ill fitting and improperly matched. On his feet were bathroom togs. On his head was an Al Tawali "baseball" cap, but he had the visor facing backwards. He was the receptionist at Al Tawali Establishment, International Sales and Purchases Division. Frank had an appointment with Mr. Doudeen here and took Debbie with him as he had taken her everywhere for the past months. Slowly, but surely, she was becoming acclimated.

"Mr. Doudeen will be able to see you very soon, sir. In the meantime, would you please sit down? Care for some tea? Cream and sugar–or straight?" When he got up to prepare their tea, they could see that he was fairly tall–around six feet, but weighed little more than one hundred pounds. Frank felt macho by comparison, a feeling he rarely had.

The receptionist brought the tea, handed a mug each to Frank and Debbie, then sat down at his desk on which was a personal computer, three phones, a large English-Arabic dictionary, piles of paper and envelopes, and a stack of old dog-eared paperback books. He resumed the typing job he had interrupted when they came in. Occasionally a phone rang and he would slip easily into Arabic or English, depending on the caller's preference.

Presently he hung up the phone and said: "Mr. Doudeen will see you now, sir." As Debbie got up to go in also, the receptionist added: "Would you kindly wait here ma'am? Your husband shall only be gone a short while. Professor Doudeen prefers it this way."

Debbie sat back down. She was quite used to the routine by now. She was either ogled or snubbed–but never treated with respect.

She was being ogled now, but this was different somehow. This man seemed harmless enough–almost desperate in a pathetic way. It was just a feeling though. She knew she could be wrong. She had been wrong about Arabs before.

"What's your name?" she asked him instead of getting mad.

"Shareef, ma'am. At your service. The sheriff of the front office."

She smiled. Bad joke–but he was cute in a weird sort of way. Despite her better judgment, she was beginning to like him.

"Hi, I'm Debbie," she said. "Where did you learn to speak English so well? I'll bet you've been to the States."

"Don't I wish," he said. "Actually I studied the fundamentals at the University of Cairo. I have a B. S. in Engineering with a minor in English. Apropos, don't you think? Since I do nothing but b.s. But seriously, the English they teach there is roughly equivalent to the Arabic they speak in Upper Egypt. In other words, real bad. So I fine tuned my grammar by watching old American movies over and over. I know Bogie like the back of my hand. I prefer Randolph Scott to the Duke, and I modeled myself after Satch in the Bowery Boys."

Debbie laughed, thinking hard to recall the actors he had mentioned from the old movies she had seen on occasion. She faked it. "I thought something looked familiar about you."

"I also got a lot of my words straight from the horse's mouth. I used to spend my summers in Sharm El Sheikh and met lots of American girls there."

"Oh?" The smile disappeared from her face. "What's it like there? I've heard of it." She had read of the glory days when Sharm El Sheikh was in Israeli hands. That episode had become but a fleeting memory.

"Great place. Nothing like this dump. They have a great beach there where you can skinny dip–a real tourist trap."

"You don't like it here?" she said, ignoring his come-on like she always did. "Then why did you come."

"Like it? I hate these people's guts. Pompous and stupid. But they have the dough. That's why everybody's here. Wouldn't you agree? To get some of the dough. How about you and your hubby? Isn't that why you're here?" The Egyptian eyed her slyly.

"I suppose you're right," admitted Debbie.

At that moment Frank walked out with Mr. Doudeen.

"This is my wife, Debbie Costello–Mr. Doudeen, General Manager of Tawali Enterprises." Mr. Doudeen took her hand daintily.

"Very pleased to meet you, Mrs. Costello. We are extremely pleased with the service your husband's company has given us thus far. And I am pleased to inform you that the Sheikh, Mr. Al Tawali himself, has extended an invitation for your husband and yourself to take a tour of his farm in Wadiya this Friday. It's not too far from here. But for your comfort, we shall provide a guide. Mr. Shareef here will have the honor.

Fine?"

On Friday Shareef showed up at the Marriott to pick up Frank and Debbie. He was wearing a new Hawaiian shirt and white slacks, but still had on the Al Tawali cap and bathroom togs. This time, however the cap's visor was facing front but was bent upward. He led them to a white Mercedes and held open the door for his charges. "Chauffeur Shareef, at you service," he bowed. Frank looked at him quizzically. Debbie laughed.

Then he drove them through Riyadh's street maze for a half hour with his hand on the horn the whole time. After that they drove at one hundred forty kph for an hour on a new black top highway, and after that another half hour on a bumpy desert trail at one hundred, until finally they reached the majestic white palace of Yusuf Al Tawali situated at the top of a mountainous sand dune.

Surrounding the palace was an expanse of several thousand acres of cultivated and irrigated farm land. Encircling the entire farm was a ten foot high stone wall. There was an armed guard at the entrance gate, but he let them through with a simple look inside and a wave of his hand.

When they approached the palace, however, an Arab motioned the car to stop and then talked to Shareef for a few minutes. He looked into the car at Debbie several times and each time shook his head. Finally Shareef turned around to her and said: "This birdbrain won't let you go in unless you cover your face with a black rag and go to the women's quarters. He said he will escort you."

"Balls," said Debbie. "I'll wait here."

Just then Ustez Doudeen came out. He said something to the Arab who then walked away from them and into the house.

"Please," he said. "My humble apologies, but there is a little problem. We have some representatives from

Joseph's Seed

the religious leadership visiting today. Normally the sheikh would have no difficulties receiving Mrs. Costello in a manner satisfactory to her. However, we can not anger these men. They have considerable influence in Riyadh.

"Perhaps if Mrs. Costello would not mind remaining in the comfort of my Mercedes with Mr. Shareef–who is an educated man and a perfect gentleman–for some short time–perhaps one-half hour only. I will have refreshments brought out and will send a servant who will show you to private rest rooms if they are needed.

"Mr. Costello can make his appearance to the sheikh and his guests in the sitting room, just to drink a glass of tea and coffee. After that, the sheikh and I will join you for a tour of the farm which will be conducted by Mr. Wolfgang Dietrich, our farm manager. Fine?"

"Fine," said Debbie. "Go ahead in, Frank, I'll be alright."

As soon as they were alone, Shareef started talking. "These damn Arabs and their laws. A guy can't even live like a human being. You know how hard it is to get laid here?–Oops, I'm sorry. I probably shouldn't say that."

"Don't worry about it," she said. "It won't go past me."

Shareef then put his arm on the seat back and twisted around to look at her for a long moment, finally he said in his best Egyptian Bogart voice, "I wish I had a sweetheart like you, but life never dealt me the cards." He stared at her for a few moments longer until she spoke.

"Forget it. There's no chance," she said.

"Too bad," he said looking sad. "Anyway," he smiled, "I get to live once in a while. I found a cute little bedouin girl once. Her husband never even suspected."

"You did? But how can you tell what they look like under the veil?"

"You have to go by their voices. A lot of lonely women call me on the phone–you know–the handyman receptionist? You learn to feel them out by their voices–of course it's not foolproof."

"Isn't that dangerous?" asked Debbie, quite incredulous. "I mean I thought they behead you for adultery here."

"They have to catch you first. But imagine how hard that would be with everybody's face covered. I mean, if I walk down the street with a lady, her husband could go right past us and never even know it. Believe me I've done it a few times.

"*Meshugah*," said Debbie.

"What?"

"Nothing."

Eighteen

Junk in Neat Rows

Around an hour later, a luxury model Toyota Land Rover pulled up next to the Mercedes. A burly man dressed for work got out and bent over the Mercedes to look in.

"Is this Mrs. Costello?" he inquired. "If so, I vas sent to pick you up. The sheikh will meet us with your husband at the rear entrance to the house–it is easier for the old man that way. Your driver can wait here." Shareef started to say something, but the big man gave him a cold, hard stare. Shareef closed his mouth.

As the man drove Debbie the quarter mile to the rear of the palace, he said, "I'm Wolfgang Dietrich, manager of this place. Pleased to meet you. We get a lot of guests here. Last week I conducted a tour for Yassar Ararat–you know of him? I must say, you are much better looking."

"Thanks," said Debbie, looking straight ahead.

The ancient sheikh was holding Frank's hand when they approached in the Land Rover. Ustez Doudeen waved. The three men got into the back seat, leaving Debbie to sit in the front with Dietrich.

"The sheikh extends his profound apologies to you, madam," said Ustez Doudeen. He wishes to make it up to you by extending to both of you an invitation to a celebration next week at his Riyadh villa. The Crown Prince Bandar will be in attendance. It will be the sheikh's ninety-fourth birthday. You will come? Fine?"

"We appreciate it," said Frank. "We'll be glad to come. And please tell the sheikh that my wife has no ill feelings about what happened today. She understands completely."

Ustez Doudeen explained all this to the sheikh.

"*Al hamdillila.*" said the sheikh.

The tour began with the circumvention of the farm's "junk yard." Piles of discarded machinery, metal parts and debris of all description were neatly arranged and stacked in rows.

"You may not think that a farm's efficiency has anything to do with how one manages refuse. But the two are intricately related. I assure you." Dietrich then drove past scores of large circular irrigated fields which were at varying stages of growth and some of which were lying fallow. Arranged neatly in rows in the spaces between the circles were numerous farm tractors, trucks, combines, and cultivating equipment. While he drove, Dietrich carefully explained his farming methods and why they resulted in outstanding yields year after year. Throughout his lecture he interjected anecdotes about his hero–another great planner–Bismarck.

"...and you may vonder why we build these dikes here in the desert," Dietrich was saying as they drove over an extended curving road that had been built up twenty feet higher than the normal lay of the land. "You may think that we must worry about lack of water when actually our biggest concern is that at certain times in the year there is too much water. The farm lies in a vadi. When the rains come the vadi becomes a river. It could wash away all of my efforts. Thus I build dikes or levies as you call them."

"Of course," said Ustez Doudeen, "Mr. Dietrich's

outstanding methods and results can not be matched yet by the normal bedouin farmers, but it is the sheikh's hope that by the example he sets our people will learn to improve."

"*Al hamdillila*," said the old sheikh.

"What grain storage capacity do you have at present," asked Frank. Our bins will not be in place for months. What will you use in the meantime? This is just too big of an operation for the Riyadh elevators to handle."

"You are correct," said Mr. Doudeen. "Of course most of the corn storage bins you are providing us will be sold to our customers–although we will use some for our farms. But Mr. Dietrich has already made considerable advances in that area. We will show you on the way back to the palace."

Soon they drove into a large asphalt paved area in which were situated seven corrugated metal buildings each roughly the size of an airplane hangar. They parked, went over to one and entered it. Inside was a mountain of wheat.

"We store the grain in this way because it is easier to monitor," said Dietrich, "to protect from rodent infestation and disease. Of course during the rains, the driers provided in your bins would be preferable, but so far we have managed to keep our grain dry for several years, and you can see our capacity is quite large. I have still enough space for one more harvest."

Then Debbie asked, "How long will it stay here before it goes to market? I imagine that sooner or later it would rot here, wouldn't it? I mean, when do you sell?"

Dietrich turned to Debbie, looked at her for a moment, then smiled and said, "Do you know the Bible story of Joseph and the Pharaoh? Joseph kept the grain of Egypt in storage for seven years, thereby protecting the people from the famine which followed during the next seven years.

"Actually the grain can be stored indefinitely. In excavations of the ancient pyramids, archaeologists have found that cereal grains preserved for thousands of years have still been able to germinate and so were still edible."

"That's very interesting," said Debbie. "I didn't know that."

Nineteen

The Inner Circle

Hijazi Bin Ashamary was proud of his handiwork. As he stood surveying the green fields around him, he thought that it was because of him that all this existed. Because of him, thousands who wouldn't have otherwise been fed might now find sustenance. Perhaps some of the grain that he had caused to grow here could be donated to help the starving in the nearby famine stricken countries of Ethiopia and Somalia. Perhaps some would be used as a tool for Arabian diplomacy. Much of it, he knew, would be stored until such time as it was needed.

There were already immense stores in the land, enough to pale those of the ancient Egyptian Prophet Joseph, and this was just the beginning. The new grain storage bins–one hundred in number–for this, the kingdom's largest agricultural project, were even now being raised.

Five hundred, quarter-mile radius circles of wheat were now green and knee high. Dark green, as far as the eye could see, where not long before had been only sand. It gave him a good feeling to watch the sun play on their green leaves as the short stalks of wheat fluttered in the gentle breeze. It was a special fast growing and hearty variety imported from America, able to withstand the harsh climate and the hot, saline water being pumped up from deep below the desert's surface.

Some said the water wouldn't last longer than a few years but Hijazi Ashamary knew, *Inshalla*, that it would always be there. Allah would provide. He had given them oil, so why not water? Hadn't He provided so much already?

He looked at the giant circular sprinkling machines. He could see a score of them from the knoll on which he stood. They moved so slowly you could hardly detect their motion. Like the growing grain, he thought–like the growing strength of his country. You couldn't see that growth either, but it was happening; was it not? Soon there would be a great harvest, *Inshalla*. And the new storage bins would be filled.

Yes he, like the great Prince Bandar, had many enemies. But this project–the job to which he had devoted the last five years of his life–was a success. JADCO was his accomplishment and today he would be praised by many princes.

He watched the festive tents being raised in the dry triangle of sand which lay between three circling sprinkling machines. He saw the hovering Army helicopters bringing dignitaries over from the tour they had just made of the newly completed King Waleed Military City nearby.

He was almost happy. Perhaps he could have been happy had he no conscience, if such a thing were possible. But he had; he was human. He knew that he had not made this. Others had, especially one other whom he had treated with malice. Then, because of trouble with his creditors, greedy men who weren't willing to sacrifice for his cause, who selfishly made problems for him, he hadn't even been allowed to complete the project. The JADCO committee had given the construction of grain bins over to Yusuf Al Tawali who had sold the contract to Mr. Frank Costello's company.

Ma'alaish, he thought, what of it. He had completed most of it himself single handedly, hadn't he? Or at least Rex Lawton had, under his guidance. As for the salesman, Mr. Costello, he was nobody; anyone at all could have provided his service. He, Ashamary was the fountainhead; he needed to feel important. He had to have something to be proud of. He tried to feel it again, but it was gone and there was no time to conjure up another illusion. The princes were coming. They had allowed him to supervise the preparation of tents and food for this important occasion, and it was almost time to start. He made haste–for in his heart he knew he was no more than the servant of his betters.

The leading princes of the land and their chief aids sat now on the ground in three circles at the center of a cluster of tents which were at the center of a cluster of circling irrigation machines, at the center of their universe. They were eating goat meat with their hands as their people had always done. Though they could easily have afforded to have a five-star hotel built on this very spot and to be served by French chefs; they preferred this simplicity instead. They liked the feel of the desert at their feet, even though it was a rapidly changing desert. They sat now in a dry oasis in the midst of miles of wetness.

This was the first meeting of the Council of Princes in some time and much had changed. Today, Crown Prince Bandar intended to defend those changes against the challenges of men who were still theoretically his peers. It was true that many of them were his brothers or half-brothers, but that no longer mattered. This was the business of government and he, Bandar, was now its effective head. After food had been eaten and many pleasantries exchanged, Prince Bandar began to speak.

"I decided on this location for a royal majlis at which my distinguished brothers might convene," he was saying, "as a symbol. It is a symbol of what has been accomplished and what we are capable of accomplishing. After the death of our beloved King Waleed, and the ascension of Muhammad as king–who could not attend this meeting for reasons of ill health–and myself as his right hand; and as such the burdens of rule have born down on me heavily. Still we are moving forward rapidly, our power is increasing beyond imagination, and our finest hour is yet ahead–of this, however, we will speak at a later time. For now, my brothers, the ministers will speak of the current state of our land and what shall be expected of each of you in the near future. There is some resistance, I know, to my programs. I have called this majlis, among other reasons, to dispel the fears which give rise to that resistance."

Then the minister of defense, Prince Rasheed, made his report.

"All of the kingdom's moneys which had been previously used for business growth and development," he reported, "are now diverted to accelerate the completion of all military projects in progress. The King Waleed Military City, the largest of these, was thus finished years ahead of schedule.

"We have just signed a new contract with Strupp Corporation, the great Brazilian armament industry. They will be installing a strategic defense system, at several of our military cities. Such a system is hitherto unknown in this part of the world. I estimate another year, *inshalla*, until we reach a level of strength sufficient to defeat the Zionists."

Next Dowi Al Harbi, Bandar's chief aid spoke. "The party of his Royal Highness Bandar Jibreen has now become more confident of success," the eminent Palestinian informed the princes. "Although Arabians have long supported the Palestinians in their righteous struggle, they have previously always been discrete in their aid to what the West called terrorist activities. Now that has changed. You are now admitting openly that you are supporting a noble cause, that it is Allah's will for you to do so."

Although the great Baal Bazz had seemed to disappear from the public eye lately and Denny Rasner had even speculated that he might be dead, several new terrorists all calling themselves "Ibn Baal Bazz," had recently surfaced, making a series of spectacular strikes. Successful hijackings, kidnappings, bombings, raids into Israel, spurring on Palestinian uprisings; all were being credited to Ibn Baal Bazz, though it was obvious that many different individuals were involved. The PRS and Yassar Ararat were becoming jealous.

"The American government has protested to Riyadh," continued Al Harbi, "and Israel has threatened to attack what it calls 'Arabian strongholds.' Therefore his royal highness, Bandar, has advised King Muhammad to declare a national state of emergency and if necessary to break diplomatic relations with the West. The only continuing link will then be oil. All else will be bought and sold elsewhere."

There was much whispering among the princes at this last announcement for large sums of money, and long term contracts and investments were at stake. Many looked to Mustapha, and wondered whether he could stem this latest tidal wave.

Throughout this process of radicalization which had just now reached critical mass, these conservatives had not been silent. Although much of their dissension was never heard in the international media, nor even given much attention in the Arab press, which was for the most part pro-radical. Nevertheless, the conservative voice under the leadership of Mustapha was being heard. It was heard by powerful sheikhs who were wary of the growing power of the radicals and who had much to lose by a break with the West. It was heard by Mustapha's allies in Egypt and other moderate Arab and Muslim nations who saw the folly of a war-like Islamic World. It was heard by a growing Arab middle class who were becoming tired of fanaticism.

Most important, the radicals still had not silenced several of Mustapha's remaining moderate brothers, first line princes who feared that Bandar would only lead them to destruction.

But these were in the minority, or if they were indeed a majority, it was a silent one–for the voice of irrationality, as it always is, was the one favored by the media, the one which makes the most noise.

The conservatives were losing ground rapidly. The cause of the Radicals, the cause of Palestine, the cause of a resurgent Islamic World was too strong. Many felt that it was the irresistible trend of history, the will of Allah.

Thus, under the pretense of celebrating both the completion of the JADCO project, and the King Waleed Military City; these had been some of the matters discussed at this meeting of the Council of Princes.

Mustapha had made it a point to sit at the same circle as his brother and rival, Crown Prince Bandar. He did so both as a gesture of peace within the family and also for another reason. He was considering murdering his brother that day. If he decided to do so, he knew that unlike his son, they would not be able to stop him. Mustapha was speaking now. The tone of his voice was gentle, imploring. He wanted peace. He was ready to pay almost any price for it.

"I have never complained," he was saying, "that my eldest son lies now in prison for months waiting for the executioner's sword. He has always been an impetuous boy. Perhaps he deserves to die. I do not know. It is Allah's choice. Not mine.

"But I do know that this proud nation which our

Joseph's Seed

father gave us does not deserve death. We cannot fight, we should not fight the West. It is folly. My brother's intentions may be noble, but his policies will lead to our destruction nonetheless. He must heed the voice of Reason. In our religion, my brothers, Reason has never been a stranger, never forbidden as it was in other religions. We must use it now. We must employ it with all our strength. Our situation is desperate."

"My brother speaks of reason," said Bandar easily, smiling contemptuously. "But the fruit of his loins has attempted regicide, even as he himself now considers it."

"My brother already speaks of himself as king," retorted Mustapha, "while our brother King Muhammad lies in bed with a mere cold."

"I, and those who join me," Bandar went on in a louder voice, "have brought great pride to our people. We do not have to fear the Great Satan. The Americans have grown fat and cowardly. They work for us like slaves. They develop our agriculture; build our factories, our office buildings, and modern highways. We have taken the oil concession from them, and they said nothing. They protect our sea lanes and we pay them nothing, refusing them even simple amenities such as the use of our bases for refueling. Still they say nothing. I say they are nothing, and will always fear to act.

"As to the Zionists, they have no power without the Great Satan. We, too, now have the benefits of modern science and technology, and much more money than they, and many, many more people. We will deal with them at the proper time."

"I disagree with my brother," said Mustapha politely. "History has shown again and again that the Americans have resoluteness when they were pushed too far. It is a common error to mistake their freedom for cowardice. My brother should know that. He spent many years in California, just as I did.

"True, we might be able to destroy the Zionists, but is it worth the price we would pay? How in fact do they hurt us by their existence? This I still do not understand. I say it is time to let old wounds heal."

At this, Bandar raged and began to stand up, but those nearby calmed him somewhat and he sat down again. "I wonder if my brother does not secretly love the Jews," he said, sneering. "Perhaps the slave Samira, his mother, was an Ethiopian Jewess and not a good Muslim as we were led to believe."

Although Bandar had once feared his younger brother, he now had much power, enough power to say what he just said–the ultimate insult–defamation of another man's mother. Still a pang of fear arose in him as he spoke. But surely his loyal servant Dowi Al Harbi would protect him. And his new aid, Muhammad Ali the Yemeni who was sitting next to him would protect him again as he had done when the young Mugrin had tried to kill him.

But it was no use.

In an instant, before anyone could blink an eye, Mustapha was at his brother's throat. With his left hand, he twisted Bandar's chin far to one side. With his right he pressed a large, bejeweled dagger against his brother's juggler vein.

Now the man who had just raged with anger was trembling in fear, eyes bulging from his sockets. No one else dared move.

"I should end your miserable life," Mustapha spat out the words with venom. He held Bandar in the death grip for several long moments. The victim's quick breathing could be heard in the silence–the only other sound was the distant clicking of impact sprinklers and the creaking of slowly moving towers–wheels crackling slowly over young stalks of wheat.

Mustapha shifted his glance from face to face. He looked to his brothers. They knew very well what was at stake. Then he held the eyes of Dowi Al Harbi for a few seconds, but the other turned away. Then he looked

Joseph's Seed

at the Yemeni, but the Yemeni merely stared blankly and did nothing. When his glance passed over Ashamary, Ashamary bowed his head in humble submission. Time was frozen out of mind. Then Mustapha broke the spell.

He said, "But I will not grant you the privilege of becoming *shaheed*, a martyr, to let your followers praise you for dying for your cause. No, I will let you live to prove yourself for what you are. Neither do I wish to destroy our father's efforts so lightly by plunging this country into civil war."

Mustapha then released his brother who fell to the floor covering his face. He strode away without looking back, returning his dagger to its sheath beneath his flowing thobe. One quarter of those present followed. Within a few minutes two helicopters were rising above the sprinkling machines, heading toward jagged peaks and the city of Jabalain. Bandar did not raise his head until the sound of the helicopters were airborne. Then he got up, dusted himself off and smiled, "The young Mugrin will die within the month," he said. "The king cannot refuse me now."

Hijazi Ashamary watched all of this in silence. At first he had been fearful, for the future of the kingdom was in the balance. But then another feeling slowly began to invade his consciousness. What manner of men were these two rival brothers? Which was the greater? Which would the people follow? Until now he had thought the answer self evident. But now doubt had arisen; he began to fight a battle within himself.

He was an educated man who had read the classics. He knew of nobility of soul, integrity, and courage from literature, but he had never seen them in real life. Could they be possible, he wondered? It was a question the answer to which he would go through much pain in an effort to discover.

Twenty

The Sheikh's Party

Frank loosened his blue silk polka dot tie. He was sweating under his navy blue suit. The powder blue button down shirt which had just been pressed for him by his valet at the Marriott was soaked in perspiration. While he drove, Debbie wiped his brow with a handkerchief. The damned air conditioner in the Pathfinder still didn't work right. He sat there honking his horn in another of Riyadh's never ending traffic jams. He was lost.

"Why didn't you bring the directions Shareef wrote out for us?" asked Debbie, who was also hot, but not in the same way Frank was.

"Because I was sure I knew the way, damn it! Now all these streets look the same. We've gone by that same green and yellow mosque five times. I'm sure of it."

"Well, that's one thing you're sure of."

"Let's see...," he went on, not seeming to have heard her. "Was that Al Jumma Street we were supposed to turn left on or Al Jamaih Street? Shit. I can't remember."

"Shmuck," said Debbie.

"What?" asked Frank. But he had heard. Debbie

Joseph's Seed

didn't answer. After that neither of them spoke for the next half hour. He shouldn't be lost, he thought, he could read the signs now, and he had directions. Deep down he knew he hadn't really want to go to this–but he had to.

Finally he found it.

"This must be it," he said with relief. "I recognize Clement's red step-side parked over there. He works in one of Al Tawali's minor divisions. Just a laborer really. I'm surprised he was invited. I told you about him, didn't I?"

"About a dozen times," said Debbie.

She was dressed in a long, black, bedouin gown with gold and blue laced embroidery. It came up to her neck and down to her ankles as prescribed by law, but when she got out of the Pathfinder, it was obvious that the woman underneath was a classic original and amply endowed. She was dressed to kill.

Her long golden hair was uncovered and bounced in unison as she walked adroitly in four inch heels over the broken cobblestone pavement toward the security gate entrance. She was wearing gold–around two ounces of gaudy, twenty-two carat Arabian gold jewelry on her fingers, wrists, neck, ears; which on her didn't look gaudy. Frank had purchased the gold for her the previous evening at Riyadh's gold souq, a place where fifty merchants in shanty kiosks weighed out and sold gold and silver jewelry by the gram to adorn women whose faces might never be seen.

But when they were admitted beyond the large steel plated gate of Al Tawali's high-walled Riyadh Mansion, they discovered that there were no covered faces inside. Dark haired women with skin ranging from fair to black, some beautiful and some plain, but all confidently exhibiting the wealth of their families, moved freely within the sanctuary of Al Tawali's expansive flower gardens.

The men however, except for a very few who dressed in European style clothing, still wore the traditional

Arabian attire: white *thobe*, white or red checked *gutra*, black silk *aghal*. Debbie noticed one man almost immediately who was dressed differently. He had on a ten gallon hat, a fancy red western shirt, Levis, and a pair of three hundred dollar, embroidered, western boots. He was short. From the stories Frank had told her, she guessed correctly who that might be, but she had thought he would be taller. He was standing by a cascading fountain holding a drink and talking to Mr. Fahad. He was looking at her too.

Ustez Doudeen approached Frank and Debbie as soon as he saw that they had arrived. He was accompanied by Mr. Dietrich.

"I was afraid you were not coming," said Doudeen. "The sheikh was very concerned that you were angry with him over the incident of last week."

"Oh, that!" said Frank after a moment's pause, the searching look on his face changing to brightness. "No, we'd forgotten all about that. There was just some unexpected business to attend to this morning. Sorry if we're late."

"Never mind." said Doudeen graciously. "Please, now you will enjoy the sheik's hospitality. Mr. Dietrich will introduce you to the guests, fine? You will find that for Americans and Europeans like yourself who care for the Arab people and their cause, which helps us in many ways, our people will always remain friendly to you, in spite of what you may have heard lately."

As Doudeen walked away, Debbie asked Dietrich, "Is this horticultural paradise your handiwork also? I didn't know that many of these varieties could bloom in this climate. It's very impressive."

"Vith the proper care," said Dietrich. "Anything can survive here. And conversely, if neglected or mistreated, anything can die." Presently a waiter offered them drinks, which were non-alcoholic. "If you prefer something stronger, it can be arranged," the German said to them, sotto voce.

"No kidding? No, this is fine," said Frank. "Anyway,

I thought it was against the law."

"The people at this party, you will find, are the law. Now, maybe you would like something to eat? But first I suggest that you pay your respects to the sheikh. It will be expected. He is over there sitting under the veranda."

It was impossible to tell if the ailing old man recognized them or not. Nevertheless, always on the lookout for new prospects, he feebly took Debbie's hand and smiled lecherously.

"Your party is very nice, and the garden is beautiful," she said forgetting to wish him a happy birthday. This was translated by an attendant, where upon the dying sheikh responded with the one phrase which had replaced his former command of his language. "*Al hamdillila*," he said.

"That's mean 'thank the God'," said the attendant. The sheikh is a holy man."

"Yes, that's obvious," said Frank as they begged off. "And a very good customer," he said to Debbie out the side of his mouth, as they walked toward the *hors d'oeuvres* table.

While Debbie was sampling something on a Ritz cracker, a pencil thin man in a shoulder padded pin striped suit two sizes too large leaned over her shoulder from behind, hands on her waist. "Classy spread, wouldn't you say, kid?" It was Shareef. "You look like Lauren Bacall in 'To Have or Have Not'."

"If you say so," she laughed.

"You want me to take you around to meet the big shots?"

Then Dietrich, who weighed around three times more than Shareef, sneered. "Uh, maybe some other time kid," said Shareef. "Talk to you later."

Frank noticed all of this. He noticed the way his wife flirted, however innocently, with Shareef. He noticed the way she was ogled by just about everybody, and it was beginning to annoy him. He was beginning to regret bringing her to the kingdom. On the other hand he knew that he had not had a choice.

Something had changed in Debbie. He feared the obvious; that she was simply getting tired of him; but he also had the sense that she was hiding something. He was determined not to let it bother him. Anyway, if it were true, what could he do about it? Still, he wanted to know. But every time he tried asking her she only said, "Nothing is wrong."

Frank separated from Debbie to talk to his past customers–many of whom were in attendance at the party–and he was presently speaking to Mr. Ashamary who was fawning profusely over Frank. He was telling anyone who would listen how Frank traveled the desert alone, "just like a bedouin," and how he and Frank had single handedly built the Al JADCO project which was now growing more wheat than any other farm in the kingdom. Mr. Ashamary was drunk.

Mr. Dietrich introduced Debbie to one of Ustez Doudeen's four wives who, in turn introduced her to a group of women who Debbie found to be personable and extremely interested in life in America. He left them to their "women talk" and went to get a drink, a real one.

"Isn't it quite chaotic to have women working at men's jobs, involved in politics, even driving?" one woman asked. "Nonsense," replied another, anticipating Debbie's answer. "I have driven myself once. It is very easy, really. "When did you ever drive?" asked a third, incredulously.

Debbie glance around while the women were thus arguing. Suddenly she froze–her heart started to pound so loudly she thought her companions might hear it. He was there! She was sure of it. Ahmad was standing with Doudeen and some other men not far from her. He was looking at her, but everyone did that. Momentarily his eyes moved on. Did he recognize her?

The talk moved on to other subjects. "Is it true," asked a young woman in hushed tones, "that girls may chose whom ever they want, and that sometimes they may even chose more than one—as the men do here?"

"It's not as easy as that," Debbie informed the disappointed ladies. Another woman asked, "What do you think of our form of punishment, cutting off the head for wrong conduct between man and woman? Do you know that a famous prince will die that way in a few more days? Although, of course it is not for adultery in his case." Then one of the braver ones asked, "What is it like—to use—the mouth—you know? We have heard that even that is not forbidden in America."

"I don't know if I want to discuss these..."

"Shhhh," said the woman who had asked the last question. "Here he comes."

A tall, distinguished looking Arab was heading straight for Debbie. He had not been introduced to her, but none of the women dared now to speak. Debbie had seen his face many times before on TV. Against all precedent he was going to speak uninvited and without being introduced—to another man's wife. Even though the man was Crown Prince Bandar, he might not have gotten away with it had the woman's husband been other than Frank Costello.

The man was breaking precedent in another way also; instead of the traditional headdress of red check or white, the head covering he wore was a deep blue. It was embroidered in white with an eight pointed Islamic star.

"May I offer you a drink, Mrs. Costello? I have heard much about you."

"Thank you," said Debbie. "But it is I who should be saying that, Your Highness."

"You know who I am then?"

"How could I not know?"

"It is gratifying," said Prince Bandar Jibreen Ibn Abdul Lateef, next in line to be king of Arabia. "It is very gratifying.

"May I offer you something perhaps a little stronger than this to drink while we talk?" He took the drink she was holding, snapped his fingers and then led her to a corner of the garden. Muhammad Ali the Yemeni came over, bearing a tray with new drinks.

While they talked, Frank watched her with his peripheral vision only half listening to the sputtering of Mr. Ashamary and the more reasonable inquiries of the other sheikhs who had joined them. As for his wife and the man she was with, he knew it was out of the question to interrupt them, so he just watched and waited.

Without being obvious about it, the sly Egyptian Shareef watched also. As for the man in the ten gallon hat, he made it a point to be able to hear as well as to watch.

Thus in the traditional, devout world of Islamic Arabia, precedents and traditions were being strained or broken, passions were felt, plots laid, and paths crossed or missed being crossed.

As these things were happening, one young Arab prince who had only recently returned with his American girlfriend from his studies at a university in the United States, had prevailed upon the orchestra to play something more lively. The couple was now dancing to a rock tune before amazed onlookers. Although they were amongst the most sophisticated members of Arabian society, still there were those present who could not accept the change.

The young Arab, although he condescended to wear the traditional white Thobe, did not cover his head. Instead his hair was arranged in the "punk" style with greased strands extending six inches into the air like a porcupine. The girl with whom he was dancing wore a white, "see-through" dress which revealed the scant pink bikini briefs she had on underneath. For awhile then, in that closing hour of the sheikh's party, the eyes of those who did not have a personal stake in matters, were not on Debbie.

Twenty-One

Mugged at the Supermarket

Debbie was totally unable to believe that there was something around her neck–pulling–hurting. She was actually choking. She tried to scream, but the thing was gagging her so that she could scarcely make a sound. She swooned. Where was she? Was this a nightmare? Was she somehow transformed to the Nazi Germany of those old nightmares she had once had, of her father's tales filled in by her own imagination, fortified by her real life nightmare of Ahmad Daweesh, killer of her brother–of so many of her friends.

Then she remembered. She was awake and this was real. The thing around her neck was a cane, and the man holding it was a foul smelling old bedouin.

She did not have to accept this. She was in a public place; at Safeway, a modern American style supermarket. Next to her were rows of products she had known all her life," Dr. Pepper," "Tide," "Wheaties," "Peter Pan Peanut Butter."

Since those things were real, she didn't have to accept this. She could fight. But why were people turning away? Why wasn't anyone helping her? Had they discovered her secret? Had Ahmad recognized her and come for her?

The man holding the cane around her neck was dragging her now, holding a hand over her mouth with one hand, the cane on her neck with the other. He looked old, white scraggly beard, wrinkled hands, but he was strong. She couldn't break his grip.

She kicked him in the shins, scratched and struggled. She was getting away. Shareef was waiting in the car. If only she could get there–escape. Then the man called for someone to help him. Help him? This was insane. Then there were two, subduing her, molesting her in broad daylight. She fainted.

Vaguely she remembered the forearm, large and sinewy. The hand grasping the wrist of the man who held her, forcing it to yield. The simple words that made the second man back away. "*Zowjati*," she heard him say again and again. She knew what that meant; she had been studying the language for months now. Reluctantly, after some commotion, uncertain hesitation, they backed down. Then she was leaving that place with him. He had even brought her groceries. She was leaning on him as if it were the natural thing to do.

But instead of going to Shareef and his waiting white Mercedes, they went to a red pick up truck. She got in and they drove away. She was conscious now but still in something like a state of shock. She knew she could have resisted him if she wanted to, but she was exhausted. She felt safe with this man who had defended her against the brutality she had just experienced. She knew who he was although she had never met him. Frank had not thought to introduce them at the party the day before.

"What was it about?" she asked finally. "Why did those men attack me? Why did everyone act like I was the criminal and not them? I don't understand."

"Far as I can fathom the unfathomable," said Clement Schmidt, "it's your physical appearance. You were attacked because you're beautiful."

"What?"

Joseph's Seed

"I mean, I see you know about the dress rules. Don't have too much ankle showing, nor too much neck. But still you were too much for them to bear for all that. They were *mutawas* you know, religious police. They have a lot of power, I was lucky to get you away from them."

"I've heard about them but I didn't believe it was possible. This is the twenty-first century."

"Not for them it's not. They were driven into a frenzy by their own lust and that made you the guilty one, by definition–according to their way of thinking I mean. It was your looks; your shape, your hair. You know."

"I see," said Debbie.

"Believe you do. I'm surprised it hasn't happened sooner. How long have you been here in the kingdom now?"

"Six months."

"Welcome to the Kingdom of Arabia."

They were silent for awhile, then, noticing that they were on the beltway, leaving the city behind them she asked, "Where are we going?"

"To the desert. It's where I go when I want to think– to be alone. You need some time to gather yourself. Then, after that I'll suggest some options and you can decide for yourself."

"What if I want to go back to Riyadh right now, back to the Marriott to call Al Tawali's, have them locate Frank for me?"

"Then that's where I'd take you. Is that what you want?" He started to slow the pickup.

"No."

Then they were a hundred miles outside of Riyadh. Clement left the road and headed for a wadi he knew where the water flowed that time of year.

Neil DeRosa

Twenty-Two

Missing in Action

Shareef sat entranced. He was listening to *Um Arkarthoom*, the Egyptian singing star, in concert on the tape deck of his white Mercedes—she was imploring him to try and find happiness in love—and if he did, Allah would be very glad.

Finally, he snapped out of his reverie, broke away from the lyrical melody and went into the Safeway where he had taken Debbie to shop; he wanted to carry her groceries or push her cart. He liked being with her. He couldn't help it. But he knew she needed some space so he had left her alone to shop, thinking it would be safe—and where could be safer than a Safeway supermarket?

As soon as he entered the store however, he knew what had happened. She was gone. The place was buzzing with gossip. He heard it in both languages. Then he sidled up to a group of women cloaked in black. He could tell by their voices which ones to approach.

"Where is the *Amerikeeya Jamilla*?" he asked one. "I am her driver. I must know where they have taken her. It is my responsibility."

"Her husband took her," said a sexy voice. "I wish he took me instead. He was a *hawaji* Cowboy, I think."

Joseph's Seed

"What?!" said Shareef, visibly shaken. "That's impossible! Her husband is far from here doing work for my company, Al Tawali. I know; I brought him to the airport myself this morning."

"All we know is what we saw," said another woman; this one had an ugly voice. "The *mutawa* was beating her and calling her 'whore,' when the *hawaji* came and took her away. He said he was her husband and was responsible. How many men can be responsible for one whore?" The sexy voice was looking Shareef up and down through her veil. He could tell.

But he was in no mood. "I wish I had time," he muttered, and left the supermarket in a hurry.

Shareef first checked at the Marriott to see if she had returned there. He waited there for an hour then went back to the office. There he immediately picked up the phone and made use of his network of Egyptian colleagues who worked as telephone receptionists at the many branches of the Al Tawali enterprises throughout the kingdom. He left word at all the offices which Frank was expected to visit in the next few days.

Shareef's boss, Doudeen was not in and he was glad. He didn't feel like explaining how he lost Debbie in a supermarket. He knew he could get deported for this– or thrown in jail. He hit himself on the forehead. How could he have allowed this to happen? He should have gone in with her.

Within an hour Frank called. "What's wrong?" he asked. "I couldn't get this fellow here to tell me anything, except that you called about my wife. Where is she? Is she still with you? I want to talk to her."

"Hold your horses, err, calm yourself, Mr. Costello. Your wife is fine. There was just some little misunderstanding and I thought I should call you."

"Well where is she now, at the Marriott?"

"Not exactly. I don't know how to say this, but your wife had some trouble with the religious police. They tried to arrest her, and your friend–the one who sounds like Johnny Cash–took her out. I can't seem to locate them at the moment, but I'm sure there is nothing to worry about."

There was a pause and then Frank said: "I'm coming back to Riyadh right now. I'll call you back as soon as I get a flight so you'll know what time to pick me up. Stay by the phone."

Shareef met Frank at the Airport at nine o'clock that night. The first thing he said when he came through the arrivals gate was: "Have you found her yet?"

"Not a clue," said Shareef. "I've checked every place I could think of and no one has seen her."

"Have you called the police?"

"Are you kidding," said Shareef out the side of his mouth.

"Take me to the hotel," ordered Frank. "That's exactly what I'm going to do."

Frank was intelligent, but he did have a propensity for narrowing his vision, of concentrating only on the subject at hand, of seeing only what he wanted to see. It was a psychological skill that had long served him well. It had allowed him to not worry about the problem of self confidence long enough to snare someone like Debbie in the first place. Later it allowed him to be audacious enough to make a lot of money when the opportunity presented itself in the Kingdom of Arabia.

Now however, his proclivity was working against him. He knew that the country he was living and working in was on the brink of civil strife–even war. But he totally misjudged the immediacy of the danger. The now familiar groups of Arab dignitaries he saw on the evening news were still drinking tea, arriving at and departing from the Riyadh Airport–to the tune of "What's New Pussycat," the same inane political occurrences that had always caused him to shake his head in indifferent disgust. But there were small differences he wasn't paying attention to. He noticed when the News-in-

English which had previously been completely non-controversial, was now criticizing, however subtly, the conservatives and their leader, the governor of Jabalain; but he missed the significance of the fact that the controversy was being aired in public.

The problem was that ever since making his stupendous sale to Al Tawali Enterprises through Mr. Doudeen, Frank could think of little else. He had all but forgotten Mr. Snead and their agreement. He rationalized by telling himself that since Snead hadn't returned his call, he wasn't going to worry about it.

Although he was still selling Agricultural equipment to the Arabs and the money was still rolling in, Frank was aware that his small customers had disappeared. He convinced himself that the gigantic Al Tawali deal had simply dwarfed all else, thus causing him to neglect the others. It wasn't true. The regular customers had just stopped coming. Frank should have as a good salesman asked himself why, but he didn't.

He had asked himself many things, such as: How had Debbie acquired a visa so easily, and what was the cause of her sudden change of personality? Why did she now ask him so many questions about people and places in Arabia without ever indicating why she was so interested, when she used to have such contempt for the "barbaric Arabs?" He had always thought it incongruous for her to want to come to Arabia at all, and had told himself that it was to be with him. But her subsequent behavior had made him question that assumption. And where had she picked up that ridiculous phrase, "be that as it may,"? Hadn't he heard Snead saying that? He hadn't previously given such questions the urgency they deserved; now he had to.

Right now he intended to do what any civilized person would do under the circumstances–call the police.

"Well hello, Mr. Costello, *shlonik*," said the man tapping him on the shoulder. It was Mr. Fahad; he was smiling broadly. He was with a rotund man in a grey business suit and a red tie. They were standing in the lobby of the Marriott when Frank entered with Shareef.

"Where are you going in such a great hurry?" asked Fahad. "Are you chasing some new deal? Soon you will be as rich as Joseph Tawali, aye? Although soon he will die and as they say, he can not take it with him."

In his agitated state Frank, very uncharacteristically for him, had no patience for this idle chatter. He started to go, making feeble excuses to Mr. Fahad, not even noticing the man with him.

"No words for an old friend," said the man. "Be that as it may, it's good to see a familiar face in this God forsaken place. 'Scuse me Fahad, just a figure of speech."

"It is no problem," said Fahad. "I agree with you. This town must be forsaken or at least forgotten by Allah for a time."

Frank looked at the man now for the first time. Then he remembered. "But I didn't think you..."

"Yes sir," said Snead. "A real pleasure–but we shouldn't gab out here in the lobby. Why don't we go up to Fadsy's suite and order room service. I hear they have a French chef here who makes a terrific Roquefort salad. I'm starved. You must be hungry yourself. I understand you just arrived from Jeddah."

"How did you. . ?"

"Frankie," said Snead slapping him on the shoulder with some force. "Let's go get that salad."

Twenty-Three

Sowing Seeds of Hate

Not far away, in the second most luxurious palace in Riyadh, Dowi Al Harbi was speaking to his master. Although Bandar had decided that it was no longer necessary for Al Harbi to personally carry out operations–and not worth the risk–Al Harbi still made regular trips to Europe and America on "diplomatic missions." Under the pretext of consulting with his publishers, he told the Crown Prince, he continued to coordinate the activities of his terrorist organization.

"The most important part of the training of freedom fighters," Al Harbi was saying, "comes before they are trained at all. First, I select only those completely devoted to our cause. They must be willing to die for us at the bat of an eyelash. Sometimes indeed I test them, and if this is not the case, they are killed immediately. Our cause depends on their unfailing loyalty.

"Then they are sent to North Africa, Iraq, Iran, Brazil–to any one of our network of training camps–just as I was, to be trained by the best professionals that money can buy. They are given easy tasks at first, such as shooting unarmed tourists or mailing out envelopes with various deadly ingredients inside. If they are successful with this, they are then moved on to more important tasks–and finally to the ultimate goal–suicide missions and to the glorious reward of Allah.

"The warriors I select are dedicated, but still at times we err, for only Allah does not err. That is why no 'Ibn Baal Bazz' has ever or will ever see my face. We have organized for us the most intricate chain of command you can imagine. There are five levels between myself and any would-be operative. They never see my face or suspect who I am. Yet I make it all happen. It is I who orchestrate all like the great maestro of the Israeli Philharmonic."

"You forget yourself, habeebi."

"Of course, *ya emir*, my humble apologies. You, of course, are the prime mover."

"Within the kingdom events are progressing nicely also," Bandar spoke now. "We have the traitor Mustapha on the run. His Followers are deserting him in numbers. In two days his son will lose his head with the king's blessing. Old Muhammad gladly allows me to direct affairs now. His health is very poor, you know. He will not last long.

"He insults me for the last time," Bandar went on, his face livid with remembered rage. He was speaking not now of the king, and the other understood this. "Perhaps he will live long enough to regret it.

"I no longer need to depend on my brothers for money, though most give of it freely now. Thanks to Doudeen, the entire fortune of Al Tawali is at my disposal. As soon as the forces are in place and the remainder of the missiles are installed, we will act. Yes, we must still import many more slaves, uh-soldiers." The crown prince smiled and took both of Al Harbi's hands in his. As he squeezed them, a numbing fear surged through his veins.

"At that time," said Dowi Al Harbi, "I myself will undertake my last and most important mission also, one which I must execute personally. For it, I must return to the city of my birth. I may even take a small holiday while there." he smiled. "After that we shall have what is ours."

"All in Allah's good time," said Bandar. "You know, I just met the most extraordinary woman. She is a blond American, but somehow she almost looks as if she could be an Arab. I would like to add her to my harem. She is married now, but these things can be arranged. She was at the old sheikh's party. Perhaps you saw her."

"What is this *hurma's* name, *ya emir?*" asked Dowi Al Harbi humbly so as not to infringe on that which the crown prince already considered to be his personal possession.

"Debbie Costello, I think. Her husband is a ridiculous salesman who I will dispose of as soon as he is no longer useful to me. She will be surprised when she finds that although we will continue to treat her well, she will never leave our kingdom again."

Twenty-Four

A Momentary Reprieve

Debbie Costello felt free for the first time in memory. The man was holding her, lying next to her on a thin blanket cushioned by the soft sand underneath. He was sleeping now, but for a long time they hadn't slept. He had possessed her in a way Frank had never done, never known how to do, and she had allowed it–wanted it. Why? She couldn't think now; she only knew that it had felt right. It felt right now.

She looked up at a billion stars. The red pick-up truck was nearby. It had everything in it needed to sustain his simple existence–hers now–here in the desert.

They were hours from the nearest road. Earlier, they had driven past a few isolated bedouin tents on their way to this place. He had stopped at one to talk to an Arab. The Arab had scarcely noticed her.

When they arrived here they had eaten flat bread and meat which the Arab had given him. It was roasted on a spit over a fire he made. She had wanted to talk but he told her, "not now," and she had complied with his wish.

Now she lay there gazing at the bright night sky. She could hear the faint sound of the water moving in

Joseph's Seed

the wadi nearby. She wanted to think, but thought instead, "not now." She fell asleep.

When she awoke he was gone, but the truck was not and there was coffee and dates by the fire. She took some. When he came back, the first thing she said was, "I want to talk."

"All right."

"I've got to tell you that last night–well, I think it must have been obvious to you how I felt–but I'm making no promises about the future. Do you understand what I'm saying?"

"Of course," said Clement.

"Do you know why I was attacked, really?" she asked then.

"That could have happened at any time. But things are much worse now. Although the government has promised safe conduct for Americans remaining in the kingdom, hostile actions, such as the one you experienced, have increased. I've heard of several, though they've not been reported in the news.

"That's not important now, however," he went on. "You're in danger for other reasons. I was looking for an opportunity to take you out of Riyadh for several weeks. Had this not happened, I would have kidnapped you."

"Oh?!"

"Riyadh is about to explode. Just how, I'm not sure yet but I know what will cause it;" and he told her.

"What about Frank?" she said when he finished. "Is he in danger?"

"There's always danger, but I think he'll be relatively safe for a time. Al Tawali perceives that he needs him just now. So indirectly Bandar needs him. He should be okay for awhile. But you're different. You ask questions. You don't pander. You're beautiful and can't hide the fact. Most importantly, Bandar has you earmarked."

"How do you know?"

"Believe me, I know. You're in danger. I want you

to stay here."

"In the desert, living out of a pickup truck?"

"I have a better place in mind. I can have your clothes brought. Your husband will cooperate. You will even be able to talk to him, though I wouldn't advise you to tell him too much."

"Don't worry," said Debbie. "I never do." Then she was quiet for awhile. Finally she asked, "What do you know about Dowi Al Harbi, Bandar's chief aid?"

"I don't know," said Clement, a little surprised at the question. "Just that he's an Islamic author who is now part of the new militant regime. He's a Palestinian, I think. There are quite a few of them here you know. Doudeen is one also. Why do you ask?"

"Just curious," said Debbie. "You know me. I ask a lot of questions."

Then Clement knew that he didn't have her. Not completely. He wondered what her question about Al Harbi meant. He was determined to find out.

Twenty-Five

First Revelations

"Debbie is on a mission," said Snead.

"I can't understand it," said Frank. But he didn't shake his head this time; he was too numb. "I brought the photos to you. I was supposed to keep an eye on things for you. But I don't understand what Debbie has got to do with. . ."

"I'm trying to make this easy," Snead proceeded patiently. "I've already told you that we can't reveal all of the details at this time. Fahad here assures me that your wife will be safe while she is under the protection of the governor of Jabalain. She knew in advance that Clement Schmidt would be abducting her—that she would be leaving the city of Riyadh with him. It was only the details of her departure that she didn't know. We find it expedient not to reveal too much. I promise you, we made every effort to insure that she wouldn't be hurt.

"The religious police were real, I grant you—planted you might say. But we had our people standing by to see that they didn't get carried away; didn't go too far."

"But Shareef said they were beating her!" Frank protested.

"Be that as it may," Snead went on, clearing his

throat. "She wasn't hurt. Clement got there in time. No part of our operation has thus far been very dangerous for either of you. But that may not be the case before long. Events may soon take a turn for the worse. Events may also dictate that we will need to rely on your present positions in the kingdom more than we have done so far. You may soon be able to be of great help to us."

"I don't know," said Frank. "This is a whole other story. I don't know if I want to risk my neck–my wife."

"Your wife may not go along with you on that," said Snead. "You may get left out in the cold if you lose your nerve now. Really, you haven't much to lose. You're already here."

Frank tried to think. But his head was spinning. Things were happening too fast, things over which he had no control. Someone very important to him, someone he loved, was in danger–missing. He couldn't accept Snead's reassurances to the contrary–and now he had to make some relevant decisions. He knew he had been selfish or at least single minded; that he had evaded reality, that he had been blind to what was happening around him. Now reality was closing in on him.

Part of him wanted to scream, "Get her out! Get us out! We're quitting!" But he couldn't do it. He was afraid she wouldn't go with him. He had let that much seep in. She was involved in this for some reason. But he didn't know what it was.

No, he had to go on, to do something. If he didn't act he might lose everything–her. He'd be out of the story, out of her life.

"When will she be coming back–here I mean?" he asked, looking up with difficulty.

"Hard to say," said Snead. "But if you're willing to go along with us, we'll tell you how to proceed, and we'll get a call to you from Debbie as soon as possible.

"How soon do you think that will be Fadsy?" Snead asked, turning to the Arab sitting next to him.

Joseph's Seed

"They listen to all telephone calls now," said Fahad," and they are closing the personal phones of the ones who they do not trust. But we shall arrange something. Tomorrow, *Inshalla*. We will tell you. In the meantime I suggest that you go back to work. Say nothing about your wife. Mr. Doudeen is out of the kingdom for a few days. Say nothing to him when he returns. I am sure he has other things to worry about.

"I suggest that you get help from your friend Shareef. He can be trusted. You will find that he will be useful for some things." Shareef had been told by. Fahad to wait in the lobby while the others talked in Fahad's rooms. Now Frank was even more confused by this new piece of information.

"You mean Shareef works for you too?" Frank asked incredulously.

"Let us just say," Fahad answered, "that he is useful to us because he hates the regime of Prince Bandar. However, he may hate us also. In his heart, he believes that Egypt should rule all Arabs. But we trust him. Just we are careful how much we trust him."

The hotel phone rang then. Fahad picked up the receiver, absent mindedly brushing the flap of his headdress out of the way to do so.

"*Aye, Naam*," he said into the phone. Then, in English, "Yes, yes. You can come up now. He is ready to go."

A few moments later there was a knock on the door, and Fahad opened it to admit a Shareef who no longer looked the comedian to Frank. "You will take Mr. Costello to the home of Sheikh Moneef Mulafic tomorrow at noon." said Fahad. "There will be a telephone call, *Inshalla*, for him. After tomorrow you will bring him to see the execution. Go early, so you can get to a good place to see everything."

"*Aye, Naam*," said Shareef.

That evening on the News in English, Yasser

Arrarat was sitting in majlis with the usual dignitaries, trying to raise money no doubt. He was sitting next to Doudeen. But wasn't he out of the kingdom? Then Frank remembered the other time he had seen Doudeen on TV when he couldn't have been there. There was no mention of Debbie's kidnapping of course. But there was mention of another of the exploits of the great freedom fighter, Baal Bazz who took credit for blowing up a 747 airliner over the waters near New York City.

   That night as Frank lay in bed trying to sleep, his mind raced.

Twenty-Six

Chop Square

Two days later they stood among the throng of people waiting at "Chop Square" to see the beheading. Riyadh's beheadings had always been carried out here–public capital punishment for a long list of crimes, from adultery to insurrection. The square itself was in an old part of the city and was nothing to see–just an open space between government buildings, dull lumbering buildings the color of sandstone. The new glimmering glass and steel high-rise structures of the city built by Western talent were not in view. Neither could Frank see Americans or Europeans in the crowd. Many of these were gone from the kingdom now, he assumed, for rumors were spreading about the new direction the kingdom was taking. He should be gone too.

He wore dark sun glasses as he often did to protect himself from the glare, but now they also hid his bloodshot eyes. He hadn't slept much in the last two days and it showed. Shareef stood at his side, his hand resting in the crook of Frank's elbow. They were about five rows from the open space ahead of them. A friendly Arab standing by them, had a notion to give the American a good scare. He nudged Frank and pointed the way toward the front row. The Arab called to some others standing in front of them to clear the way for Frank. Shareef protested, harshly telling the Arabs to leave him alone. But Frank, understanding the gist of the conversation said: "No, I want to get closer." Then there was only the open square in front of them.

When he had talked to Debbie on the phone the day before, she had told him that she was alright and not to worry, but not to ask questions. She would see him soon. When? She couldn't say just when. They were in this now, she had said, and had to see it through. She hoped he would understand, but right now, she couldn't help him. When he asked simply; "Why?" all she would say was; "Not now."

He had been standing in the hot morning sun for an hour now, his sweat drying and caking under his button-down collar. "Nothing's ever done on time here," he muttered. "Not even beheadings." Shareef gave him a sidelong glance but said nothing.

Finally, after another hour's wait, the gate opened at a nearby high-walled, windowless building complex which looked like an old palace, or a prison. A motorized procession came through it and moved slowly toward the square in front of Frank, which was cordoned off by many soldiers wearing red checked headdresses and army-green uniforms. The procession was led by other soldiers on foot accompanying the three white Mercedes cars, which constituted the motorized procession. All of the soldiers had automatic weapons.

When the procession reached the center of the square, it stopped and several bearded Arabs got out of the first Mercedes. One of them spoke into a microphone which had been set up for the occasion, and it was soon obvious to Frank that he was leading the throng in prayer. Shareef nudged Frank. "You better not attract too much attention today, boss," he said. "The natives are restless." He pulled Frank down with him to the prostrate position to simulate devotion.

While they were thus laid out, several other ve-

Joseph's Seed

hicles approached from the opposite direction on a road cordoned off with iron railings and more soldiers to keep out the crowd. Toward the rear of this new procession was a gold Rolls Royce. After it entered the square, the driver, Muhammad Ali the Yemeni, got out and opened the rear door. Three men got out. They were: Ustez Doudeen, Dowi Al Harbi, and Crown Prince Bandar who was the only man in sight wearing a blue headdress.

When the throng began to rise and saw who was now among them, there went up a sound of awe, and the people returned to the ground to continue their supplications. Frank followed.

Then after some moments with a wave of the hand by Dowi Al Harbi and a command into the microphone, the execution ritual began.

The door of the second Mercedes then opened and a large black man got out carrying a leather case of the kind in which one might keep a musical instrument. He took off the cloak he was wearing to reveal white pantaloons and huge, glistening black muscles.

"Who's that?" asked Frank in an incredulous whisper.

"That's the heavyweight champ of Arabia," said Shareef. His name is Muhammad Ali too, no doubt. Just watch and you'll see." Presently, the Nubian executioner opened the leather case and took out a large curved sword. As the blade waved above the eunuch's head in a warm-up swing, it reflected sunlight into Frank's eyes. Frank winced.

Then, from the third and last Mercedes there appeared three other men. All three were dressed in Arabian garb except that the one in the middle had on no head covering. He wouldn't be needing it today. The two on either side seemed to be holding up the man in the middle—or more accurately, the boy in the middle. The boy was the condemned, Prince Mugrin Ibn Mustapha. The boy was hanging his head. His hands were tied behind him.

"Why does he look so sleepy?" asked Frank.

"They gave him downers," said Shareef, "to take the fight out of him. Maybe he does not care what is to happen to him right now." Then the two men led Mugrin to the spot where the executioner had set up a chopping block, and forced the condemned to his knees.

The crowd became silent. Moments passed. Anticipation grew as the final act grew nigh. Then, Prince Bandar who was seated in a chair provided for him while all others stood, waved his hand. It was the command to proceed.

But just as the Sudani pricked the back of Mugrin's neck so as to get a clean sweep as he had done so many times before, something distracted his attention. There was an immense explosion. First the sight of it reached them, and then the piercing sound cracked. The brick wall of the structure next to the square from which the Mercedes procession had come–around fifty feet in height–blew apart.

The drugged Mugrin held his head high for some moments–waiting. Then he dropped it lazily.

Blocks and debris flew everywhere; a dust cloud descended upon the crowd with the debris. Panic struck. The white bearded *Ulema* at the microphone pleaded for calm, but before he could restore order, a large green fire truck approached at high speed–bells clanging, sirens blaring–from the same road on which Bandar had just made his entrance.

People and soldiers dove out of its path, for surely it was on official business which had to do with the explosion they had just witnessed. Perhaps there was a fire also.

Then the truck came roaring and clanging into the square, en-route to the site of the blast. Everyone jumped clear of its path into the safety of the crowd. As he leaped for safety also, Bandar wondered dimly if his chief aid had some reason to create this new spectacular. When he gave Al Harbi a questioning glance, the other understood and shook his head. Then the truth came to them both simultaneously, but it was too late. They began shouting orders to nearby soldiers, but in the confusion they reacted slowly.

Mugrin, who was too drugged up to think of running for cover, was already in the truck—dragged aboard by one of the Filipino "firemen." As the fire truck made a screeching u-turn in the square, some of the soldiers began to react to the orders they had just been given, and opened fire on the truck. But they were counter-attacked by a watershed. With a signal from the driver, who was wearing his *gutra* more in the manner of a bandit from out of the Wild West than a marauding Arab, the Filipinos trained the truck's high pressure hoses onto the enemy, and the truck made its getaway in a cloud of misty spray and dust.

Those nearby heard the driver hoot and holler something, but few had any inkling as to what it meant.

"Atta boy, Alex ol' hombre, that was one hellatious roundup!" he yelled. The man to whom he was shouting then made the 'thumbs up' sign. "Texas number-one," he replied.

Just as the fire truck rounded the corner on two wheels to exit from "Chop Square," two successive explosions louder than the first, erupted from other adjacent buildings. After that moment pandemonium struck in earnest.

When order was finally restored hours later the authorities found the fire truck abandoned a few blocks away. Witnesses said that the firemen left in cars. "What kind of cars?" they were asked. "Red and white Datsuns like all the bedouin and workers drive." "Which way did they go?" "Only Allah Knows," said the witnesses. It was later discovered that the fire truck had been taken from a nearby firehouse the night before. The sleeping Yemeni guard at the firehouse was given a mild injection to insure that he would remain asleep.

Twenty-Seven

A Shadow Descends upon the Kingdom

There was one person who, if he did not quite understand the dialect of the driver of the fire truck as it fled from "Chop Square" on two wheels, he was close enough to the thick of things to hear the voice of the driver and recognize it–and to be haunted by it. The last time he had heard that voice was when its owner had said to him; "I quit you son-of-a-bitch . You kin take my pay and shove it."

The last time he had seen him was still vivid in his mind and the arrogance of that man irked him still. He had been insulted by that crude American once too often over the years. He who was almost royalty did not have to take such abuse. Now he would see to it that he paid. He would relish seeing the first American ever led to the chopping block.

He tried to push past the guard at the entrance to the emergency majlis being held at the king's Riyadh palace, to determine what to do in the wake of the catastrophe which had just occurred hours earlier. The order had already gone out to place road blocks on all of Riyadh's outgoing roads, but so far it had not been implemented, for the leadership was in a state of confusion.

Joseph's Seed

"You can not enter this day, ya Sheikh." a guard said, barring his way. "Bandar has ordered this session closed. The king is in attendance also; only his top advisors are to be admitted."

"I must enter," insisted Ashamary. "He will demand to know what I have to say." Ashamary's voice was loud and the guard feared lest he be blamed for the disturbance. He was about to call to his fellow soldiers to assist him in evicting the persistent sheikh for he had strict orders that no one was to be admitted. Besides, he knew that this particular man was not as welcome as he once was. He had overheard the prince say recently that Hijazi was becoming a "pest."

Just as the guards began to manhandle the sheikh, Muhammad Ali the Yemeni came out of the majlis and tapped the lead guard on the shoulder. "Let him go," he said with quiet authority. "Come with me, *ya Sheikh*."

The Yemeni, who once worked for Ashamary as a driver, now led his former boss into a meeting of the most powerful men in Arabia. When he entered the room he saw no cameras or electronic equipment as was usually the case. About ten Arabs were sitting on the floor around the room. These were the highest ranking officials of the Rasheedi regime. A few standing attendants were serving them coffee and refreshments.

Muhammad Ali motioned Ashamary to sit, then he went and whispered something to Ustez Doudeen who then whispered to the prince. Knowing well the tradition, Ashamary sat quietly on the floor, crossing his legs. Arabic Coffee was brought to him in a tiny cup. No matter how urgent his message, he knew he must finish three cupfuls before he dared to speak.

Meanwhile, Bandar was speaking to the king, who although he was now more of a figurehead than a real king, could not avoid attending this majlis. Major decisions would have to be made today, decisions that would require a king's stamp of approval.

"*Ya Muhammad*," continued Prince Bandar, "only

when the rebellious emir of Jabalain is stopped will order be restored to our land."

"But we do not know that Mustapha was responsible," said the king. Do not forget, he has publicly honored my order to proceed with the execution of his son. He respects the law. I do not believe that he would do this. Why don't you ask him Bandar Jibreen, he is your brother."

"His palace has been contacted, Your Majesty," answered Dowi Al Harbi, knowing that Prince Bandar would never again speak to the hated Mustapha. "His aids have denied responsibility for what happened. In fact they told us that they did not even know it had happened, for we have not yet allowed it to be in the news. Mugrin's brothers, they said also, could not have freed him. They are all too young to undertake such an action. The emir of Jabalain himself is in Egypt at present–on a business trip, they said, so he could not have done it."

"He must be punished," said Bandar with finality.

"But we do not know," said the king. "We have no proof." Although he was weak and sickly, the king was reluctant to give total power over to his crown prince. Being king had given him a new feeling of duty–a love of his people. He could not simply give Bandar a free hand.

"We must take action to arrest him. I can subdue the city of Jabalain in one day. King Waleed City is prepared."

"I will not condone it," said the king, afraid of Bandar's wrath, yet suddenly determined not to let him do this. "Our great father gave us this kingdom. He unified the land–the holy places. There must be another way to settle this, another way short of war. Talk to your brother."

"I will not," said the only man who could refuse the king.

"Your royal majesty–your highness," interrupted Ashamary at that point. "Perhaps I can shed light on

Joseph's Seed

this discussion."

"*Yalla*," said Dowi Al Harbi. "What do you have to tell us?"

"I know the man who committed this act of violence against our government and our holy laws. He is an *Americee* who once worked for me. . ."

"*Walla*, an American!" said Ustez Doudeen. "The CIA?"

"I do not think so," said Ashamary. "Although it is possible."

Bandar held up his hand for silence; then asked the newcomer. "Who is this American, Hijazi? How could a *hawaji* accomplish such an act as this in our city? Who is his sponsor?"

"Actually, your highness, er, I am still his sponsor—although I have not seen the man for several months. A cooperative farm from Jabalain tried to buy his contract from me but I refused, since the American had not fulfilled his obligations to me."

"You mean you did not pay him," said Bandar sarcastically. "But never mind that. Where is this man now? Where does he work?"

"I am not sure, your highness, but I believe that he must be under the protection of the emir of Jabalain or else he would have already been arrested. You see I submitted a complaint about his failure to report to work and..."

"You see!" said Bandar excitedly, turning to the king. "The traitor has hired someone to disgrace us, to destabilize our regime. Perhaps there are American spies in the kingdom right now undermining our efforts with the blessings of the traitor."

"I do not think..." said Ashamary.

"Silence Hijazi," said the prince who looked at the king once more, waiting for him to speak.

"Still," said the king after some moments. "There is no proof."

Then the Yemeni, who was standing by the entrance, leaning against the wall, spoke. "I too recognized some of the intruders," he said. "They were Filipinos who once worked on the JADCO project. There leader is one called Alex. Perhaps they can still be found."

"I suggest then," said Dowi Al Harbi, "that we attempt to locate this Alex, and even if he can not be found, there should be a general internment of trouble makers of that nationality. We now have the facilities to do so. A few beheadings to restore them to the fear of Allah."

"I agree that we should search for these renegades," said Muhammad.

"So ordered," said Bandar looking away from the king. Then he turned to the minister of internal security who was present and said, "If there are to be no hostilities at the present time, there will at least be readiness for such time as they are needed. Ordered also is a state of military readiness at all of our facilities and military cities. Ordered also is a search for this American–in fact, we will bring in for questioning any Americans still remaining in the kingdom." The king did not object this time. He was tired.

Bandar turned to Ashamary, "What is this man's name, Hijazi?"

"Rex Lawton," said the sycophant. The male secretary in attendance wrote the name down.

Then Bandar turned to Ustez Doudeen. "You must convince the sheikh to release now new funds. Preparation must begin."

"It will be done," said Doudeen.

Although King Muhammad had not agreed to an attack on the province of Jabalain, nor a formal declaration of hostilities against the emir Mustapha and his followers, he had acquiesced to all of the rest of Bandar's demands saying only to the crown prince, "I don't know, Bandar Jibreen. I don't know, still–if you think it is best."

The king was weak and in ill health, and not suited for such a job during these troubled times. By disposition he saw only the best side of people. He revered the noble tradition of his family: the House of Rasheed, and could not believe that it was capable of evil doings.

He felt guilt over the death of his beloved brother Waleed, the former king–and somehow responsible. Had he been duped? During the world Islamic convention, at the Ambassador Hotel in Tunis, had the telephone call which took him out of the convention hall just before the explosion, been some kind of a plan? He had told himself that it had been the will of Allah; but perhaps the other–the Satan–had a hand in it? The king did not know anymore, but there was a growing feeling within him of impending doom.

He had supported his younger militant brother Bandar, because he believed that the Arabs needed pride in themselves and should not simply be, as he had heard Ararat say once, "stooges of the West." But he had never before thought his brother evil.

When Bandar had insisted on the execution of the boy Mugrin for what amounted to nothing more than a fit of bad temper, he was bewildered. He had agreed because he had not wanted to appear weak to his people.

Now Bandar was talking of warring on his brother. How had his country become so divided suddenly? Why was so much money being spent now on the military? The entire fortune of Al Tawali, it seemed, was now being used for that purpose. Although many of Mustapha's allies still controlled the oil money and kept it safe in foreign banks, Al Tawali seemed to have an endless supply of it and it was at Bandar's disposal.

Was there to be war with the Zionists? With the Americans? –but that was insane. With some other Arab nation then? The king did not know. He was tired. He went into his harem and tried to forget.

When he left the king's majlis, although he knew he had been insulted and abused, Hijazi Ashamary felt vindicated for his feelings of jealousy and his desire to strike out at the unruly American, Rex Lawton. But his feeling of doubt which had first taken root at the meeting of the Council of Princes at the JADCO reservation was beginning to grow.

Would they succeed in capturing Rex? He wondered now if that was what he really wanted. And what of Frank Costello? Would they kill him too?

Frank was getting used to being without Debbie again, but he went about his duties now with the feeling that something vital was gone out of him–like a missing organ; and Shareef, although with him almost constantly now, provided a poor substitute.

He dressed this morning in a hurry for he had overslept and Shareef was picking him up in a few minutes. They were going to Al Kharge to supervise the unloading of another shipment of grain bins, arriving on a fleet of tractor trailers from Jeddah. The trucks were already waiting at the site and Mr. Doudeen had called him at five a. m. to say that he had to be there. He had fallen back to sleep and now he had to hurry. The phone rang. It was Shareef. He was waiting in the lobby. He quickly finished dressing, forgetting to button down his collar.

Twenty-Eight

Arab Jail

A road block was set up on the Riyadh-Al Kharge Highway at the halfway point between the two cities which was around forty kilometers from downtown Riyadh. The withering palms lining the road were either dead or dying. A steel tower from the electric distribution line which follows the highway was leaning like Pisa after having taken part in a recent collision with a fuel oil truck. A mammoth oil refinery could be seen in the desert a few kilometers off the highway, its pungent smell co-mingling with the untreated exhaust of passing diesel trucks. It was another hot and stultifying day in the kingdom, but there was work to be done.

Shareef slowed the white Mercedes to a halt when the soldier standing in the road ordered him to do so. He expected this to be no different from the many checkpoints he had gone through in the past. He would show his Al Tawali identification papers, and he would be allowed to pass without a word.

The guard examining his papers was about to do just that when he heard a shout from another soldier standing on the road side who had been conferring with some men and talking loudly on a hand held two-way radio at the same time. The soldier, apparently an officer, had alertly noticed the white man, a *hawaji*, probably an *Amerikee* judging from his clothes, sitting next to Shareef, and he had strict orders.

Frank heard the shouts and saw the Arab soldiers running toward him. "What's going on," he asked Shareef, more curious than worried–for he too had driven through many check points and had always managed in English by simply showing his papers, telling jokes and making small talk which he was sure the soldier wouldn't understand. The guards would then allow him to pass, if not courteously then indifferently. Frank had always previously gone through check points with the feeling that he had pulled the wool over some dumb Arab's eyes. Today things were different.

"They want you to remove yourself from the car," said Shareef.

"What for?!" asked Frank, astonished. "Did you tell them who we work for?"

"Of course," said the Egyptian. "But it did no good; they don't care."

Frank was leaning over Shareef now so he could make eye contact with the officer. "I just spoke to sheikh Tawali's business manager this morning," he said emphatically. "Mr. Ustez Doudeen? –He insists that I go to Al Kharge immediately. He would be very angry if he knew I was being delayed." Frank was speaking English, but the officer made no effort to answer him in that language. Instead, he shouted an order to another soldier who opened the door of the Mercedes on Frank's side and began to drag him out.

"Hey!" yelled Frank. "What the hell do you think you're doing!?"

"I don't think he's impressed with who you know, boss," said Shareef. "He says you're under arrest. He wants me to keep your appointment with Al Tawali for you. In other words, I can't go with you. He said he'll shoot me right now if I argue. I suggest you go peacefully–but don't worry, I'll do what I can."

An hour later at what seemed to be a police station somewhere in Al Kharge, Frank was thrown into a room with bars on the window. It was a jail cell. The cell already contained over fifteen men, all of whom seemed to be Arabs or "third worlders" of various nationalities. Frank surmised this to be a kind of waiting room where he would have to stay for an hour or so until Shareef made the necessary calls to get him out.

There were no beds or other furniture in the room, but there were filthy foam mats and blankets strewn helter-skelter over the floor. The room smelled foul. Frank sat down and tried to think.

That night, still having heard nothing from Shareef, he faced the fact that this was where he was going to sleep.

As he lay on a thin mat shivering, he wondered what in the world had happened. Had Agricultural International's luck in the kingdom suddenly turned sour? He had heard stories of company men being jailed when there were money problems at higher levels. Or maybe the Authorities found out about his relationship with Snead–but he had never really done anything for Snead. Frank did not know about the general roundup of Westerners, for it was not advertised. If Shareef knew, he hadn't told Frank about it.

Was this about Debbie? Had she started mouthing off about hating Arabs again like she used to do? Snead had said she was "on a mission," but Frank could make no sense of it. What could she possibly be up to?

"Nah!" thought Frank, denying his fears. "She's just out for adventure. Nothing more to it. She knows which side her bread is buttered on–probably fooling around with Clement that's all–what could she possibly see in him though? The muscle-bound cowboy." A flush of jealous anger surged through him; "–nah, couldn't be," he shook his head.

He shivered again. The desert night was colder than he had expected. The unfinished cinder block building he was in was damp and dank. There was no glass on the jail cell's window—only iron bars. Insects could come and go at will. Someone threw a stinking blanket at him. He wrapped himself in it with relish. "Shukron," said Frank, using one of the few Arabic words he knew. "You're welcome," said a voice from over in a corner.

The next day after he estimated it to be late enough for the business day to begin, he went over to the window and called to the armed guard who was standing outside.

"Uh, excuse me," he said to the guard. "Would you please call someone in authority. I'd like to make a phone call."

The guard either didn't hear him or pretended he didn't, or else he didn't understand English. In any case he made no response. He continued to lean against a wall, holding his automatic weapon casually, looking away from Frank. Frank tried to elicit help from someone–anyone. "Does anyone here speak English?" he asked looking back at his comrades in the cell. There was no response.

Frank grew determined. He should be allowed at least one phone call. As soon as Mr. Doudeen found out he was here, he'd be released immediately. He wondered what had become of Shareef. Something should be happening soon. It couldn't hurt, though, to speed things up from this end.

"Hey! com'ere!" he shouted a little louder to the guard. "I want to make a phone call–you know, telyphone?" Frank pantomimed the motion of dialing a phone. The guard looked over lazily. Then he walked toward him. "Finally," thought Frank. He was holding the bars desperately without realizing it.

"Move from window! Sit down!" ordered the guard harshly. He then rattled his gun barrel back and forth across the iron bars catching Frank's fingers. "Oww!" screamed Frank.

"*Yalla!* Move back!" the guard ordered again. This time Frank's fingers were off the bars as the barrel

Joseph's Seed

rattled by. He sat back down on his mat rubbing his smarting fingers.

It was much later before he remembered that he was hungry. The day before he had seen his fellow inmates eating chicken and rice from a communal dish, eating with dirty hands and without utensils. It wasn't very appetizing. In fact, it looked downright disgusting, so he wasn't much interested in food at the time. He wondered now when they would serve more. They never did. He wasn't about to ask the guard about it though.

After awhile a boy came to the window and several of the inmates went over to him and gave him money. Frank surmised that they were placing their orders for food. Someone tapped him on the shoulder and said, "*akel*," mimicking the motion of eating to Frank. "Sure," said Frank. "I want to eat."

"Ten riyals," said the boy at the window. "What you want?"

"Let's see," said Frank, taking out his wallet. "Get me an omelet, some toast, juice and coffee." The boy took the money and left.

An hour later the boy came back and handed several packages through the bars. The inmates took them and handed one to Frank. It contained some cookies and a can of banana juice made in Japan. All of the other packages contained the components of a chicken with rice dinner which was then laid out on a platter and eaten communally.

After a few such days had passed, Frank began to learn the ways of survival in this particular hell. He learned that he had to eat with everybody else if he wanted to eat something besides cookies and juice. He learned that he had to pay for his meals, but that he could get "desserts" if he paid extra. He learned that there was a bunghole of a room attached to the cell where he could wash and take care of his bodily needs. It had no door. There was no toilet paper or other amenities in it, just a hole in the floor, and a faucet six inches from that. But there was a box of "Tide" which could be used as one saw fit. He learned that there were to be no phone calls, and no getting out of the cell for exercise or any other reason. He did isometrics and stretched several times a day to keep from going lame.

Occasionally he had conversations with one or two inmates who had a smattering of English. They told each other of their plights as jailbirds do. Frank often said too much, but he figured that no one would understand him anyway. He almost forgot about the voice that had come from the man who had thrown him the blanket.

One of the guards, he learned, was not as cruel as the first one he had spoken to and would at least reply to his request for a phone call. *"Baad shawaya,"* the kindly guard would answer sympathetically. Frank learned that this was the equivalent of "soon."

The kindly guard also allowed Frank to acquire another blanket after he had been interred for a week. In addition the guard allowed the food boy to purchase something for him to read. The boy brought him a paperback novel about the love life of a lady speech writer for a fictitious Italian governor of a New England state. It was terrible; poor narrative, no plot which he could discern, and the dialogue was pathetic. But Frank was desperate. He read and re-read the novel until he knew it by heart.

Frank had been in the calaboose around two weeks before Shareef finally showed up. He brought Frank more cookies and a handful of dog-eared books from his own collection. They were Dashell Hammett and Mickey Spilane novels–a lot better than the story about the lady speech writer. He also threw in an Arabic/English dictionary. Shareef's first comment when Frank came up to the window was, "You don't look American anymore boss, you're one of us now."

Frank had a two week growth on his face and he was filthy. He had made an attempt to wash his body with the Tide a few times but he hadn't bothered with his cloths. There was no place to hang them, and he wasn't too enthusiastic about leaving them off while they dried in any event.

"Where have you been?" asked Frank. He was almost desperate, but still controlling himself. Can you get me out of here? I can't take much more of this."

"Sorry Frank," said Shareef. But this was the first time I have been allowed to visit you; although I knew where you were.

"I spoke to professor Doudeen," he went on. "He told me to tell you that his lawyers will have you released soon and to be patient. He sends his regrets. I have also been in contact with AIC. They in turn contacted the American Consulate in Riyadh, but the Consulate said that although they were sorry for you, they could do nothing. You would have to take your grievances through normal Rasheedi channels, they said.

"I'll be here to see you more often now until you're out. Keep your chin up Frank. Speaking of chins, you need a shave. Want me to bring you a razor?"

"Sure," said Frank smiling. "Thanks."

Shareef returned almost every day after that. He brought clean clothes, a decent blanket, more books, and cookies. Hope returned to Frank's eyes. He began to button down his collar again. Then one day he heard the good news.

"You'll have a hearing tomorrow, Shareef told him."After that you will be released on condition that you stay in the kingdom to finish the installation of the grain bins."

"Sure," said Frank. "I planned to stay anyway. You know why."

"Yeah," said Shareef. "I know why."

That night one of the inmates tapped Frank on the shoulder. Frank looked up from the book he was reading.

"Please, Mr. Frank," said an oriental. "Save me."

"What can I do?" replied Frank. He recognized the voice as the one that had come from the man who had thrown him the blanket when he was shivering. It seemed like ages ago. "I'm as miserable as you are. How can I help? I have a little money left. You can have that if it will..."

"No," said the man. "I do not want money. My problem is they are killing many Filipinos now–cutting off our heads. They will take me away soon. Please we need your help. You are American."

"Killing Filipinos," repeated Frank dully. He was not astonished because he was not able to take in what he was hearing. "Why would they do a thing like that? What have you done?"

"We have done nothing, yet they are killing us. You do not believe me." said the Filipino. "I can see the truth on your face. It is because you are American. You can not believe that there is such a place like this. Even after you sit in this shit hole for many weeks, you still can not believe it. Still you do not understand what is going on here. You think you are in jail by some kind of mistake."

Frank was a person who had spent his whole life living by his own pat answers, whose plan was basically how to get rich, closing his mind to anything that might distract him; in a dogmatic slumber, as someone once said.

"That's right," he said. "It must be a mistake."

"Maybe they will kill your wife before you wake up," said the Filipino. Frank turned away.

The next day Shareef waited while Frank cleaned himself as best he could and put on the fresh clothes Shareef had brought him that morning. Then the kindly guard unlocked the cell and let him out. They walked to a conference room of some sort in the building next to the cell where Frank had lived for the past three weeks. Several men sat around a table. Some were dressed in army clothes and some, including Shareef, wore the traditional Arabian garb. The officer who had arrested Frank was present but another young officer seemed to be in charge of the hearing. He had seen this man before but did not mention it.

"You will be free to go today," said the officer in decent English. "But first we should like to ask you some few questions. Is this acceptable to you?"

Shareef had already cautioned Frank not to act outraged about being detained under these horrible conditions for no apparent reason. "It wouldn't work this time," he had said. "Just keep cool and be polite no matter what they say, and they will let you go." Shareef's warning was unnecessary; it was already clear to Frank that the rules had changed.

"Sure," said Frank now. "I'll answer your questions. I'm always glad to help in any way I can–always have been."

"That is very sensible," said the officer. "In that case we shall begin." He took out a sheet of paper on which was written a list of questions in Arabic. The officer translated them freely as he went along.

First, Frank was asked his name, religion (to which he answered, Italian Catholic), the name of the company he worked for, the name of his present sponsor–this was Ustez Doudeen. Before that it had been Hijazi Ashamary, and before that Moneef Mulafic.

"Very impressive portfolio," said the officer. "You have been employed by many important men in our country. I understand you were also employed by the Governor of Jabalain? Emir Mustapha?"

Frank knew that this particular customer was now considered an outlaw.

"I've never actually met Prince Mustapha," answered Frank. "I did however make a small sale of five grain bins to his business manager, Mr. Fahad. But I really don't get involved in politics," he added. "In fact I know very little about what the issues are in your country. I'm a businessman."

"Yes, yes," said the officer. "We understand that

you are a business man. But still you must realize that we are living in a dangerous time here. We are facing the danger of a revolution."

"I didn't know that," said Frank.

"I believe you," said the officer. "However, let us proceed. Are you acquainted with an American named Rex Lawton?"

"Rex? Yeah, I know Rex. I know a lot of Americans who work in the kingdom. I met him at an agricultural fair in Riyadh two years ago. I see him once in a while at Friday brunch at the Marriott. They serve American style food there."

"Yes I am aware of this," said the officer impatiently. "Do you know his–how do you say–his where he is about?"

"You mean his whereabouts? Actually I don't. I had heard he was fired from the JADCO project before it was completed, and I haven't seen him since. I figured he went back to the states for awhile–but don't worry; he'll be back. He's lived here a long time, you know."

"When was the exact last time you have seen him?" the officer persisted.

"I'm not sure. But I think it was at the Marriott around four months ago right after my wife arrived..."

"Where is your wife now?" asked the officer, apparently no longer interested in Rex Lawton. Frank gave the name of an American woman and her husband who managed prince Razi's farm, as Shareef had instructed him to do should they ask.

Then the officer moved to a chair at the other end of the table where a wealthy looking Arab had been sitting in silence the whole time. The two men conferred in hushed tones for some moments. Frank thought there was something strangely familiar about the rich looking Arab. But he couldn't quite place him; something didn't fit. Suddenly it came to him. It was the clothes. The other times he had seen this man he had been dressed gruffly in jeans, a tee shirt and a sloppy red checked headdress. It was Muhammad Ali the

Joseph's Seed

Yemeni, Mr. Ashamary's driver. Then the Yemeni spoke.

"Mr. Frank," he said. "We have very difficult times now. You must be..." He was groping for a word which he did not know in English. He said something to the officer. The officer turned to Frank.

"Sheikh Muhammad Ali apologizes for the inconveniences you have suffered," said the officer. "But he fears you may yet have more sufferings. For reasons of security we may have to detain your wife, Mrs. Debbie Costello." There was a pause, but Frank said nothing. "When you are released, you must not try to contact her. This is an issue of utmost importance to our government. It seems that perhaps unknown to you, your wife has become involved in attempt to overthrow our government.

"We apologize; but any Americans now remaining in the kingdom will be considered under the arrest of the house, as you say. You may continue your work. There is no reason to stay in a prison since you can go nowhere anyway. Mr. Shareef will continue to be your guide, but he will take you only where it is necessary for us to allow you to travel.

"Do you understand, Mr. Costello? You are free to leave now. You must behave in a sensible way. Stay cool, as you say. As to whether you shall see your wife again soon–it is in the hands only of our great king Bandar."

Twenty-Nine

The Prince of Um

The golden grain stretched out into the vast emptiness; its color blending with that of the sand dunes of the Nafood and the color of her hair. Beyond the dunes, shrouded in the morning mist and barely discernable were the peaks of Jabalain.

Nearby, two Filipinos were in a field working on a large pea-green combine. They were setting it up for the wheat cutting which would soon begin. It was early May and nearly harvest time. On the combine was the emblem of Agricultural International. The machine had been sold to the American farm manager here by Frank Costello on the day he had climbed the butte.

Debbie tied back the tent flap she was holding and stretched. Then she pulled the draw string on her pink robe and waved in reply to the Filipinos who had just noticed her and were waving. It was Alex and one of his men.

By now she knew the reason for the desert mystique; the reason why Arab women kept themselves shrouded. It was the openness. There was nowhere to conceal oneself in the desert, thus modesty became a necessity. She thought now, that it was not men who had forced their peculiar manner of dress upon the women, but it was they themselves who had initiated it in their own self defense. Still, she couldn't agree with the lengths to which they had gone.

But she was among friends here and not worried about that. It was the future which worried her. She knew this could not last. It was not for happiness that she had come to Arabia, it was to stop Ahmad Daweesh.

She turned to look back into the tent. Clement was still asleep but would soon awaken. They would be traveling today, making their weekly trip to Jabalain and Mustapha's palace, and after that to the farm to see Rex. This would be her last trip.

But she still had time. In awhile they would dress and go to Razi Al Atebbi's farm to the house of Craig and Mary Johnson from Nebraska. Craig was Razi's farm manager. Nearby also was a small Arab town called "Um," where they could get gas and provisions. It was a town a hundred miles removed from the nearest paved road. Um was on the ancient caravan route to Kuwait. Razi Al Atebbi was the emir or "prince" of Um.

The Johnsons had invited them to share the comforts of their modern farmhouse, but Debbie had declined preferring this tent. She wanted to experience the desert. In a little while they would stop at the house before making the four hour, off-road trip to Jabalain.

She had thought she might like an early walk before he awoke. It was not yet six. But then she changed her mind, she decided to get her exercise in another way. She sealed off the tent again and got back into their foam rubber mat bed. Then she snuggled up and put an arm around him. He stirred, and after a moment he turned.

"Frank hates to be awakened so early," she said.

"Shh!" said Clement, and kissed her.

Two hours later when they knocked on the door of the Johnsons' modern pre-fab home. Mary greeted them warmly as she always did. "Come on in," she said.

"Coffee's ready."

At breakfast, Craig said, "Two of Bandar's agents came by yesterday after you left. They said we would have to market our grain through Riyadh this year instead of Jabalain and Kuwait like we been doing' since we built this farm. In other words, they want us to give it to them. The hell we will.

"When I told Razi the news, he laughed and said we'll just harvest a little sooner this year. The grain's still wet, but in this climate it should be safe enough. Alex says he can get it out in less than a week. He's the best hired hand I ever had–sure appreciate you and Rex steering him my way.

"I expect the Rasheeds will be back soon enough but the wheat will be gone by then, and inshalla so will we."

"What if they come earlier–or send the Army?" asked Debbie.

"We don't think they'll be here again for at least a few weeks," said Mary. "First, they don't want to inflame the desert bedouin like Razi until they've got Mustapha locked away. They know they won't have any trouble taking Jabalain any time they want to, so they're in no hurry. It was in the news last night. They're trying to get him to surrender his son to the Riyadh authorities along with the 'renegade American'. That's what they call Rex. They also want Mustapha to publicly endorse Prince Bandar's policies. They challenged him to prove that he is still loyal to his country and a good Muslim."

"He'll never endorse them," said Clement.

"Mustapha don't have much of an army," Mary went on. "In fact, he's not supposed to have one at all."

"But he has friends," said Craig. "At King Waleed and a lot of other places. He's stalling Riyadh for time now. Mustapha needs that now more than anything else. The only thing preventing his being arrested by Bandar is the old king and a few friends."

"Friends like you," said Debbie.

"And Razi," said Mary. "He stands to lose everything he built here if the Rasheeds come."

"Oh, I don't know," said Clement. "This is a long way off the beaten track. If the Rasheeds take his wheat this year, next year he just won't grow any. They'll lose interest in him. Not much out here really, just a small town with a lot of donkeys in it."

"He was supposed to be here by now," said Craig. "He's got to decide whether to start cutting."

"That sounds like his truck now," said Debbie who had pulled back the kitchen curtains to look outside. "Why does he drive such an old beat up pickup? I thought he was supposed to have money."

"He does," said Clement. "Just doesn't do much good to drive anything nice out here–no roads. Anyway, he wants to be like the rest of the bedouin and that's what they all drive–red and white Datsuns."

Just then the door opened and a frail old Arab walked in, a shaggy, white bearded apparition who looked as if he hadn't bathed in months. But his smell was not foul, it was that of jasmine and goat's milk.

"*Sabakh al kher,*" said Razi Al Atebbi.

"*Sabakh al nur,*" replied the American Farmer.

"Good morning," said Clement, who then got up and gave the old man a bear hug in greeting. Then Debbie, who had grown fond of this good hearted man who had extended his hospitality to her against the criticism of some of his people, did likewise.

The old man beamed. "I know your husband." He winked. The English words sounded strange coming from him.

"Yes I know," Debbie smiled, for Clement had told her the story of the time Razi jumped on Clement's back and pretended to try to wrestle his camera away. It was an amusing joke the old man had wanted to play on the strange newcomer. Clement had gone along with it having briefed Rex beforehand.

Then Razi said something to Craig in Arabic. Debbie heard a word she knew. It was '*Khatar.*' It meant 'dangerous,' but it was more than that. It was a term of foreboding. Craig turned to Debbie and said gravely: "He told me that Bandar's men have killed King Muhammad by slow poison. Bandar is now king. He said also that the Rasheeds know you are out here. It's your hair. You stick out like a sore thumb in this part of the world. He says for you to be careful. He's worried about you."

Thirty

The Nazi

The palace guard admitted them informally, for he knew them well. "Mustapha is in the garden," he told them. "He is expecting you."

They found him sitting with Rina whom he had gotten out of Riyadh before it became dangerous for her there.

"Welcome," she said, and she got up to embrace Debbie. "How was your trip? How are you feeling?" Her concern was real, and natural for all present knew what Debbie was going to attempt. She took Debbie by the hand and together they walked into the arboretum.

As he watched them walk off Mustapha said to Clement, "Mr. Snead was here yesterday with Fahad."

"Oh?"

"You know that my brother has made himself king?"

"Razi told us this morning–I'm sure it will be announced soon enough."

"Yes. They tell me that he will have me arrested soon–within the week it seems.

"I have also been informed by my sources that another shipment of strategic equipment has arrived at King Waleed City. Troop levels there alone have now passed the eight hundred thousand mark."

"Pakistanis, Somalis and the like," murmured Clement.

"You underestimate them," said the prince. "They are being well trained–and well fed. More important, they believe in him. When and if they are mobilized they will have vast numerical superiority and state of the art military equipment."

"It's not a question of 'if' anymore. Is it?"

"By the way," said Mustapha, ignoring the question. "Debbie's husband has been released from jail. He is being assigned to work at JADCO. But they will allow him to see her first."

"It doesn't matter," said Clement. "They won't be together for long. Afterwards, she won't go back to him again–if she survives that is."

"Yes," said the prince; "if she survives."

The next day at the farm, the Indian cook, Abu Baker served his best cinnamon flavored mutton stew to the prince's company. Mustapha and Rina sat at opposite ends of the table. Abdullah and some other men stood outside the small dining hall, apparently with nothing to do.

At dinner with the governor and his wife were several children. Among them were some of the prince's elder sons from other wives, including his son Mugrin. Present also were Debbie, Clement, and Rex.

Mugrin was arguing with Rex, speaking half Arabic–half English.

"*Ya, Mohandas,*" he insisted. "We can not take the diesel off of well number fourteen this day. There is still much sand."

"Okay then," said the Texan. "We kin wait another day. But I say it's as clear as it's gonna' get."

"No, no," insisted the boy. "I do not think you are right."

The prince laughed. "You are making quite a farmer out of my son," he said. "I remember it was not long ago that he despised work, just like all of his friends at Riyadh University. I thank you for inspiring him to change."

"It ain't nothin'," said Rex. Then the older man turned to Debbie and asked, "When are you goin' Deb?"

"Tomorrow morning," she answered.

"I'll take you in," he said.

"Thanks, but Mustapha has arranged for it. I'll be back at the Marriott by evening."

"You realize," said the prince, "that you could become trapped there during a war with the Jewish State. It could be very dangerous for you."

"I'll have to chance it," she said.

Then Clement said something she had never heard him say.

"It wouldn't be such a great loss," he said. "If that country was blown away before this thing gets settled. Might bring things more in line with the way they aught to be."

"What do you mean?" asked Debbie, her eyes narrowing.

"Why I guess I mean that a final solution that's fifty years too late is better than no final solution at all," answered Clement quite seriously.

Debbie stared a long moment at the man with whom she had been intimate for the past month. As her eyes narrowed, she went from love to hate in the time it took her to process what he was saying. "That's very interesting," she said. "I thought you knew. I had assumed that Snead would have told you."

"Told us what?" inquired the prince.

"That I'm Jewish," replied Debbie.

"Oh?" said Clement. "Uh, no he didn't."

Thirty-One

You're a Dreamer

"We thought simply that you were an American agent," said Mustapha, "under the jurisdiction of Mr. Snead. We didn't really consider your religion, though now that I think about it, it doesn't surprise me. Is your husband Jewish also?"

"Half," she said, "his father was Italian."

He was sitting across from her now in his private office at the farm, his expressive eyes sympathetic but otherwise noncommittal. The others were gone, politely excluded from further involvement in the matter. After her revelation an hour earlier, Clement had maintained his predictable poker face, refusing to disclose whatever emotion, if any, he was feeling about the news—or about her. As for Debbie, she was infuriated and upset, and let him know by becoming cold as ice toward him.

It was no act. For a second time in her life she had grossly misjudged someone for whom she had cared a great deal. First it was Ahmad, and now this. She had been strongly attracted to both men—and both had proven to be evil. It was clear to her now that Clement was a hardened anti-Semite—probably a neo-Nazi. She despised him.

The prince waited patiently for her to talk. "So where does that leave me?" she asked finally, holding his gaze. "Are you going to throw me in jail?"

He did not smile. "You misunderstand me," he said, "and many of us–most of us, I suspect. The proper question, I think, is where that leaves me with you. Do you still want to help me? Did you ever? Or do you hate us too much for that?"

"It's my people," she said, looking away. "So many have been killed and oppressed–for so long. We've lost the ability to trust."

"I did not kill them," said the man with compassionate eyes.

She looked at him for a long time, and then said simply, "I know."

"I want to tell you something," he said then. "Your people and mine, we are cousins, both of the Semitic race. I know this is not news to you, but I wonder if you really ever considered what that means."

"I'm not sure if I know what you're getting at," she said.

"I am referring to all of the things we have in common. If you considered them you might agree with me that we shouldn't be fighting at all. There are other, much worse enemies to be fought."

"Such as?"

"Such as ignorance, and disease, for starters."

"Everyone is against those things," she said.

"Okay, then what about fanaticism, or the power lust of men like my brother? Surely you'll agree that these are common enemies of ours."

"I don't mean to be belligerent, Mustapha. You have treated me well–better than I ever expected–and Rina is dear to me–but I have to say that your people are known for their fanaticism. It's common knowledge. I don't know if it's your religion or just some forms of it. Look at the terrorists. They are almost always Muslim Arabs." She thought of Ahmad and felt vindicated by her statement. She thought also, but didn't speak it, of the power lust that inflicts all males. Would the man in front of her be immune from it if he were to win? Wasn't it probable that he was pretending to be a moderate, simply because he was the underdog?

"Is that your knowledge speaking now, or your prejudice?" he asked. It was as if he were reading her thoughts.

"As I said, it's common knowledge."

"As you wish," said the prince. "I could argue that all three major Western religions have had what you call their 'fanatic' stage–even your own–and each has fanatic aspects even today. Look at the terrorists of the Irgun for example. I could point out that many other peoples have suffered massacres and even holocausts, just as your people have. Did you know that during the Mongolian invasions, for example, countless millions of my people were exterminated, wiped out–including the great civilization in and around Baghdad. I could say that the problems of your people did not begin with the creation of the State of Israel. No, there were problems with the ancient Greeks, the Romans, the Christians and many others. We do not, and have never persecuted you as many of the others have.

"I could say all these things, but I won't. You may believe as you wish about me; though I hope to change your mind some day. "What I want to talk to you about now is much more important."

"What is it?" she asked.

"Would you mind if we went outside while we talk? I don't like to discuss important matters indoors. It gives me a cooped up feeling. Maybe it's because I'm a bedouin."

"Sure," said Debbie with a thin smile. "But I don't want to see Clement again."

"You won't have to. He is gone by now. And please, try to trust me." He squeezed her hand as they got up to leave.

"We had a President who used to say that. And he

wasn't very trustworthy."

They both laughed.

As the Land Rover negotiated a desert trail between the Nafood and the more habitable terrain of Jabalain province, they spoke of many things. While he drove, Debbie watched the jagged peaks play against the sunset. He was telling her of the miracle of his country's recent growth and modernization, of its pains and its blessings. She thought of another miracle she had seen.

They passed an alfalfa field being watered by a circular sprinkling machine owned by an isolated bedouin who had been brought, perhaps reluctantly, into the new era. Its spray formed a rainbow against the setting Sun. His family still lived in a goat hair tent.

She agreed as they spoke that she should remain a few days longer on the prince's farm before embarking upon her mission. She was too unsettled now to begin such a dangerous undertaking just yet. Mustapha would not remain at the farm however–he had pressing business elsewhere–but would try to come back to see her before she left. Until then, Rex would be there if she needed anything and, after that, the prince's men would see that she was safely returned to the Riyadh Marriott. Frank, Mustapha told her, had been released from jail and had been notified by Shareef who had been told by Fahad that her return was imminent. Funny, but she looked forward to seeing him again.

He turned to her then and asked, "Why are you really doing this?" When she made no reply he went on. "If you get close to my brother, as your friend Shareef claims is now inevitable, he may never set you free. If he finds out who you are, he will kill you. He knows now only that you are involved with people who are sympathetic to me, and he is still trying to win them over.

"You don't have to do this. I can get you out of the country now if you want to go."

"I can't leave. This is what I have to do," she said.

"Why? There must be more to it than just the obvious."

"What's 'the obvious'?"

"Because you are Jewish," he said, "you are fighting my brother for his military ambitions and for what you call his terrorist activities."

"You don't believe it's terrorism?

"I'm not as sure as you." he said. "To me there is some justice on both sides."

"At least you're not totally against us. That leaves room for hope."

"Yes, I have hope. There are always solutions to problems–even problems as seemingly unsolvable as the Palestinian question."

"What solution would you propose?" she asked, not really expecting to hear anything new.

"I read a book," he answered, "about the problems in South Africa. Israel's situation is very similar. It is very difficult when the problem is both economic and racial; but if both factors are addressed, I believe a solution is possible.

"There are several keys: One is in an absolute separation of powers–not just autonomy, but not complete independence either. No, the parties must learn to live together–for they both want the same land! But each must be able to live in freedom and dignity at the same time.

"What I would propose is that each community be almost completely responsible for its internal affairs, that representatives of each area take part in the central government, that private property be inviolate–that is a most important factor.

"But to have property rights, you must reduce drastically the power of any central government. It cannot be allowed to tax or take property or income, for example, neither Jewish nor Arab. Keep the government weak and the people will be able to live together."

"You, a monarchist, making such suggestions?" she challenged.

Joseph's Seed

"Who said I was a monarchist? Anyway the biggest problem is of course the army. Whoever controls the army controls the land. The Army must be strong or it faces destruction from the outside. But it can not be dominated by only one faction, for the rights of the other faction would then be canceled out.

"I would suggest that the army remain in Israeli hands for the time being but that Palestinians be gradually assimilated into it–at all levels. What's more important is that it never use its force against its own people.

"The key to all this, of course, is that the people first have the will to find solutions–it would take an iron clad constitution. But before any of this is possible, of course, there must be a renunciation of violence on both sides."

"Would your side–the Palestinians–ever agree to that?" asked Debbie skeptically.

"First there would have to be a shift of opinion–official opinion at the highest levels–in the Arab world. But I believe that can be arranged. Men like the President of Egypt..."

"Are you suggesting an Israel-Palestine federation then?" said Debbie, interrupting Mustapha's train of thought.

"Didn't I say that?"

"You're a dreamer," she said.

"Can you think of anything better?" He waited for her answer but she said nothing. He was quiet awhile and then said: "But first we must solve the immediate problem."

"Which is?"

"What I wanted to ask you is this. If you lose contact with Snead, will you work with us? I will have trusted contacts in my brother's government long after your country's agents have all gone home. Even the mysterious Mr. Snead can not long survive my brother's thorough scrutiny. Soon he will have to flee or he will be caught. Even your Shareef is not immune. He takes quite a few risks I understand. But what you might not realize is that you won't even be able to communicate with him without my help. You will need me; there is no question of it. The only question is whether you will help me in return."

She considered for a moment then turned to face him in her seat and asked, "What do you want me to do?"

He told her on the way back to the farm.

A week after Debbie had been safely returned to Riyadh and reunited with her husband; Bandar's army stormed the city of Jabalain.

They came with a company of elite troops of the National Guard. Hundreds of armored vehicles rolled into the city. Scores of helicopters landed in the fields nearby. Within a few short hours all of the city's strategic locations were under Bandar's control. Aside from a small number of skirmishes which were more a matter of temper flare-ups than organized resistance, few shots were fired. Everyone was relieved. From the young, untried officers who led the assault, to the seasoned soldiers who were reluctant to open fire on their countrymen. All were gratified that the assault had been executed without the need of a massacre.

But the commanding officer knew that if one had been required, he would have ordered it and he would have been obeyed.

The commanding officer was Momduh Ibn Bandar, eldest son of the king. At thirty years of age he had recently been placed at the head of the kingdom's key security force, the National Guard.

Mustapha's two palaces and palace guard surrendered without a shot. Shortly thereafter, as soon as they were judged to be secure by the commander, a white Mercedes pulled up to the gates of the new pal-

Joseph's Seed

ace. The gates were opened to admit a dignified Arab dressed in white. An honor guard stood at attention with their weapons at bay. He was Muhammad Ali the Yemeni, commander Momduh's immediate superior.

All had gone well, except for the fact that Mustapha, his family, and his entourage, were not to be found. Word soon leaked out that they had fled to Egypt on the previous day.

When Momduh arrived at the prince's farm north of the city, no one was there save a group of Sri Lankan farm hands and Abu Baker the cook. Momduh was disappointed, for he wanted to see his old friend Mugrin– and of course to have the honor of arresting him again. But he had to settle for the Sri Lankans. These were rounded up and taken to King Waleed Military city where they were interrogated and drafted into the army. Later, when asked about the whereabouts of the renegade American, Rex Lawton, Abu Baker answered only: "He go with prince to Egypt."

Back in the desert near the town of Um, a contingent of troops arrived shortly thereafter only to find a sleepy town with nothing in it except a few illiterate bedouin and lots of donkeys. As for Prince Razi, and his farm; all that was found were bare fields, some sand covered farm machinery, and an empty farm house. When questioned, the townspeople of Um said that sheikh Razi was in the dessert with his clan, which was natural, since he was, after all, a nomad. No one was looking for Alex, for it was not known that he had been there.

And what of Clement Schmidt? Why was he not sought out for arrest, or at least under suspicion owing to the fact that he was a hated American? The answer was simple. As far as his supervisor at Al Tawali Enterprises knew, Clement had gone to the States on vacation a few months previous, before the crackdown had begun. It was simply assumed that he would not be back.

Thirty-Two

The Prince of Riyadh

The crystallization of an idea can be a slow process sometimes taking years before its form is complete. Thus the idea for the current political agenda developed over the years in the minds of Bandar Jabreen Ibn Abdul Lateef Ibn Rasheed and his chief aid and long time co-conspirator, Dowi Al Harbi. It can not be said that the idea was originated by either one of them, although the intelligence of the Palestinian exceeded that of the prince. But neither could it be assumed that Al Harbi was the mastermind, pulling the strings behind the scenes as it were, of the man who was now King of Arabia.

It is more accurate, if not logical, to say that the idea here referred to, was crystallized somewhere in the space emanating between them, made possible by the words they had heard their whole lives and the realities of the part of the world they lived in.

Before they met in London on that fateful day many years before, Bandar was an ambitious young prince with little to be said for him except that he was a minor member of the house of Rasheed, the rulers of the Kingdom of Arabia; with scores of brothers and cousins ahead of him by both age and reputation and already filling most of the key governmental posts. Given his own resources and abilities, he might never have become more than dean of the University of Riyadh.

Al Harbi for his part would surely have been an active terrorist in any event for he was already hardened by his hate. But he would have been incorporated more than likely into one of the many clandestine tentacles of the Palestinian Restoration Society. Had he been successful, Yassar Ararat and not Bandar would have basked in his glory and used him to his own advantage–but that was not how it happened.

As a young man, Bandar had become champion of a most noble Arab cause–namely, the restoration of Palestine to Arab control. But upon meeting Dowi Al Harbi it became possible to pursue that goal in the most effective way and to a much greater degree.

Then gradually–almost imperceptibly, Bandar had become champion of another cause. It was the cause of spiritual unity, which had become in his mind, the actual unity of the Islamic world. It was this, not to mention the untimely deaths in quick succession of his two predecessors, Waleed and Muhammad, which allowed him to outstrip his many senior brothers, and become king.

Was Bandar qualified to be king? Is any man, ever? The question should rather be whether a leader can rise to the occasion once the reins are placed in his hands. What Bandar did with those reins brings us back to the crystallization of the idea mentioned earlier.

Working together over the years, Bandar and Al Harbi learned that in order to gain support for their agenda they had to nurture those traits in the Arab people which could make it possible. They had to teach it to people who would otherwise be complacent, selfish, or lazy. In other words, they had to teach normal people to be zealots and haters. To do so, they began where the process always begins–in the schools; they spread the latest Arabian scholarship; they nurtured the Wahabi tradition of militant Islam, they led the never ending drumbeat for the death of Israel. Once their seed of hate was sown, they knew it would fester and grow in the very place where it should have been condemned–in the mosques.

From his position as dean of a prestigious Arab university, Bandar was able to encourage the spread of Al Harbi's books and all they implied. Together with the works of Dr. Wahan Al Muhless, they became standard texts in schools throughout the Islamic world.

To inspire and educate the adult population moreover, they made skillful use of the media. In this area they got much help from the Western media especially that expert of Middle Eastern affairs, Denny Rasner. Whenever Baal Bazz made another strike, he was praised and glorified in the Arab press and sensationalized in the Western press. He became an invulnerable mystery man–a Zorro, a Jessie James, a Robin Hood of the Arab world. The Arab people loved him; and Bandar, at first quietly and later openly, took the credit.

Gradually, as we have seen, as his position became more secure, Bandar began to turn a more militant face toward the West. In his speeches, Bandar began to speak of the "manifest superiority" of the Arab people over the decadent West. It was a tactic which had already been taken, to be sure, by such "outlaw" Arab nations as Syria, Iran, Iraq, and Libya, but for the staunchly pro-Western, pro-business, fabulously rich Kingdom of Arabia, Bandar's new stridency was unprecedented.

He made it clear that he believed that Allah wished him to use the kingdom's wealth to spread the True Way to the world. And to achieve that aim, he worked quietly behind the scenes. Hidden in the vast empty desert, at such place as the King Waleed Military City, he precipitated the growth of a military machine never before seen in the Middle East.

The only thing that could have stopped Bandar at

home and the exploits of Baal Bazz abroad was Reason and Enlightenment. But such concepts were in retreat from the world at large and especially from their part of it–the Middle East. They understood this very well, and they strove, each in his own way, as they grew in power and stature, to prevent Reason and Enlightenment from ever rearing their ugly heads again. To achieve this end, they had first to eliminate Mustapha from the picture. Not long ago they had tried and failed to do just that.

He had to be eliminated, for Mustapha was a dangerous anomaly–if not within the context of Islamic culture and history writ large, then from what Islam had become in modern times. A thousand years ago, in the days of the Islamic Empire, when Europe was in its Dark Ages, great Arab philosophers; Averroes, Avicenna, and others had saved for the world the wisdom of the ancient Greeks and improved on it. Were it not for them, it might have been lost forever–and with it the possibility of a modern era. Reason in those days was not the enemy of Islam, as it was in the Christian World. Mustapha was a man of that Islamic tradition– if not the present one. But Mustapha had fled to Egypt. Now, with the help of a large foreign aid check to the Egyptian government, the "traitor," Mustapha would soon be delivered into the hands of his enemies.

Thus the mystique which had grown around them; the invulnerable Baal Bazz, and the Great King, who would lead his people to a great destiny, was coming to fruition.

The king's reputation grew naturally from his earlier reputation as a famous Doctor of Islamic History and Philosophy, and master of Baal Bazz. He was both religious leader and political zealot; a lethal combination.

He developed a "one greater than Baal Bazz" aspect. Although he didn't encourage the association, neither did he discourage it. The name of "Mahdi," the Muslim Messiah, was increasingly being used in connection with him. But privately, Bandar preferred the historical approach to the strictly religious–rather he preferred what might be called, for lack of a better name, "historical mysticism."

To this end, he encouraged certain images to be applied to the growing mystique surrounding him. The first was the theme of Dr. Wahan Al Muhless which Dowi Al Harbi, in his guise as scholar had preempted and helped to spread. This was the theory that the holy land had originally been located in the Hijaz region of the Arabian Peninsula. It was there, they reasoned, that the climax of world history would be enacted. After Palestine was reconquered, the center of all of the world's great religions would again revert to its rightful location; the House of Abraham in Mecca. This would bring the dawn of a New Age of world peace under one religion–Islam.

The second theme, flowing naturally from the first, was the millennial idea which put the final battle between good and evil in the Holy land on the mountain of Har Megiddo or Armageddon. There was still some dissension among Islamic scholars as to whether Har Megiddo, was located in the mountains of the Hijaz near Mecca, or in Palestine as was traditionally believed. Bandar favored the traditional approach because he intended soon to conquer that land. The details mattered not to him in either case since he knew that he would triumph over the evil Zionists on that day.

How did he know? It was a well guarded secret that Bandar had long been a student of astrology and the Medieval See Nostradamus. He had long believed that One would rise out of Arabia to world Domination–a man in a blue turban. He could not remember when he began to understand that Allah had ordained that

Joseph's Seed

he was to be that man. But he did not advertise this secret knowledge. The world would know soon enough.

The third theme, which became clear to Bandar and Dowi Al Harbi once they began to see the possible scope of the modern agricultural miracle of development in the desert, was stranger still. After they had seen the vast stores of grain that Tawali and other sheikhs and princes were accumulating on their desert retreats, Bandar had decided to back and then eventually to take over the JADCO project and other large cooperative farm development projects in the kingdom. He had a plan for the enormous surpluses which the small population of Arabia could never consume.

The kingdom had a long tradition of importing armies of slaves. In modern times this became vast armies of imported third world workers, paid subsistence wages from the government's coffers. Now this vast army of near illiterate Muslim workers would gladly follow the Mahdi King as enlistees into an ever growing Islamic Army.

This army, which now numbered in the millions, needed food. The food would be provided by Allah with the help of JADCO, Al Tawali, and the Arabian bread machine. It was a desert miracle which Bandar believed he had caused to happen.

Yusef Al Tawali, the richest man in Arabia, had long been associated in the folklore of Arabia with Joseph of old–sharing a common name and an uncanny ability to succeed where others had failed, and now to grow and store wheat for the difficult days ahead. Thus the term *Bazratuhu Yusuf*, "Joseph's Seed" became the code word for the secret weapon which would triumph over all odds.

To enhance his new mystique and in keeping with the Nostradamus prophecy, Bandar, as was noted by Debbie at the Sheikh's party, took to breaking a long standing tradition by wearing a new form of dress. He continued to affect a *gutra*, and *thobe*. But he altered the coloration and design markedly.

On his head he wore a sky blue *gutra* with an eight pointed Islamic star on it. This was to fulfill the Nostradamus prophecy, but to those who inquired as to the reason for his new manner of dress, he said, "This is what will become of the Zionist Flag after the Jihad."

His *thobe* remained white, but for special occasions he had one made with an insignia on the back of three green concentric circles representing irrigation machines in the desert. Under those were two crossed chaffs of wheat to represent "Joseph's Seed."

"My Brother is insane," Explained prince Mustapha Ibn Abdul Lateef the exile.

"But the People love him," said the President of Egypt, "even many of my own."

"Nevertheless." said Mustapha.

"I know, I know." The President smiled wryly and shook his head slowly. Between his fingers was a ten million dollar check drawn on the bank of Joseph Tawali. "He must be stopped, but it won't be easy.

Thirty-Three

A Determined Woman

Debbie sipped a Pepsi and absently watched an Arabic rendition of Sesame Street on T V. She had on the oversized peach colored tee shirt with a picture of a Beagle on it, which Frank had given her once–and nothing else. Frank wasn't watching her though. He was working on a laptop in the other bed. He didn't seem to be noticing her presence for they were together again.

The valet wouldn't be coming to the door this morning and Shareef wouldn't be there to pick them up for several more hours; still she pulled the sheets over her, up to the waist. Here she could never be as carefree as they had been in their home in Spring Valley.

Would they ever get back home? She wondered. A pang of fear struck her heart–then she remembered and the fear went away. She had come to this God Forsaken place to stop the man who was all of what she knew to be evil. She had believed that aside from her personal desire for revenge for the murder of her brother and her friends, that the world would be a far better place without Ahmad in it.

But something had changed in her mind since her recent discovery about Clement. She had always been sarcastic and blunt because she had been brought up that way; but underneath had always been the feeling

Joseph's Seed

that the world was still a good place–that people would be loving and kind and fair if only you gave them a chance. Now she doubted that assumption. Were most people like Clement at heart? She wondered.

She knew when she came to Arabia that it would be dangerous for her here, but somehow that hadn't struck home. Somehow she had felt immune to the danger. After all, she was a beautiful woman, she was American, and she was smart. Although the training and instructions that Snead and Sadya had given her had instilled her with confidence in her ability to succeed, confidence was a trait that she had never lacked.

Then she had been brutally attacked by those insane religious police, and fear had struck her. They had molested her–contaminated her–but worse, they had given her the feeling that she was in a place where no justice, especially not the kind that she understood, was possible.

Had she been naive? Had Sadya and Snead made her believe that she could really make a difference? "With your husband's business connections," they had told her, "you will be able to get near to the sources of power and that's where you will find him. All we need is advance information about just one of his strikes, and we will have him." She had wanted Sadya to have him, and she believed Snead; so she went.

Would he somehow recognize her first and kill her? They had talked of that possibility too and came to the conclusion that there was not much chance of it. She had been a child of sixteen when she knew Ahmad; fat, (she didn't like to remember that) mousey brown hair. Now she was a beautiful blond woman of thirty. They had looked at old photographs before she had embarked on the mission. He would not recognize her even if he had noticed her as a child, they decided. But in the event that he did, they gave her a contingency plan. She was ready to kill him–they had shown her how, with a poison prick which she would inflict on him. The weapon was hidden in her make-up–in a lipstick. It would work instantly, and then she would kill herself rather than face a horrible execution.

But this scenario was unlikely, she hoped. He had glanced at her at the sheikh's party and there was no sign that he had recognized her. In addition there was little to fear because of Dowi Al Harbi's activities. He spent the majority of his time abroad, practicing his avocation.

She knew from the beginning that in order to accomplish her mission she would have to be separated from Frank, but she hadn't known how it would be arranged. After being attacked by the religious police, she had given herself to Clement because she knew this was it, and she wanted the break to be complete But she also did it for another reason–he exuded masculinity. She had never had that before and she needed it–needed some of his strength and courage. He was absolutely sure of himself. He hadn't a hint of fear in his body. He could come and go, it seemed, even in these dangerous times, without ever being stopped or challenged. She had asked him how he did it, and he had told her it was because he knew many people who were friends of Mustapha. Those who weren't, he knew how to avoid.

And then she discovered that she hated him. She had to, how could she love or want someone who desired the destruction of her people? Still she couldn't just shut herself off like a valve; there was still a leak. But she would stop it she knew–in time.

Now here was Frank again; meek natured, but intense with new determination, and with his new worries. Frank had told her about how, when he was released from jail, he was told that Debbie was to be arrested and he might not ever see her again. But then, both Shareef and Snead had mitigated that trauma by telling him that if he cooperated, he and Debbie could still both get out of this safely when the proper time came. With most of the American and European expatriates gone, they explained, Frank's abilities would

Joseph's Seed

be desperately needed. They couldn't keep him in jail; things were falling apart on the outside and people like him–there weren't many left–were at a premium.

When he first saw her in the lobby a few days ago, Frank whispered a prayer of thanks–and he didn't even believe in God. But now he had to concentrate on the serious task of somehow getting them out of there.

Frank was sitting on his bed now working on his laptop. He was mulling over plans for a factory to be constructed by third world engineers and labor. It would be a food processing plant built on the JADCO reservation to provide supplies for the King Waleed Military City nearby. Frank was not a fully qualified engineer but he had taken many math and engineering courses in college and he had training as a computer specialist. He knew how to make use of the latest engineering software such as the CAD 2000 program he was now using. He shook his head, these plans were a mess and he would have to straighten them out. He couldn't finish the job here, but at least he could map out a plan.

They would be leaving for the site with Shareef this afternoon; and, he was told, they would be leaving the hotel Marriott for good. Well at least Debbie was going with him. He had to get her out of this place–this country–somehow. He knew it wasn't going to be easy.

Debbie got up, pulled off the beagle tee shirt and turned to face her husband. He looked up and smiled, but there were lines of worry in his smile. "I can't," he said. "I've got to do this." She shrugged and began to dress for their trip.

🐫 🐫 🐫

Shareef, Frank, and Debbie arrived in a white Mercedes at the JADCO site just before sundown. A new black top highway with a bright yellow line down the middle was now complete all the way to the large chain link fence gate of the entrance. A six foot high fence with razor wire now surrounded the entire reservation. Inside, the highway continued through the reservation for many miles, dividing the irrigated fields, the grain bins, and some new factories and agricultural facilities which had sprung up. In that direction also, out the back door of the JADCO reservation, so to speak, the road continued on, Shareef told them, to the King Waleed Military City.

An armed guard stopped them at the gate and ordered them to wait. After a half hour, another white Mercedes pulled up to the gate from inside the reservation. It was Ustez Doudeen driving himself. He got out and approached the waiting car.
"How do you do," he said graciously in his sing song voice, leaning toward the opened window. "Mr. Costello, Madam." He took her hand daintily. "Much has changed has it not?" He extended his hand toward the reservation. "Yes, certainly," he went on without waiting for anyone to answer. "Much has changed in many ways. But I am being impolite keeping you here. Please follow me. I have had adequate quarters prepared for you. And then you will have dinner with us, let us say in two hours? Fine?"
At dinner with Frank and Debbie was the manager of the reservation, a man who looked somewhat like, but was not, Mr. Ashamary. Present also were Doudeen and an Arab dignitary who Frank recognized as Muhammad Ali the Yemeni. The Yemeni was staring intensely at Debbie from behind dark glasses. Shareef was waiting outside.
"We are very proud of the progress which has been made, Mr. Costello, said the manager."As you can see, it is quite impressive."
When no one spoke, Doudeen said cheerfully, but at the same time affecting concern, "Yet we have many problems. We have had difficulty finding men with your qualifications to manage the technical aspects of our

operations. Now we are having serious problems with expediting the parts and repairs needed. We expect that your company, Agricultural International, will through you, be able to help us in some of these matters? Perhaps you will be able to contact them again soon?"

Now Frank hadn't, since the start of his troubles, been able to contact AIC at all. All communications had been halted by the Rasheedi government. Most international business activity, except the commerce in oil, had ceased. All imports had been subject to seizure. He wasn't sure if he even worked for them anymore.

"I'll try," said Frank.

"Fine," said Mr. Doudeen. "Your helpfulness will be appreciated. You can be sure of it."

"Thanks," said Frank. Then the Yemeni said something in Arabic and after a moment Doudeen went on.

"You understand, Mr. Costello, that this is not a very suitable environment for a woman to live in. It is true that we have improved the infrastructure here somewhat, but there are still few of the conveniences that–Mrs. Costello, for example, would expect, such as modern shopping plazas and the companionship of other women–whereas in Riyadh she might be much more comfortable."

"I'm sure Debbie doesn't mind," said Frank. But he knew it was no use; he knew what was coming.

"Let's hear what he's getting at," said Debbie, looking at her husband. "I want to hear this."

"You are very perceptive, Madam," said Doudeen. "What we propose is this: We are trying to become a more modern nation. We have a girl's school in Riyadh. We would like you to work there as a teacher, and on weekends perhaps, you can be driven here to spend time with your husband who will be far too busy to come to see you."

"I don't..." protested Frank. But Debbie cut him off

again.

"Frank," she said. "It's very important for us to be cooperative at this time. You've told me that many times. If this is what we have to do, then I'm ready.

"When do I start?" she asked Doudeen.

"One week from now will be sufficient. I understand that you have been separated from your husband for some time. We do not lack compassion. In any case, we will need some time to prepare for you—your quarters, your schedule and so forth. You understand."

"Perfectly," said Debbie.

The next day, when Frank was out with some of the other engineers getting briefed on his new assignment, Debbie talked to Shareef in the privacy of his white Mercedes while he was ostensibly showing her around the reservation which she had never seen before and didn't want to see now.

"Who gave the order?" she asked him.

"If it came from Muhammad Ali the chauffeur, then he got it from the boss himself. Looks like you'll finally get your chance to fuck your way to the top."

"Shut up or I'll smack you," she said.

"Sorry," said the Egyptian. "I just wish it was me."

"But you're not king," she said smiling.

Thirty-Four

The Character of a King

"Morality," said the king, "is nothing but a moment to moment decision making process." He said this as he was considering what it would be like to give the command that would bring about the Great Day Of Reckoning. Although his father and six of his brothers had been king before him, he himself wanted to be remembered as a great king, perhaps the greatest of them all. He knew that when the time came, he would need only to say the word and it would be done.

But he felt now inclined to ponder the question yet again–for the pangs of fear were stirring up in him again, and with them, the fear of doubt and uncertainty. He told himself he was sure. He knew he was right. All the signs pointed in only one direction–yet what if something went wrong? His mind drifted. . .

"With your permission, your Majesty," the voice came through the dark hole between his consciousness and the abyss in which he was sinking. He struggled to pull himself back–out of his private hell–back into the world.

The man was standing behind him, resting a hand on his shoulder. It was a warm and familiar feeling. He looked up from the chair he had been sitting in, only now becoming aware of the other's presence. He squeezed the hand.

It was his chief aid and de facto Prime Minister, Dowi Al Harbi, just returned from yet another of his many trips abroad. He would order him to stay home from now on, thought the king. Now he needed him more than ever. The other's outside activities would no longer matter soon. But they would talk of that later.

"With your permission, your Majesty," said Al Harbi again. "I would point out that the responsibility which you are about to undertake has been predestined from the beginning. It is the will of Allah."

"Yes, yes, I know all that," said the king impatiently, feeling himself once again. "But it's the others I'm worried about–the Americans and the others. What if they don't respond as planned? I mean they do worship different Gods than Allah. And the Chinese; they claim to have no God at all. Can we truly trust men who don't believe as we do? What if they don't agree to back down when the time comes?"

"Really, your majesty!" responded Al Harbi. "Please get hold of yourself. Now is not the time to falter. Everything has been planned down to the smallest detail. There is no room for doubt. Moreover your people, no the whole Islamic world, are depending on you. You can not turn back now. Your opponents would not allow you the luxury of second thought. Your armies would lose hope. And you, your majesty, would lose face, and that you must not permit, for that is the worst fate of all."

The king stared into the face of the man who had been with him for fifteen years; his aid now, but really his spiritual partner, for they had always given each other strength. But it was he now who needed the other more than the other needed him. He could feel it.

He wondered which of them was really causing this thing to happen. Which of them was the one making history? Which of them was really the man who had been created by Allah to fulfill a great destiny? The king felt weary. Was this the kind of feeling with which to enter into the greatest triumph of his life?

But then another thought slid through his brain and he felt his strength returning, if only momentarily. The thought brought hatred, a bright intense hatred which he felt only for one man in the world. It gave him all the meaning he needed–if he could only sustain it.

The other, noticing that his master was drifting again, tried a new tact. He could not let the king fall apart now. Much still remained undone.

"And what of this *hurmah, ya emir*? Have you made arrangements for her yet? If you'll permit me to be personal–but I believe that she would be a great help to you just now–for I have seen that she is an unusual beauty. In fact she reminds me of someone I knew in my youth, but of course that cannot be...You have many wives, but which one can give you strength in your times of trial?"

The king looked up and searched the face of his chief aid for some moments. But he could find nothing in it. What he said was true. He needed the thing that this *hurmah* could give him; he needed to feel that he was alive again.

"Yes, yes the *hurmah*–Debbie Costello. I have not forgotten her, but I have not allowed myself to think of it. There are so many important concerns..." He knew his aid was about to speak again–to object, if ever so politely, to offer more advice. He was sick of it.

"Muhammad Ali has taken care of it," he went on with a casual wave of his hand. "She has been removed from her husband who is in our service now–and placed in a suite here in Riyadh. She will work as a teacher at one of our girl's schools. She has been told that I will visit her and that she must understand that it will be a great honor for her. I am told that she has agreed willingly. I will dispatch Hijazi to make the arrangements, and then I will go to her when I am ready. But right now I have many things on my mind—many concerns.

"Yes, yes," he went on, not wanting to speak of it further. "I will go soon."

Joseph's Seed

Thirty-Five

A Kept Woman

Debbie paced the lush pile carpeted floor again, in her apartment on the fifteenth floor of an ultra modern building in Riyadh called the Twin Towers. When she looked out the window she could see the Safeway below–the place where she had been attacked and molested.

She knew the Arab guard was there outside her door as he always was. Except for the girls, her routine was dull now. She spent most of her free time waiting and pacing the floor. She knew what was to come and her only thought was, "let's get on with it." But so far he had kept her waiting for two weeks.

She was teaching English, plus a course called "American Studies." The text for the course was a horrendous book ostensibly about America, its political system, its sociology and culture. But mostly it was a potpourri of misinformation intermingled with out of context and outdated "facts." It was a translation of a work by the Lebanese scholar, Wahan Al Mukhless.

When Debbie read from it, she shook her head, a thing she had never done before. She had to read it to the sweet, innocent teenage girls in her class who she knew would be destroyed by men before they ever had a chance to make any kind of use of the information she was giving them. The best among them were destined to be the teenage wives of old men.

She was no teacher, but she knew the harm she could do; so she tried to ameliorate that harm by steering a course closer to the reality she believed in. But she had to be careful for her superiors at the school had been very explicit as to what they expected her to teach. They were watching her; she had to be careful–and patient.

She was able to be patient because she never forgot why she was there. So she waited. Her personal guard, who was also her driver–they would no longer allow Shareef to drive her–had hinted several times that someone would come soon–someone important. She doubted whether he was actually privy to any real information to "leak," but she listened. He hinted as much again tonight.

She paced back and forth again. "People really do this," she thought. She had never done that before either.

The doorbell rang.

A serene looking Arab stood at the door when she opened it. She was not sure if she had ever seen him before but thought that perhaps she had seen him. Was it at the sheikh's party? Was it on television at one of the many editions of "the king's majlis"? She looked at him more closely. She should be more observant, she chided herself.

Upon looking closer she noticed that he was bleary eyed through his tinted glasses. Had he been drinking–in this "dry" country? "Good evening madam," said the man. "I have been sent by the government of his majesty, King Bandar Bin Abdul Lateef. May I enter?"

Debbie stepped aside and made a partial bow and an *entree vous* gesture with her right arm. "Please do," she said. She led him to the plush living room and bade him sit in a comfortable chair.

"His majesty offers his warmest greetings and hopes

Joseph's Seed

that you are comfortable in your new surroundings and have a sense of your value in your new position at the Riyadh girl's school. We are told that already, your students love you. I myself was once a teacher and so I understand the rewards which teaching the young can bring."

"Thank you," said Debbie. "Actually, I am enjoying the experience. I have never taught before. Though I look forward to a time when the political climate will allow me to return to my own country."

"Of course," said the man, bowing his head. Though she knew that she could be mistaken, he seemed to be apologetic–perhaps because he was on a pimping mission and was not proud of it.

He seemed sincere. "Incidentally, I know you husband." He said. "We have worked together many times, and believe me, I respect his work."

"Thank you," said Debbie again. But not wanting to inquire further into the matter, she said nothing else and waited for him to speak again.

Then the man cleared his throat and recited the king's proposition. When he finished, Debbie said, "I'll agree to do what you say, but only if he will agree to certain conditions of mine. I understand that a man in his position could force me to do his bidding unconditionally, but what then would I be worth to him?

"Yes of course," said the Arab, looking down. "I am not insensitive to your feelings. Please tell me these conditions, as you put it, and I will relay what you say."

"First, tell him I'll do it for six months and then I want to go home. If he can't solve his problems by then, it won't be because of me. Second, I want Shareef, my driver, back. What difference can it make to you? He works for you anyway doesn't he?" To the Arab's look of curiosity, Debbie answered, "It's no big deal, really. He makes me laugh, and I'm bored silly here. It's not too much to ask. That's all I want, and then I'll be your king's whore."

"Please, Madam!"

"I'm only kidding, but do tell him of my conditions."

"Of course," said the Arab. "Still one thing troubles me. You have not asked for your husband's freedom. Though there is good chance that the king would be moved by your devotion to your husband and grant it. Loyalty is a trait most respected among our people."

"He made his bed," said Debbie.

"I beg you pardon?

"I said I don't give a damn if he lives or dies. That will not be one of my conditions."

"I see," said the Arab.

Two days later in the evening, the same Arab returned. Shareef was with him.

"You see madam," he said without fanfare. "His majesty is not insensitive to your concerns, however he prefers to look upon the matter as a favor that he is bestowing and not as you put it, as 'conditions.' After all, he is the sovereign. You have his solemn word that six months from today you will be allowed to leave the kingdom.

"Also, as you can see, your old driver has been restored to his former position. However, he will not act as your guard. It has been decided that the normal building security is adequate to insure your safety and that no further guard would be needed. Mr. Shareef will now be available to take you to your place of work and to shopping as you wish or to socialize with any women friends you may have. Other than that, on certain designated evenings as we have already discussed, you will be available at one hour's notice of the telephone, by which you will be informed of his coming. Are we in agreement then, madam?"

"It's a deal," said Debbie.

As the two men were leaving, Debbie asked, "By the way, what is your name. You look familiar, but I'm not sure."

"Hijazi Ashamary, at your service Madam."

"Of course," said Debbie.

As he pulled the door closed behind him, Shareef stuck his head in at the last moment and said, "Pick you up at eight, kid," and he winked.

Thirty-Six

In The Hands of Allah

Clement Schmidt lounged back in a bamboo recliner by the edge of the pool. He was sipping a tall drink through a straw. It was sweet and cold, and filled about halfway with gin. Beyond a nearby fence, he watched an elephant plucking fruit from a tree. Further in the distance were herds of grazing zebra, gazelles, and a few stalking cats.

But he turned away from those scenes for a better one. A voluptuous black bosom was staring him in the face. It belonged to the scantily clad waitress who was offering him something from the tray she was carrying from guest to guest. He preferred her first treat to the pastry he now selected and let her know it with his eyes and a few well chosen words. He tasted it; he would taste the other also, he hoped, before the day was out.

Then a watershed hit him, the pastry too; but he finished eating it anyway.

"God damnit, you old buzzard!" he said to the man in the pool who had just splashed him with a paddle board. "You got my hat all wet!" He took off the straw cowboy hat he was wearing and shook water from it.

"Always said you was all wet," said Rex Lawton laugh-

Joseph's Seed

ing, pulling himself up over the edge of the pool. "Besides, she won't care if your hat gets wet. Won't even care if your money's wet for that matter, long as it's green. That right, honey?" But the waitress just smiled and moved on to the other guests.

His eyes glued to her backside as she walked away, the older man sighed. "We took too long a'gettin' out this time old buddy."

"That we did," said Clement. "That we did."

"Too bad we got to go back," the Texan went on. "I about had enough of it."

"Except for the fact that he needs you. You know we've got to go in one more time."

"Yep, I know, I know."

Two weeks later, they disembarked on a Kenya airlines flight from Nairobi to Cairo, well rested and ready to face new challenges. But soon after landing they were stuck in a taxi in a traffic jam to dwarf any they had ever seen in Riyadh. They were hot and close again and the sweat poured down. A riot of car horns had replaced the call of the wild. They wished they were still in the bosom of Africa where they had been vacationing, but they had an appointment at the Cairo Hilton in another hour or as soon thereafter as they could get there.

They asked the driver to please hurry, and upon slipping him a bill, the man, who drove just like Shareef, turned sharply down a narrow alleyway and not long afterward, having turned perhaps twenty corners, he pulled into the Hilton. The first thing they did when they entered was to go into the bar.

They looked around through obstructing indoor palms and large plants until they saw them in a corner, past the end of the bar.

A man in a grey summer suit was eating some kind

of a salad. Next to him was a very old and frail looking man with a full crop of tight, curly white hair who looked as though he could have been an Egyptian. He was eating a melon with a spoon. With them also was a dark, handsome man dressed like a tourist and wearing shades. He was speaking with great animation to the man eating the melon.

"I am convinced," he was saying as the Americans approached, "that the turning point came with the fall of *Andalus*. That precipitated the decline more than any other single event."

"You are mistaken, my friend," said the old man in a thick accent. "The decline was much more closely associated with the Orientalization of Islam and the subsequent fragmentation of the Khaliphate."

"Be that as it may," said the man in the summer suit looking up. "Look at what just came down the Nile."

"I need a drink," said Rex Lawton, sitting down. Clement, after shaking hands three times, sat down also. The tourist called for a waiter.

"We were discussing," he said, turning to the newcomers, "how an empire which lasted for hundreds of years, one which once extended from the Atlantic to India, could have declined so completely, erased from the pages of history, as it were, leaving in its place only an assortment of so-called "third world" nations which have been equated by many, in terms of their present level of cultural development, with that of aboriginal peoples, or American Indians, if you prefer. How could such a thing have happened one wonders?"

"You know as well as I," said Clement, "that such concepts are relative to the criteria employed in their determination. Were the desert bedouin, for instance, more civilized in the past when they washed their hair with camel's piss, ate curds, and used dung chips for fuel; or now that they drive Datsuns, send their children to American Universities, and take vacations on the Riviera?"

"It's an intriguing question, of course," said the tourist. "We may never answer it. I do, however, know which you prefer."

"Maybe we should be more concerned," said the man in the summer suit, "with the question of whether the present phoenix which is rising from the Arabian desert will be more or less civilized–or a gigantic bird of prey–an unmitigated catastrophe."

"Can there be any doubt," said the old man with the curly white hair, "that it will be, as you say a 'catastrophe,' unless we are successful in our intervention? Can there be any doubt that we must act, and soon?"

"If we're goin' into action, let's do it," said Rex Lawton. "I'm ready."

"Patience, old buddy," said the tourist. "There is still some time. There are still preparations to be made."

"Preparations, I'm afraid," said the old man with the curly hair, "are being made on both sides. The London papers have reported a certain act of sabotage which my government has known of for some time. We have taken action, as you say, but the true extent of the damage we still do not know. I have good reason to fear the worst."

"Are you referring," asked Clement, "to the spy who released photos to the press, of the Atomic installation in Damona? But he's behind bars now. Surely the information he gave out is not that hot. Anyway, who could ever make use of it, if it were? Your country's security is the tightest in the world. No one could ever penetrate that installation. Bandar's the real threat, not some misguided spy."

Then the old man looked to the man in the suit. "He does not know?" he asked. But no one spoke. Then light came into his eyes. "Yes, yes, of course. I remember now. 'Spy versus spy,' you call it. *Nu*, as you wish."

Clement said nothing. He knew the game, for he himself had played it also.

He had joined the agency many years before and knew the game well enough by now. He had been an ex-social worker, ex-civil engineer, disillusioned with both—with the rat race—with life in the fast lane, with the workaday world where no one advances but every rat runs on a treadmill biting the next rat's tail. He had jumped off the treadmill long ago and never regretted it for a minute.

When he was younger they told him that his I. Q. was 170, but it wasn't long afterward till he asked himself: "How far can I throw it?" Of what use was intelligence to someone who wanted out, who hated the world around him?

So finally he narrowed it down to a few choices. It was to be either auto racing, or a life of crime—to get away with as much as he could and live as dangerously and outrageously as possible for as long as possible—or else.

He decided to join the "company" instead and become a government agent, a spy. It was almost the same thing to him as a life of crime—and he could race to his hearts content on the kingdoms roads.

He had successfully completed several assignments before being sent to the Middle East to monitor the progress and intrigues of the "oil sheikhs." Early in his tenure there, he witnessed first hand the Iraqi invasion of Kuwait and its aftermath—Desert Storm. The experts had expected the Kingdom of Arabia to be next. He knew first hand of the militancy and fanatic enthusiasm possible in that part of the world and believed also that the kingdom would follow suit.

Then he had gotten to know the desert bedouin and changed his mind, if not completely, then with certain qualifications. He now saw that Arabia, "Al Jazira," as the Arabs call it, was a special place, and the bedouin were like no people he had ever known before. He had fallen in love with the desert. That was the reason for his passion for photographing it.

Regularly, he had sent in his reports and met with his superiors. When he learned of the political rivalry between the princes Bandar and Mustapha, he had tried to approach the former and his supporters more than once but never succeeded. But in Mustapha he found not merely a source, but an ally.

The Emir of Jabalain had never known of Clement's connection–that is, not until very recently. They had become friends because they seemed to share values and ideas. Clement had honored and respected the prince as much as any devious man can feel such feelings for another.

Then when Rex, who was not an agent, but simply what he was, decided single-handedly, with help only from his trusted Filipino friends, to rescue the young prince Mugrin from the executioner's sword, Clement made his move. His superior, Snead, concurred and did his part.

First, plans were made to kidnap Debbie, and then Clement convinced Mustapha to go to Egypt on a "business trip." But the latter did not need much convincing. He knew what was in the wind. He could do nothing for his son. But he was determined to challenge his brother however possible. He went to Egypt to solicit help for his cause.

Next Clement took his old friend Fahad into his confidence. But to his surprise he discovered that Fahad was already part of an intricate organization himself, one dedicated to the overthrow of Bandar's regime, and to the restoration of sanity to the region and the institution of a more moderate Islamic government with Mustapha at its head.

It was never a case of one side being the dupe or "stooge" of the other. It was a case of two sides sharing a common cause–more or less–and working together as allies. This they did, from the days before Rex's rescue mission took place up to the present.

He thought back to when Snead had first given him instructions to maneuver Frank into bringing his wife into play. He hadn't been given the real reason. Now that he knew the right question to ask; he would corner Snead about it at the first opportunity. His mind flashed back to the strange question Debbie had asked him about Al Harbi. He knew of course about the latter's rumored connections with terrorism, but he had been at a loss to imagine what Debbie could have to do with it. He would find out.

But for now, five men sat in a hotel in Egypt plotting the impossible: How to overthrow a powerful regime which had at its disposal a vast new arsenal and millions of men armed with state of the art weaponry and at the command of a madman.

Neither did Clement know exactly how the old Israeli agent now sitting next to him fit in to all of this, except for the obvious concern that country would have in the matter of its own security against a neighbor arming itself to the teeth against it. He sensed, however, that something else was in the wind, something to do with Debbie. He would find out about it all right. Or perhaps he would read about it in the papers–after the fact.

"Have you heard from our girl lately?" he asked the tourist.

"She is my brother's consort now, but I am told that she is well and her spirits are high. She is an exceptional woman; and I needn't tell you that I don't make such statements lightly."

"I knew she would hang tough. You know, of course, that I plan to take her out of Riyadh again when we go back?"

"When we do. For now, we can do little more than watch and wait. Events, as we say, are in the hands of Allah."

Thirty-Seven

Juggling Act

Shareef was worried. His present juggling act was becoming too much for him. In the past he had always prided himself on maintaining his composure even under the most dangerous–or ridiculous–circumstances, but this time he couldn't quite do it.

He had always felt that he had an edge over those around him and could handle almost anything. Maybe his wits were quicker, maybe it was just a matter of being awake while others slept–or maybe it was the fact that he had grown up on the garbage heaps of Cairo, and having survived that, he could survive anything.

He wasn't sure what it was and had never before cared. Whatever it was that drove him, it had always served him well; but now he felt like he was losing it. Why? Because now for the first time in his life he actually cared about someone and wanted to survive this. But it had not always been so.

He thought back to the time he was almost caught red handed with the wife of a sheikh who was then a customer of Al Tawali International Sales Division, where he worked. He had struck up a friendship with the customer's fifteen year old wife in the usual way, when she called inquiring about the particulars of some furniture they were buying for their new villa.

Then after a walk to the souq with her one evening, (she was veiled like all the other women so no one was the wiser), he had secreted her back to his room–which wasn't much of a room really–just a cubicle beside the front gate of Tawali's Riyadh villa. Doudeen himself would often take customers there to sit in the garden on hot evenings, to drink cool drinks and close deals. If Shareef was in his room, he could hear the details verbatim.

That night while he was there with the bedouin girl, he heard Doudeen coming through the gate. That was bad enough, for Doudeen sometimes came looking for him in the evening to work overtime. He couldn't refuse. Doudeen would simply walk into his room and get him.

Then, realizing what could happen, he had installed a small latch on the inside of his door. Doudeen shook it on a few occasions and was annoyed at the inconvenience, but he had accepted the lowly Shareef's right to a little privacy. He was good at his job and Doudeen didn't want the bother of finding someone new.

That night Shareef and his guest were making a little too much noise when they heard someone coming. It was Doudeen. Maybe he had heard them and would demand to know what was going on? Then they heard the other footsteps and the voice; it was the customer–the husband of the girl in his bed–coming to chat with his boss. In a cold sweat they listened to the two men talking amicably in the still air of the Arabian night. They were eating *shwarmers* and drinking orange juice cocktails. He could smell the pungent aromas from where they lay naked in the darkness of his room a few feet away.

Then there had been the knock on his door. Silence–panic heart beats–and finally, after a few more persistent knocks: "Perhaps he is asleep, *ya ustez*. Well, we can draft the contract in the morning, fine?"

Joseph's Seed

Shareef thought back on that night. He knew he could have been beheaded if he had been caught. But since he wasn't, he decided to tempt fate again and keep the girl with him a little longer. She was supposed to be visiting her relatives and her husband wouldn't be the wiser.

They had just started making noise again when he heard Doudeen's voice again. He was back, but it soon became apparent that someone else was with him this time.

"Be careful, *ya sheikh*, no one must know—not even the king."

"Do not concern yourself," said the other voice. Shareef recognized it. It was the Yemeni. "It shall never go past my lips. Had I not a brother working in the security force of The South Yemen with which you once negotiated, neither would I have known. Your secret will be safe with me."

"*Shukron*," said Doudeen.

"Do not think, however that you can dispose of me so easily—there is still the matter of a sealed envelope."

But what was this? Shareef in his agitation over what he was hearing, suddenly knocked an ashtray on the floor.

"Who's there?" called Doudeen. "Shareef?" Shareef dared not make a sound. Again quiet. "Shareef?" It was the Yemeni this time. Then a hand was on the door again. When it felt the hasp, it gave a hard jerk and the hasp popped off. The two men walked in to find Shareef and his guest in their glory. They knew. But he knew something now also. What exactly, he wasn't sure.

They let him live. He might prove useful to them, he thought; but who was he kidding? More likely they simply thought that a ridiculous little man like him could be of no danger to them. But he knew that permission could be revoked at any moment.

Shareef decided to keep this unexpected bit of information out of official channels. It might work to his advantage if the tide turned the wrong way. But he was not strong enough to stand completely on his own; he needed to tell someone. He thought of Debbie but decided better of it; she was in too much danger already without adding this. He decided to tell Frank.

He smiled and pulled his shoulders back at the thought of being killed. He remembered what Bogey had said in "Casablanca:" "Go ahead and kill me. You'll be doing me a favor."

But he didn't want to die. He wanted Debbie. "What if?," he thought. Then, after awhile his mind drifted back to reality, to the task at hand.

Not long after that while he was at JADCO on an errand for Doudeen, he told Frank. Shareef was inclined to think that the hammer the Yemeni had over Doudeen was some knowledge that the latter had embezzled Al Tawali funds–a crime punishable by beheading. When he told Frank as much. Frank said only, "No kidding." But he didn't think so.

Months later Shareef left the office early to pick Debbie up at the Twin Towers which was in a newer part of Riyadh. Traffic was lighter than usual and he arrived there quickly. He was taking her to the desert to see Frank. It would be her first visit with him since their separation. She had not wanted to go, but Shareef prevailed upon her. Frank was falling apart, he had told her. The authorities had sanctioned the visit. Frank was no good to them as he was. Shareef felt sorry for Frank; another new emotion for him. Besides, Shareef's boss, his other boss, had told him to take her there.

When she got into the Mercedes and they were far enough away from the guard at the Twin Towers gate, he turned to her as he drove and said, "You look devastating today Your Majesty."

"Fuck you," she answered.

"Don't I wish," mumbled Shareef, and in a louder voice, "Seriously, if he marries you, that's what you would be–well kind of. Has he asked you yet?"

"Yes, many times."

"Well, what do you say?"

"I tell him that I'm already married. He says that it can be arranged. He'll even divorce a few of his wives for me. I remind him that we have a deal. He sulks."

"He sulks?"

"Yes, he's not as confident as people think he is. I think he's afraid of what he's doing. But I don't think he can change, or wants to. He keeps talking about his 'destiny.' But I haven't pressed him about what exactly that means. That wouldn't be a good idea."

"No it wouldn't. What's he like–in bed I mean?"

She looked at him for a moment considering whether to answer. She didn't want to encourage him with that kind of talk. But then she decided, "This is business."

"He's very proud," she said. "And visionary. He's an intellectual, well read but not overly intelligent if you can understand the difference. He's not very good in bed, but only because he's so preoccupied with his own thoughts most of the time–his megalomania. Sometimes, when he forgets himself, he's not bad. He seems to hold me in high esteem. At least he acts that way. That's probably because he can see that although I give him what he wants, I don't care about him, or what I'm doing. It makes his blood boil. But it's the edge I need."

"You have a way of doing that," thought Shareef, almost out loud. But he didn't say it out loud.

"I'm not a psychiatrist," she went on. "but I think he's crazy."

"Why?"

"Well, it's the way his moods swing, and the way he

often drifts off, into kind of a trance, 'spaced out' we'd call it. Sometimes an hour goes by and he'll just stare, at some talk show on TV, or at a book without turning the pages. I say nothing; just watch while I pretend to be doing things–puttering–you know. After awhile he revives and starts talking to me–or he suddenly gets interested in me.

"Sometimes he talks about his 'mission'–about history and his place in it, about prophecy, Nostradamus–stuff like that. He talks about religion a lot, but it's a weird kind of religion. I don't think it's Islam. I've learned something about that since I began teaching. This is different. More like the crap in one of Wahan Al Muhless's books. Or Dowi Al Harbi's. Doesn't make much sense to me. Tell you more when I know. You get everything?"

"So far," said Shareef. They talked further as the thoughts came up during the remaining four hours to the JADCO reservation.

When they arrived and saw Frank, Debbie thought he looked like what he was: a prisoner, not the kind she imagined he had been after his month in the calaboose, but worse. He was clean shaven now and his clothes were still neat but worn; he hadn't been able to buy anything new for some time. They were tight also, for he had gained weight.

When he got her alone, with only Shareef driving them around the reservation in his Mercedes, he turned to her and there was a flicker of hope in his eyes; but then an ill wind came and blew it away.

It was her face. It held nothing for him. She looked at him, and then through him, surveying the scene around them.

"How have you been?" she asked absently. And then, when he didn't answer immediately; "holding up, I hope. You know, you have to. You have to do your best; we both do." She smiled at him cheerfully, doing the best she could.

Joseph's Seed

But he wasn't listening to her or responding to her smile. His face reflected nothing but the hurt he felt. All he could say was, "Why?" She knew what he meant.

"Don't ask, Frank," she said. "Look! If you want me to stay for awhile you'll have to forget how it was and what might have been. We are here, both kept against our will, both prisoners, and we have to make the best of it. It's the will of Allah. Maybe some day—but I'm not going to talk about that. I want you to just consider that we're separated. When and if we get out of here we can make it legal. But I'm not going to dwell on that right now and I don't think you should.

"Now if you want me to stay for awhile, just stop feeling sorry for yourself and try to be sociable. Tell me about this place. What are you doing here? What's going on? How are you feeling? You look fat. Just be yourself."

So he did.

Later, after he left them, Shareef was seen talking to one of his countrymen as compatriots do whenever they have a chance. People, who in their home country might have nothing in common, are often drawn together when they meet in a foreign land because that which they share suddenly seems more significant.

The other Egyptian was a truck driver who made daily runs from JADCO to Jabalain delivering the freshly grown produce from the reservation's greenhouses to the city's markets. They talked of old times they had never shared and of the love for their city which they had a hard time distinguishing from hate. They also talked of other things. The dialect they used was difficult to understand for anyone who was not a lifelong inhabitant of Cairo. That is—almost anyone.

"You see over there, my dear, the bedouin dog who stands not far from us watching so carefully?" continued the truck driver. "His name is Hijazi Al Ashamary. He is new here. Don't talk too loud; they say he understands all the dialects and many other languages as well. They say he will be the new manager of the reservation soon. The old manager is finished. He broke his ass, but he couldn't make it. They say this new manager is smooth as your sister's pussy, and very tricky. Watch him carefully."

"I know him," said Shareef, careful now not to say more than was needed. The truck driver need not know any more than he had to. He was just another messenger, a conduit for information to get from here to Jabalain. Someone else would take it from there.

He told the driver, "I have seen him before. He is not new here, just reinstated. He was in charge when they built the place." But he did not tell the driver why Ashamary was reinstated. He did not need to know that. He wondered what effect the change would have on Frank. But he didn't mention that either.

Thirty-Eight

Co-conspirators

Frank felt like the same person he had always been. But more often now than in the past, he thought about just who and what that person actually was. During the past few months, he had a lot of time to think about it.

If indeed he was a prisoner, he was not prevented from moving around freely in his Pathfinder, with certain restrictions. For one thing, he was not permitted to travel to Riyadh. He was aware also that he wasn't free to leave the kingdom. They had taken his passport. Moreover, there was now no way for him to communicate with the outside world or to obtain the necessary visa. No one, he was told, could travel outside the kingdom without special permission from the government.

But he wouldn't have left even if he could–not unless he could take his wife with him; and that possibility seemed to become more remote from the realm of the practical each day. He knew that for reasons of her own she had become involved with Mr. Snead. She had never told him why, but he could come pretty close to the truth by now. He only lacked the details. Still, Frank wondered what anyone–even someone like

Snead—could possibly do about what had happened to the kingdom recently. What could Debbie hope to accomplish?

He thought back to their years together. Those years he now remembered as the best of his life. What had changed? Maybe she had decided of late that she liked the attention after all.

It had started with Snead. That was when he first noticed the change in her. Then she had run away with Clement. He couldn't accept that, couldn't understand it; but what could he do? He knew that with a woman like Debbie the answer was that he could do nothing and never could. She had come to him voluntarily of her own initiative. If she chose not to stay with him voluntarily, there was nothing—absolutely nothing—he could ever do about it.

Now she was with—he couldn't believe it when first he heard the rumors months ago. He had confronted Shareef about it, and Shareef had told him. It was crazy—but in a way, ironic. He had always felt that she was a queen—in fact, it had once been his pet name for her.

Frank didn't have all the answers. How could he? He knew only that his wife was—well, doing strange things. He still did not know why, not really. He knew only that she was there and he was here—a prisoner.

But even in prison life wasn't all bad. He was keeping busy and under the circumstances, doing productive work. He was even picking up quite a bit of Arabic, which was the language of most of the workers; though he still spoke only English to the Powers That Be. Also, Mr. Ashamary was back at JADCO, and they had become friends. The pompous sheikh he had once known in his early days in the kingdom was gone. In his place was a gentler, almost refined man. Frank welcomed the change. For the first time in his life perhaps, he had someone–another man–to confide in. They became like fellow travelers–or co-conspirators–in the world in which they were now both confined; for it didn't take him long to realize that Ashamary was a prisoner also.

Soon after Mr. Ashamary assumed his duties as general manager of JADCO, Frank was summoned by his new boss.

He entered Mr. Ashamary's office that day as he had done before when JADCO was being built; but this time there were no pandering, Pakistani secretaries, no shouting, and no ominous Yemeni leaning against the wall; only an efficient looking Sri Lankan working on a computer at a corner desk. After talking to his new boss for some moments, Frank noticed the change. Mr. Ashamary looked mellower, almost serene.

Perhaps it was his own selfish need for someone to talk to, or perhaps it was just an impulse, but Frank did then two things which he never before did with a customer: He said something personal; and he was honest.

"You seem different for some reason" he said. "More peaceful than I remember you. To tell the truth I'm glad to see you, especially after the jerk of a manager they just fired."

"Yes, peaceful," said Ashamary in a voice not as confident as it had once been. "Many things have changed; however, one bad habit I have not been able to overcome is my taste for Turkish coffee. I still drink far too much of it. You, too, it seems, have changed. You are not trying to sell me something–are you?" The two men laughed. It was a slightly strained laugh, at a joke made–and heard–by men in pain. But the attempt had been made, and ice was breaking.

Thirty-Nine

The City

Over the next months Frank Costello, the shallow American salesman, and Hijazi Ashamary, the Arabian sycophant, became friends. They shared meals, talked of past experiences, of books they had read, of the current state of affairs in the kingdom and the world. When Ashamary, discovered that Frank was making an effort to learn his language, he showed him ways to speed up the process and to learn it the right way. Hijazi was an excellent teacher; in fact, it was his natural avocation.

They had both, they came to realize, been greedy in the past; but this was not what they had wanted: to be held prisoner in the regime of a madman. "Perhaps," Hijazi had said one day, "we are also to blame. Better men might have refused to take any part in building this."

Frank shrugged.

Together, they seemed to develop a new perspective. They accepted the fact that although they could not change things, they still had a right to live with a certain dignity. They also had a right to try to understand the world around them. To the extent of their abilities they tried to do a good job. They tried to make

JADCO a productive organization despite the lack of resources and spare parts, despite disrupted markets and lack of communication with the outside world; and with no better than sporadic cooperation from the Rasheedi regime.

In their free time, they discussed the kind of ideal world they envisioned, but realistically, never expected to see. They talked of peace between Arab and Jew, between America and Islam, between rich and poor. They played chess.

It was, in spite of its shortcomings, a period of growth for both men. In short, they had become philosophical, as defeated men often do.

Occasionally, they drove together to Jabalain, the nearest city, for supplies or for various other reasons. That day, they had been summoned to that city by its new governor.

The city of Jabalain was no longer a pristine garden. Weeds had overgrown the arboretums. The date palms were dusty and neglected; litter had accumulated against their trunks.

But the town still bore some resemblance to what it had once been. When Frank and Mr. Ashamary passed between the Two Mounts that day, he noticed that the giant urn still stood. Its brass was tarnished, and a vine was creeping up its side, but it loomed majestic in the sun nevertheless as they passed; as if it were beckoning them to enter a magic kingdom; as if a friendly genie would soon peer over its top and grant them wishes. But there were no genies in the land at the moment.

The governor they were going to see was Prince Momduh Ibn Bandar, the man who had occupied the city when Mustapha had fled.

Frank had never seen the inside of the palace which the former governor had built. They were led now through spacious anterooms, rotundas, vestibules, and corridors on their way to the rooms which had once served as the Prince Mustapha's office and were presently occupied by Momduh.

The building was constructed of glass, marble, and a granite-like stone which was the color of desert sand—not a dull sandstone but a golden sand. There was natural light everywhere, emanating from the skylights—but refracted somehow to avoid the Sun's direct glare. There were large windows through which Frank could see neglected gardens. Trash had begun to pile up in the hallways and he could detect a familiar scent as he passed through them. It was a combination of urine and some kind of spice—jasmine, he had heard. The structure had obviously been very expensive, but it was also obviously quickly passing into that state of neglect which Frank had come to expect as commonplace in the kingdom.

The edifice was modern; it had been constructed, Ashamary had told him, by a company from Colorado. Its theme was classical Arabian but with unusual differences, among which were domes made of glass, and several minarets resembling the jagged peaks of Jabalain. Through sheets of glass Frank could see a large outdoor garden enclosed on three sides by the palace, and on the fourth side by a mountain. It was a desert garden, including only varieties indigenous to the region. In its center was a goat hair tent. It was the place where the first owner had held his daily majlis.

The new governor welcomed them cordially, in almost adequate English. He wore an army uniform. There were several other officers in the room.

"*Salaam,* Mr. Costello," he said. "I see we meet again."

Prince Momduh, Frank realized, was the officer who had presided over the hearing at which he had been released from jail. But he said only: "How do you do, Your Highness."

The prince went on: "You remember me of course.

Joseph's Seed

It has not been very long ago. You have been very cooperative, I understand. Is that not true *ya sheikh?*" he said to Ashamary.

"Yes, Governor," replied Ashamary in their language. "Mr. Costello has long helped our cause."

"Hmm. I knew him also when he 'helped us' as you say," he replied in English. "But I wonder if he remembers the other times we met."

Frank looked again at the prince. "No," said Frank slowly. "Just the time you let me out of jail."

"You do not remember the 'boy prince' who accompanied his friend Mugrin to your sales presentation when my father was constructing JADCO?"

Frank squinted: "Was that you?"

The prince nodded, smiling: "We have come a long way. No?" Then he grew stern again: "But there were still other times. One was when I arrested Mugrin at the Marriott where you were eating with your friends. And the other–the first time? Do you not remember when I found you trespassing near Waleed's City? When you were seeing visions. You were–how do you say? Delirious? I gave you water and sent you on you way. You remember now?"

"I can't quite remember. It seems so long ago." Actually, Frank remembered but he saw no point in reminiscing with Momduh.

"I believe you," said the prince. "But I think that now you should see more. It makes no difference anyway; it is almost time."

Soon after that, they were leaving the palace with Momduh and some young officers. When they passed through the anteroom again, Frank noticed Shareef conversing with the receptionist. But he said nothing and went out the door.

They drove through the fence on a new blacktop highway, the one which led directly from the JADCO reservation. An unusual kind of city lay before them. He had glimpses of it before, now he was there.

Forty

Waleed's Tents

"My brother was a fool."

Debbie wondered to which brother he was referring this time. She knew it couldn't be his hated "ex-rival," as he liked to refer to Mustapha, because he said "was," that brother was still alive.

She was facing away from him, propped up on a pillow, reading a magazine–naked. He was lying next to her in her bed, contemplating the curve of her back, the golden flow of her hair; caressing her buttocks with his hand as he was inclined to do. But his mind was elsewhere.

"Hmm?" she said absently, as if she had barely heard him. "I said, my brother was a fool."

"Which brother? You have over forty."

"Waleed, my dear. Sometimes, I imagine that he still lives–that he is still king–but he was a fool no less."

"Why?" Still reading, she snuggled gently against him almost unconsciously.

"Because he thought he could civilize the bedouin," he began loudly, angrily, and then toned down to a normal voice again. "He wanted to harness them, take them out of the desert and place them in cities. He was a fool."

"Why?' she asked again."That has happened, hasn't it? Riyadh alone has over a million people. Doesn't it?"

"You are right, perhaps two million; we do not count them. But you are also wrong."

"I don't understand," innocently.

"It is simple. True, there is a large population in this city, in many of our cities. But for the most, they are not bedouin. They are a mixture of many things—but not bedouin."

She half turned toward him. Leaning back against him she put a hand on his leg. "I don't get it." She inched it upward. "I thought that all Arabs were bedouin; the words are used almost interchangeably. Aren't they?"

He smiled. It was a patronizing smile. He was becoming sure of her. He knew she loved him now. How could she not?

"No, my dear. They are *hadhar*, city dwellers, Arabs who have always been city dwellers—very different from the bedouin. But even they are but a small part of the population of our cities, certainly no more than one quarter. The rest are a mixture: Arabs from other lands—mostly Egyptian, but also Syrian, Palestinian, Yemeni, and others. Once the majority were others still who, although they were Muslim, they were not properly to be considered Arabs. But these, for the most have been removed now."

She said nothing. He was babbling. "It doesn't matter," she thought. "Let him talk—let him keep talking."

She turned to him completely now. Wrapping her arms around his neck, she kissed him deeply and slid in closer.

"You are not interested in these matters," he said. "Do I bore you, my darling?"

"Oh, no!" demurely now.

"But you are a woman."

"That's part of why you have me here, isn't it? Because you can't talk to your women—but you want to?

Tell me, please! I'm interested, really." She kissed him again. "Where have they been removed to?"

He resisted her advances and went on, for he was in control now.

"Waleed built thousands upon thousands of modern units for the bedouin all around the kingdom. He wanted to house them, to take them out of the desert, for he loved them and wanted them to be happy.

"But they would not come. For years, his project, immense tracts of habitation scattered around the kingdom, lay unused and empty. It became a joke. The houses became to be known as 'Waleed's tents.' The largest group of these 'tents' he built in the desert itself–near Jabalain–to have them closer to the bedouin hamlets and the proposed JADCO project. Many moved to Mustapha's city, but to him they would not come.

"Finally Waleed had to admit his failure. That was when my brother Muhammad at my suggestion–I was still a young man then, just beginning as dean of the University–encouraged the king to use the housing as the core of another project–a military one. The kingdom needed to build up its defenses. We had the money, but we were weak. We all knew this had to change if we were to fulfill our destiny. The greatest of these cities was named after Waleed himself, although he was not the cause of it and did not really want it."

"And what about the Muslims? The non-Arab ones you mentioned–the ones that were removed–what became of them?"

"What?" said the king as if awakening. He looked at her strangely for a moment, and then continued. "They are now our army, the major part of it, led by a few trusted and loyal men–my followers. They now fill the housing projects–the tents. There are millions. It is funny, no?"

"And the bedouin?"

He looked at her again; but she was so close. He could not think. "They are still in the desert. They will not come out. But they will come out soon. "Soon we will have the complete respect of their tribal leaders. Prince Razi Al Atebi of Um, the proud Moneef Mulafic; and all the others. Soon they will all join us willingly. Even now, my chief aid Dowi Al Harbi is in the land stolen by the Zionists making preparations which will bring all of our plans to fruitfulness–soon.

"What is wrong my love; you are shaking?"

"It's nothing–just a chill," moving closer. "Come in me now," she whispered. "I want you."

Later, when she was telling all of this–most of this– to Shareef, he said something that surprised her: "He's wrong about one thing kid, and it's about time we cleared the air about it. If my people weren't such great liars, we would have done it a long time ago. Egyptians aren't Arabs–never were and never will be.

Forty-One

The Secret Weapon

"How does it feel to be the first American ever to lay your eyes on our treasure?" asked Prince Momduh.

"The secret weapon," said Frank Costello.

"Secret weapon? Oh, yes, I see what you mean. Yes, you could call it that."

They were underground, hundreds of feet below the giant sand dunes above. They had descended in a shaft, and then walked down what seemed to be miles of corridors, entering chamber after cavernous chamber in which huge weapons–long range ballistic missiles–were in their silos, aiming skyward.

"That is precisely what they were," Momduh had explained, "caverns–discovered by the Brazilian scientists who assisted us in this project. It was something about the geology of oil bearing rock. But alas, I am not a scientist. Anyway it is here. We at first considered building all this above the ground, and indeed we did put some small missiles above for everyone to see with their satellites and AWACS planes. And when they would be convinced that our weapons were harmless enough, they would leave us alone. They would laugh and say: 'Well, it is just the Rasheedi Arabs wasting their money again. ' But as you can see this is a little different."

"Amazing," said Frank, almost to himself. "What I heard about Mulafic's sons working on underground silos was true."

"Mulafic? Moneef Mulafic? Do you know him? Anyway, it is no matter. Yes, his company has worked here. It still does, in fact. Perhaps you have heard that he is not our friend? But you misunderstand the minds of our people. Many of our so-called enemies do us great service. In fact, we have even purchased assistance from certain Israelis for some of this. 'Money talks,' I think you say.

"Even you yourself have helped us in many ways you know."

"Yes," said Frank. "I'm beginning to believe that."

They came to a huge steel door at the end of a corridor; but Momduh did not lead them in. "What's inside?" inquired Frank.

"This room is *momnuah*, forbidden. Even I cannot open it without my father's permission."

They went above ground again and then made a tour of the 'city,' although 'city' may not have been a proper name for what he now saw. It was a fenced in section of desert some fifty by seventy five miles. All but a small portion of it remained barren. There was no landscaping of any kind inside, only buildings, equipment, and desert.

In many locations however were, for lack of a better way to describe them–towns. In each 'town' were thousands of small housing units capable of holding ten men–mini barracks, thought Frank.

There were administration areas, huge corrugated warehouses, military equipment, tanks, armored personnel carriers and many other types of vehicles. There were numerous roads crisscrossing the entire complex. Frank saw regiments training everywhere in the desert sand. As they drove, they passed an air base like the one Frank had seen from above with Clement and Rex, perhaps the same one. Frank's impression of the whole scene was that of an empty desert teaming with activity. It was clear–thought Frank–that they were preparing for war.

Suddenly, Frank came to the realization that what he was seeing was probably not understood by the Powers That Be in the West. The great Snead probably knew nothing more than what he had seen in the photographs Frank had given him. If so, then this–what they knew was above ground–was all a joke to Snead, to Clement–and to Debbie? If Mustapha and his men knew of it, Frank guessed, to reveal the fact would not be in their interest, for they would then have to watch their own country being destroyed.

Why had Momduh shown him the secret weapon? "Because," said the king's son, "I thought it would be fun, and really Frank, you will never tell about it until it is too late. Frank understood: He was a just a pawn in something very big and very ugly.

When Frank and Hijazi returned to the reservation later that day, Ashamary told him, "You realize that I have known about this for a long time, almost from the beginning, but I must tell you that only recently I have come to think of the king's plot as wrong and gravely against the will of Allah."

"What made you change?"

"What made me change? Many things: I believed that my religion was being wrongly used. I saw the corruption of small children and fellow Muslims from other lands who are poor and do not understand. I saw the flowering of the desert by your great irrigation machines being used only for evil purposes. I believed the renaissance of my country was going sour. I saw a pure soul forced to sell herself to the Satan. I saw a man who I love lose his innocence in this place.

"Finally, when I witnessed the gentle Prince Mustapha threaten to murder his brother for a righteous cause, but then spare him–this happened at a great majlis held right here at JADCO–I began to see the truth. I had been greedy and arrogant, but I was nothing compared to him. Even the renegade Rex Lawton had more honor than me.

"At first I took to drinking alcohol, but then I discovered an easier way. I too, like you, had to wake up. It was not easy to see these things. I had some help. Once, a man named Fahad came to speak to me–perhaps you know him? He is in the employ of Mustapha."

"I know him," said Frank.

"Yes, he helped me; and that made me decide to help you."

"What did he say to you?" said Frank

"Many things, but if you want me to give it to you in a nutshell, as you say, I'll tell you this: He made me realize that I could be proud to be an Arab and a Muslim without taking part in this present insanity or sanctioning it in any way. He proved his point in many ways, but we do not need to go into details now. Let's just say he is a wise man–or a philosopher–rare in this country or in any country I suspect. I'll tell you more about him when we have the time."

Frank considered these things for some time and then asked: "What will the big missiles be used for–the long range ones?"

"That I do not know. Believe me, I do not know."

Forty-Two

The Rose

"*Et ha mangina ha zot, e-efshar lehafseek.*"

The triumphant song kept pace with the tempo of the bus's wheels meeting expansion joints between geometric sections of highway. He was absorbed in his thoughts, almost too absorbed to notice the tune. But part of him heard. It was an old song he had once liked–a song about a haunting melody which was impossible to silence. The music, he knew, was about the land–it was the land.

"*Et ha mangina ha zot, e-efshar lehafseek.*"

The words entered him without his participation; he couldn't stop them. Neither could he ignore the many different fragrances assaulting his senses through the open windows. His body unconsciously responded to them. He felt warm, warm and secure, and full of energy. He was home again.

Nowhere else did the sky seem so blue. Nowhere else did white clouds form such contrast against it. Nowhere was the breeze so refreshing. Nowhere did the hills roll just so, fruit trees so inviting, the combination of living colors with the brown and yellow hues of the desert's edge. In fields he passed he saw the ancient goat herds and sheep of the land grazing rocky pastures. Now there were large modern farms as well,

Joseph's Seed

like those of his adopted country, but different. He noticed a few of the great circular watering machines of the kind he had come to know so well–even here in this tiny land.

Somewhere he had read that every soul has its special place–only one place–that it can call home. A singular place where the senses come alive, where things take on a special meaning, a certain quality of realness. They become things-in-themselves, archetypes of the imitations which otherwise fill our lives. If so, then this was his place.

It had been many years since he had been here. It was different now, yet the same. He could have rented a car of course, but he wanted to feel the land, like a worker, like the people of the land, like his ancestors. He had dressed simply. He fit in; he knew it.

They had not known when he arrived at the airport on a forged passport, that he was a stranger. His command of the language was still perfect. He was nothing more than a tourist to them, coming home from a short, cheap holiday in Greece. He left his black curly hair uncombed, the top two buttons of his short sleeve shirt open, as was the style of the men here. He answered the routine questions as naturally as if they were the truth. In a way, they were the truth. Afterward he had taken his luggage to someone he knew who would send them ahead, and he walked to the central bus terminal. It was easy. It had been many years but this was his land, and he was coming home.

He got off the bus at Beer Sheva–his home town. It was much larger now, many more immigrants had arrived. They were the strangers here, not he. He took bus number "eleven." He chuckled as he walked. It was a joke he used to play as a child on newcomers who were lost and asking how to get to such and such a place. "Take bus number eleven," he would tell them.

The streets of the city were dark when he finally made his way down a familiar alleyway and into a house that he knew well.

The next day, he stood on a precipice in the desert. He could see the rugged terrain of the Negev in the distance. The hot summer sun baked down on him but it was a pleasant feeling. He felt the tranquility of home again. . . Slowly his mind turned back to his task. Not far beyond, to the South, he knew, his people would be waiting, and he must act. Then he had a strange thought: He imagined that just beyond the expanse of land below, lay the enchanted city of Jabalain. He seemed to see the jagged peaks in the haze just beyond the horizon. But that couldn't be, he knew, for Jabalain was hundreds of miles away.

There was a new monument a few feet from where he stood, commemorating lives given valiantly in the latest of many wars. There was a list of names. He knew some of the names. They had been his childhood friends. There was a flower garden around the monument. He picked a red one. It was beautiful. *Shoshannah*, it was called. Funny, just now he couldn't think of its name in his native tongue. Then he thought of it: It was *al wardah*, the rose.

He stood in stony silence for a long time, holding the flower, almost forgetting it. Then he remembered.

Slowly, imperceptibly, his hand closed around the flower. Rose petals fell on the newly laid patio stone beneath his feet. Then he let the dead thing slip through his fingers and walked briskly away.

Forty-Three

Egyptian Express

Shareef found Frank in Mr. Ashamary's office. They were going over a list of spare parts they would order from the new ministry of procurement. They had little hope of getting what they needed but they had to try.

"Hi," said Frank, looking up from his lists. "What's up? Looking for me?"

As he did every week, Shareef dropped the mail bag on the desk where the Sri Lankan secretary was busy typing. The secretary looked up but he didn't stop working.

"No letter from Debbie, but she says to tell you she's fine. She sends her regards."

"Thanks," said Frank, knowing the Egyptian had just lied. He hadn't seen or heard from her in six months, and he didn't expect to–ever again. Still, he enjoyed hearing the lie. Besides, he was beginning to look forward to Shareef's weekly visits. "Be done here in a minute, want to come with me while I make my rounds?" "Why not?" said the Egyptian, shrugging his boney shoulders.

Shareef rode as Frank chauffeured him around in his Pathfinder from a small construction project, to a maintenance repair procedure, to a production glitch;

at each stop Frank conferred with expatriates of various nationalities, made suggestions and otherwise offered whatever help and guidance he could.

"What are you doing this for?" Shareef asked after several such stops.

"I don't know. It's the way I am I guess. I can't make money now but I still want to do some good. I see these fellows need help. So I try. Besides, what else would I do?"

"Get the hell out of here," said the Egyptian.

"How?"

There was no answer. Frank went on. "Mr. Ashamary says there will soon be a war; but exactly when he won't say. I doubt if he knows. I've told you what I've seen. It'll be bad. I feel so damn helpless. I know I'm just a nobody; there's nothing I can do. Maybe that's why I try to keep busy."

Then Shareef asked, "Frank, do you want to die?"

Frank didn't answer, but his look told.

"But will you help us? Help Debbie? Even though she's gone? Even though you'll probably die?"

Frank looked at the other for a long moment then said, "I'll try."

A few miles away the king sat in his console in a cavernous room deep below the earth. He was being instructed by experts who believed that the information they imparted would bring them great wealth. They had been lecturing him it seemed for hours. He was bored.

"Yes, yes," he said waiving them away tiredly. "Each target city has its own button, so to speak, these are the long range and these are the short range strategic controls, these are the verifications, here are the fail-safes. The computer's instructions are simple. Even a child could read from this menu, as you call it."

Joseph's Seed

"But your majesty," an aid suggested humbly. All of these procedures are crucial to achieving a glorious victory on that day..."

"Do not trouble yourself," the king interrupted impatiently. "It is the will of Allah, but Allah has already preordained."

"Perhaps you should rest now, *ya Bandar*. It has been a difficult day," said another Arab. His voice was not obsequious; he spoke almost as to an equal. He was frail, and furtively cloaked in his gutra; yet he seemed somehow more powerful than the king.

The king glanced at this aid, the man who had virtually replaced his trusted Dowi Al Harbi since the latter had left the kingdom for his final mission a month earlier.

"Yes, you are right, Muhammad. I am tired. I would like to see my concubine. My private jet can have me there before nightfall; can it not?" The king looked at the aid again–a little guiltily this time.

"You disapprove?"

"Of course I would not think of questioning your personal preferences, your majesty," said the Yemeni. "But considering the *hurma's* past, perhaps it would be safer to have her placed within the confines of your palace– with all of your other wives."

"She doesn't want to," protested the king. "Besides, my wives would become jealous. She is too beautiful."

"I suspect you underestimate your good wives. They are virtuous Muslim women. In any event, it is becoming too dangerous to leave her on the outside. She is too free–Mustapha's men could interfere."

"That problem will end soon. The President of Egypt has promised me he will deal with the traitor. He will cooperate with us. It is in his self interest. Have arrangements been made for his arrival next week?"

"Everything is prepared," said the Yemeni. "But it would be advisable to take no more chances. The time is drawing near. You must confine her."

"Very well," said the king finally. "I shall tell her

tonight. But she won't like it. Now, you have one hour to get me there. Are preparations complete?"

"*Tahkt amrak*, ya Bandar; at your command.

A week later, an Egyptian driving a fruit truck from the JADCO reservation to Jabalain, hummed a tune by *Um ArKarthoom*. Between the lines of the catchy if erratic Arabic melody, he chanted the facts he would have to relay to his contact at Jabalain, who would then relay them to his contact in Kuwait, who would then relay them to a certain tourist vacationing in Egypt. He sang:

> "And the Beautiful *hurma* went to the harem;
> And the Great Baal Bazz went to Philistine;
> And deep beneath the sands of King Waleed;
> The day grew near for holy Jihad;
> To the Old City will visit ten million;
> And to New City will visit the Phoenix;
> Will the great king become Mahdi;
> Who can lead the bedu from their tents?
> Or be slain by his brother who hides in Masr."
> They said Muhammad could move a mountain;
> But who will move the mountain this time?
> Maybe Nobody.

Forty-Four

The Harem

The thinner she spread herself, the more she felt her will deserting her only to be replaced by something alien. She had the feeling that something had been growing slowly within her, almost like a pregnancy–or was it a cancer? She was nurturing something evil, and now she must get rid of it or die. But what would the "birth" be like? Would she survive it?

For awhile, she had felt as if she had almost complete control over him; he could refuse her nothing. But she had lost it.

Now she was here. She lied on the satin pillows with the other women, in her blue satin harem pants, the scantiest lace covering her top. She was eating a juicy pear. The smell of frankincense was heavy. She was caught in a sensuous hell.

Why had he brought her here? Did he suspect her? Or did he simply want to own her now? He had already told her that he could not honor his pledge to allow her to go home. He said he loved her too much to ever let her go.

She knew that she had succeeded in getting valuable information. Had her mission been successful? She hoped so, but she wasn't really sure. Each time she had pulled something out of him and had given it to Shareef; she felt vindicated. Then, just days before he had ordered her to come here, she had managed to pass on the last crucial news.

Ahmad Daweesh, aka Dowi Al Harbi was now in Israel. His main objective was to blow up the atomic installation at Damona, the heart of Israel's strategic defense system. All of the critical scientific data needed to accomplish the feat was in his possession, stolen and supplied to him by a top level Israeli who either believed in their cause or loved money too much. In addition, Ahmad had a network of operatives of the highest caliber working for him on the task at this very moment; Germans, Italians, Americans–all the best in their fields.

But Ahmad had refused to turn over control of this crucial mission to anyone else. Bandar told her he had insisted on masterminding and directing the entire operation. First Dimona would go, and then the key missile defenses. Then there would be a general black-out when the power grid dependant on Damona was destroyed. And when the "Zionists" were in a state of panic and confusion; that is when Bandar would strike in force.

But try as she might, he would not tell her just how he intended to strike. She assumed it would be a mass invasion. For Snead had often told her that the kingdom's air force and strategic capabilities–despite the huge fortunes spent on it–was still third rate. So it would be a conventional land invasion. The Arabs intended to beat Israel by force of sheer numbers, by overwhelming odds; much like the Romans had done in ancient times.

She thought of killing herself. She still had the poison. Her job was done and she would never get out. She could no longer even see Shareef. Bandar hadn't told her why, but she knew he must suspect something by now, even if he couldn't admit it to himself.

Joseph's Seed

She didn't care. Israel would win; she could now rest in peace.

She asked one of her new "sisters" for something to drink. The king refused her nothing and she knew she could get it. The sister called a eunuch who brought her a strong fruit drink. Was that Amaretto in it? She wasn't sure. She had another. She began to be giddy.

"Tell him I want to see him," she announced suddenly. "I want him," she made a sexual gesture with her body.

"You know he can not come now," said the sister. "He is in Majlis with the King of Jordan and the President of Egypt. He will come later. You know he takes only you now; but you must wait."

"I want him NOW!" she demanded in a loud voice. She began leaving the room, now walking stridently, now voluptuously, now stumbling in a near stupor. "Wait," said the sister, "You must not." Then turning to the big eunuch who was about to restrain her. "No, do not touch her! The king will kill you."

A few of the sisters followed her out of the room trying to dissuade her; trying to hold her up. There was a general commotion in the palace. The king, hearing unusual noises in the halls from his nearby Majlis asked an aid to see what the matter was. The aid left the room to inquire. Upon returning he whispered something to the king who said, "Bring her in. But instruct her that she must not speak." The king knew that Jordan's monarch, who also had an American wife, would be jealous when he saw her.

The cameras trained upon her as she entered the room. Breaths were drawn in. She was a queen, a movie star, a whore. She sat on the floor by his side and buried her head in his knees, saying nothing. Then the king continued speaking to his guests in Arabic, but his guests had lost interest in politics.

Da'ud the Palestinian watched Egyptian news in Arabic from his home in Beer Sheva, every night at six. That night was no exception. Tonight, the president of that country was sitting in conference with the great king of Arabia. Perhaps it would be a momentous meeting. Most likely it would be nothing new, just more talk. In either case, he would watch.

What he saw however was not at all what he expected. He was used to seeing scantily clad women on Israeli television and in Egyptian movies, but such a thing on a broadcast filmed in the Kingdom of Arabia was unprecedented. It was one of the king's concubines no doubt. She looked like an Egyptian belly dancer, but her hair was golden and she was very beautiful. Then the camera zoomed in on her as she moved across the room to take her place next to the kings.

Something inside of him froze. It was her. He was sure of it. Although many years had passed he had never forgotten that face. It was the American Jewish girl who had written about Ahmad. He remembered because those weeks had changed his life. Before that, life was so simple. He was a simple workman and happy to be one. But now he was a killer–now they were all killers. Could it have been any different?

For a moment he thought that perhaps he wouldn't tell what he had seen, but then he realized he must. Ahmad must know. This could change many things. Da'ud picked up the phone. He forgot himself. He was not supposed to use the phone to speak to Ahmad, but surely something like this couldn't wait until he saw Ahmad as planned.

A few moments later a telephone rang in another part of that country. A little old man with tight white curls picked up the receiver. "*Ken*," said the old man. "Yes, this is what we have been waiting for. . . no, they have not given us much. . . yes, we knew he was here but still we could not find him. He is master of many faces... now we have him, *habibi*, almost. No, do not pick up the operative who took Da'ud's call. When the Lord of the Hawks moves, we will be ready. He must act first. But watch the ones we have pinpointed. Watch them very carefully. Soon they will lead us to him."

The old man hung up the phone. He sat silently for some time, thinking. He too had watched the news from Egypt. He had waited many years for this day. He dialed the phone.

"Give me Cairo," he said into the receiver. "Hotel Hilton... Yes. Mr. James Snead."

A few moments later a voice cracked through the wire. "Hello James... Yes, yes, I have found what you have been searching for. I suggest that we meet as soon as possible to discuss the matter... yes, and please tell your tourist friend that it is time to return to Phoenix.... yes, and I am also pleased to tell you that Dvora has said that she would like to come home now. Do you think that you can arrange it?"

"We'll give it our best shot," said Mr. Snead. Snead hung up the phone and turned to the man on the bed in his hotel room. The man was lying on his back, a straw cowboy hat over his face.

"What are you going to do now, buddy?" he asked.

"Oh," said Clement lazily. "Guess I'll go and get her."

"You'd better hurry," said Snead. "She won't have much time now."

Forty-Five

The Yemeni's Methods

Shareef's lines of communication didn't end when he lost contact with Debbie. He still had his network of Egyptian clerks, functionaries, bureaucrats, and drivers scattered throughout the kingdom. Although it wasn't aired on the Riyadh News, he knew what she had done and he knew why. Now, she would want out but alas, there was nothing he could do about it. He might be smart, but he was not a physical man. He could not save her. He might not even be able to save himself, for as soon as Dowi Al Harbi was apprehended by the Israelis, they would know. The king might not think of it; he was blinded by his own passion. But the Yemeni would know, and so would others.

Neither did he think that Frank could do anything. To Shareef, Frank was just an ordinary person who was caught up in something much too big for him. But Debbie was his wife. He had a right to know. That was why Shareef, when he made his mail drop for Al Tawali this week, decided to tell Frank the whole story–well almost the whole story. They might all be dead soon. What was there to lose?

"I can't believe it," said Frank. "An international terrorist? The king's chief aid? Debbie?"

Joseph's Seed

"You knew about her brother, Sam, being killed by terrorists, didn't you?" said Shareef.

"Sure but that was just some distant tragedy–in the past. I knew she was spying, but never thought."

"Anyway, they have not caught him yet," continued the Egyptian. "But it looks like a sure thing–thanks to your wife. Afterward, the Rasheeds will probably kill her–maybe you and me too. There is nothing we can do, but I thought you should know. Your wife, Debbie is a great woman."

"I wish I could do something," said Frank. "Save her somehow."

"You can't."

"I know."

Then Shareef said, "Who would have thought that someone like Debbie, a little American princess, would be the one to bring down the great Baal Bazz when none of the professionals could touch him?"

"What?" said Frank. "Baal Bazz? That's who she thinks this guy Al Harbi is? But it can't be!"

"What do you mean?" asked Shareef.

"Because I think I know who Baal Bazz is. I'm almost sure of it." Then Frank told Shareef what he knew or thought he knew. Later that day, Shareef Returned to Riyadh. He wanted to be with Debbie more than ever–and if that was possible, tell her what Frank had said.

The king looked deflated, and his greatest hour had not yet even come. The Yemeni was standing over him. He had just received a coded message from Dowi Al Harbi. Debbie was a traitor–worse–a Zionist. She must be dealt with. She must be executed publicly, to make an example of her. As for the great Baal Bazz; there is no cause for worry. He is a man of mystery, a man of many faces. He would triumph in his greatest hour.

"*Bismalla*, I can not believe it," said the king. "But alas, I am just a simple bedouin. I must believe my trusted friend. He has never failed me.

"Do what you must, *ya Muhammad*. Do it in my name. Make an example of this *hurma*. It is the will of Allah. Yes, and arrest this troublesome Egyptian also. If he is a spy, cut off his head; but find out what you can from him first. Anyway, they can not stop us now. It is too late."

That evening, several hours after orders had been given to isolate Debbie, and to place a guard at her door, Muhammad Ali the Yemeni went to see her.

"You have too much to tell me," he said to her in halting English. "If you would like to live."

Debbie laughed. "Sure," she said. "How can I be of service?"

That night a huge Arab quietly put a vise-like hand over the mouth of the guard at Debbie's door. Equally quietly, he slit the guard's throat and lay him down in a heap. There was a string of such heaps in the palace already.

"Always sleeping on the job," mumbled the other "Arab" in Mid-Western English. "Find the key, Abdullah?"

"*Ayewah*," said the big Arab.

They found her sleeping on the floor, shivering fitfully for she was still dressed in her harem pants and had no blanket.

"Nooo!" she began to moan when she sensed the presence of men in the room. Then, awakening, she saw him. "What? It's you?" She tried to move away from him.

"Shhh!" said the man, picking her up and wrapping her in a blanket he had taken from the "sleeping" guard.

"Not now."

Then they went to a nearby room which Abdullah opened with another key. There was a pencil of a man lying on the floor. He had no headdress or skullcap and his *thobe* was bloodstained. Effortlessly Abdullah slung the unconscious figure over his shoulder and left the room.

Neil DeRosa

Forty-Six

Joseph's Seed

The President of Egypt was standing before the group. He was a man of only fifty or so, but he had a weariness of expression that was beyond time. Still, a faint smile of hope played on his lips.

He said: "My people have been through this business for five thousand years. Why do you think that Egypt is called the mother of all nations? –It is because she has been fucked by everyone. But still she cares. It is for me to say that we sympathize with your aspirations, but we can do nothing to help, except to wish you well and to offer our hospitality and sanctuary should you fail.

"Am I worried of attack by the king of Arabia for my support of you? Yes–and no. Of course, thanks to Al Tawali's money and such oil revenues as the king now enjoys, he is very wealthy and could destroy our country with his new weapons. But then who will keep his books, and count his money, and administer his kingdom, and do countless other tasks for him?

"There are many Egyptians in Arabia. We work for him for we need to work in order to live, yet his own people, the bedouin, refuse to work for him, preferring to stay in the desert.

Joseph's Seed

"Yes, we would like to see a better leadership for that country. That is why I have taken the risks which I have taken, such as granting sanctuary to my friend, the Emir of Jabalain.

"And yes, it is time for peace with Israel. We must recognize that our cousins, the Jews, have come home to stay–and welcome. But just because I say that does not mean I don't want justice for the people of the land, the people who were there first–the Palestinians.

"I have had many conversations with Mustapha during his stay in my country. At first, I must admit that I was very skeptical of his ideas. I thought that either he was pulling my leg in order to gain an ally as part of his quest to wrest power from his brother's hands, or that he had simply picked up too many strange new notions during his stay in the United States as a youth. I myself, you see, am a traditional man. In other words, I am extremely cynical when it comes to any ideas designed to improve the human condition.

"But I have given his words much thought, and I can now see merit in them. His so called 'Libertarian Solution,' namely, a Palestine-Israel federation, may indeed be the only lasting hope for that land. But maybe I'm a dreamer also.

"I pledge therefore, to lend my support to his position on the Palestinian issue. Of course, he must first succeed in dealing with the present king–and that, my friends, is no small task.

"Joseph Tawali has planted many seeds with the power of his money. Some of those seeds have born evil fruit, such as the present regime in Arabia, and the many murders which his money finances. But some of those seeds have brought forth good things also. Many people, including my own, have benefited from his great wealth. The same, of course, can be said for the oil wealth; it has created a military machine, but it has also improved the lives of many people."

The President talked on for some time longer for he was an orator reminiscent of his hero the great Egyptian dictator of years gone by, Muhammad Diab. Finally after some time, he concluded with these words:

"There was once a prophet in our land by the name of Joseph; namely, he of the striped pajamas. He was a man who could see the future in his dreams. I also have had dreams. I dream that all of the peoples of the Middle East may one day live in peace and prosperity, and that this region, which was the cradle of civilization, and has always been the home of prophets will once again rise to glory–but it will be a peaceful glory this time.

"We have done our part by making peace with the Jews. One of my predecessors gave his life for that effort. This is now your struggle, so I wish you good luck. But that is all I can give you, for we are a poor nation."

The President bowed his head for a moment and then said: "I sometimes forget that there was still another Joseph in our land. An unsung hero in my opinion. He brought his family to Egypt to escape the Roman tyrant, Herod. In that way his seed was able to survive. Some have called that seed a prince also–the Prince of Peace. That seed has born much fruit. "

Then the president smiled and left the room.

Around the room sat the remnant. The "tourist" was by now a "resident" of Egypt, for Mustapha had been in exile almost a year. He sat in a comfortable chair. His trusted friend, Abdullah who had returned not many days ago from his mission with Clement in which they brought back Debbie and Shareef, stood behind him by the door. Except for their foray in Bandar's palace, which could not have been accomplished by men of lesser abilities, it had been an easy task, for Mustapha had many allies. There had been a helicopter waiting in the desert nearby–with a pilot who could land without crashing.

Joseph's Seed

All were present today including Jim Snead and Sadya Bar Kama the kibbutznik. Present also were a few loyal supporters from Arabia, influential Sheiks who were purportedly out of the kingdom on business trips. Among them were Mr. Fahad, and a man of many millions named Moneef Mulafic. Rex Lawton stood by a window looking out. The building they were in was a mansion in which Mustapha, his family, and his entourage now resided. It doubled as the headquarters for the resistance movement–courtesy of the President of Egypt.

He turned now to the old Israeli.

"How much time do we have my friend?" he inquired.

"Our agents are scrutinizing them with the greatest care. But still there are some missing links. For one thing, we have not yet pinpointed the mysterious Baal Bazz. He may be one of several men now in our view, but we are not entirely sure if he is even in our country. He may have felt the ill wind and vanished, or he may have never been there at all, for he often uses proxies.

"His organization is under close surveillance, but as yet, they do not seem to have committed any acts of sabotage. We do not plan to interrupt their activities until they do, since it is the Lord of the Hawks that we seek. We will inform you of any change."

"How can we be of help?" inquired Snead.

"You can not," said Sadya. "We have all the necessary tools at our disposal."

"Be that as it may," replied Snead. "We will continue, of course, to monitor troop movements. If anything unusual happens, you will be the first to know. I am sure, in the event it becomes necessary, that my government would be willing to. . ."

"As always, we appreciate what you do; but let us hope it does not come to that."

Mustapha then turned to the Egyptian, Shareef. "My friend," he began, "you have done a lot for us already. Fahad's people in Kuwait have told me repeatedly that without your efforts, the lines of communication might have been broken. I am sorry for the pain which has been inflicted on you. Of course you have no further obligations to return to the arena of danger."

Shareef, who appeared badly shaken from his recent experience with the Yemeni's interrogations, and even thinner than usual, said only: "I want to go back, Mr. Mustapha. In fact, I insist–with your permission of course."

"*Taffadel*," said the prince. "As you wish."

"Very well, then," he turned again to the others. "Tomorrow we begin regrouping in Kuwait. That government as you know, although sympathetic to our aims, just as are the Egyptians, will not engage in any hostile acts against my brother's regime. They feel that they will probably have to live with him. They do not share my confidence in the wisdom of my people– the wisdom of the bedouin. But that remains to be seen–*Inshallah.*

"So that's it, then," he said brightly, smiling optimistically, "We all have our different tasks –until we see each other next time."

As he rose, he looked once more toward Debbie, who had not spoken during the meeting, for all of the information she had to give had been known for days.

"We can not thank you enough, Mrs. Costello, for what you have suffered for our cause–and your own. You need rest now more than anything else. If I can ever be of service."

"Thank you," said Debbie and she rose and began to leave the room.

A strong hand took her elbow just then. "We need to talk," said Clement Schmidt.

"Not now," said Debbie. "I need time to think." She turned to leave again, but this time the old Israeli tapped her on the shoulder.

"May I buy you lunch, Dvora? A road side kiosk?"

"I'm not very hungry, but I'll walk with you." said Debbie smiling. She took his arm and they went out

Joseph's Seed

together.

They walked through a crowded open market, across the boulevard stood the ubiquitous desert palms, well groomed flower gardens, and the Nile. The sound of car horns was ceaseless.

Debbie was still holding Sadya's arm. She felt warm; he was like a father–the father she hadn't seen for so long. He was eating a falafel in pocket bread.

"*Nu, hamooda,*" he said. "What do you think now? Was it worth it? You have seen much. You have changed?"

"In what way?"

"Your view of our people? We Jews have survived the Nazis only for this?"

"From the kettle to the frying pan," she said.

"Yes. It has been going on throughout our whole history. One wonders if it will ever end. Is it still worth the effort to be a Jew?"

"Are you waiting for the Messiah?" she asked almost without connection.

"We kibbutznicks are atheists, you know." He smiled at her. "The King of Arabia claims to be the Messiah. Perhaps he is."

"A false Messiah maybe–more likely just a deranged man. I don't understand what they're waiting for–I mean my government–why don't they just get rid of him?"

"Things are not done that way any more, my dear," said the old man. "Especially were immense sums of money are concerned. No, his own people will have to deal with him in their own way, if they have the will."

"What do you think of him," she asked then stopping. "The brother, I mean. Is he good? Will he make peace with us if he wins? Or will it be more of the same?"

"You have become quite fond of the Arabs, some of them at least. You are not as you were."

"You haven't answered my question," she said.

"Your question? My answer is; who knows? Still I

have hope."

A moment later he spoke again. "You are aware, of course, that we can have no peace as long as Ahmad is still free?"

"Yes."

"And you are still willing to help?"

"Yes, he must be stopped."

He took her hand and they walked on.

That night Clement called her at her room in the Cairo Hilton. "Can I come up?" he said. "We need to talk."

"Where are you?"

"In the lobby."

"I'll come down."

They walked where she had walked earlier that day with Sadya. Now she was with him. They walked a long while saying nothing.

"Look," she began finally. "You saved my life–probably twice. I can't deny that. I was attracted to you. I can't deny that either. But you hate everything I am–everything I stand for. The truth is I don't think we have anything to talk about."

"You're wrong," he said. "We have a lot to talk about."

"But–what you said in Jabalain–you can't get any more anti- Semitic than that. To want us all dead–I shouldn't even be talking to you–but somehow..."

"I..." He was about to say something when an ill wind passed and he fell silent. Finally he said: "I had a reason for saying what I said. But I can tell you this. You are still in great danger."

"From you?"

"That too, possibly," and he walked away. She watched him go, confused.

When she placed her key in the lock of her hotel room, she was struck numb by the feel of someone's hand over her mouth. He drew her to him.

"Make no sound," said the figure of a man.

Joseph's Seed

Instinctively she turned and ducked, but it was too easy. She kicked him in the groin. "Oww! He screamed. As he doubled over, the *gutra* he had on his head fell off.

"You! What the hell!"

"I thought it was now or never," said Shareef.

"It's never," she said. "What do you want?"

"I had to talk to you. It's a matter of life and death–yours. I'm not kidding. Let's go inside." After she shut the door he said. You're in danger kid–mortal danger. The man you're hunting is. . ."

Just then the door burst open. It was Clement.

"Don't you two think it's about time we cleared the air around here?" he asked.

Later, when they were gone, she called the only person for whom she still felt total trust. He had left his hotel number with her just in case she felt like talking.

"Sadya," she said into the phone. "I'm afraid."

"What is it, *motek*?" When she told him, he said: "I too am now afraid. Our enemy is much more dangerous than I have long believed. I must think this out. *Elohim*, I pray there is still time enough. Will you be alright tonight?"

"I think so. I have a gun."

"Then we shall return to Tell Aviv in the morning to begin our preparations."

Forty-Seven

Not the Hero Type

Shareef was the first back. When he saw him at the gate, Frank thought it was the fruit truck driver, but then he saw that he was too thin. He had a grubby beard. His hair was different. Somehow he looked different. But it was him; Frank was sure of it now. He got into the truck as the "driver" continued on his way to make his pick-ups at the green houses.

"What are you doing here?" asked Frank. "Don't you know it's dangerous? We saw it on the news. They're looking for you. They showed your picture."

"What about you boss? Isn't it dangerous for you? Do you know about Debbie?"

"Yeah, I know. But that wasn't in the news. They never mentioned her, but Momduh told me. That's the king's son, you know. They made him governor of Jabalain."

"I know who he is," said Shareef.

Then Frank asked, "Did you see her? Is she alright?"

Shareef told Frank what had transpired in Cairo, but left out a few details. Then he asked, "What else did Momduh tell you?"

"He said that at first the king wanted me killed–you know, because I'm still her husband. But then they

sand nearby.

"*Ahalan Wa Sahalan,*" said the withered old Arab, Prince Razi Al Atebi. "Welcome."

"Your brothers in Kuwait and in Egypt send their greetings," said one of the visitors, after he embraced his host and kissed him on both cheeks many times.

"Your brothers in Arabia send you two greetings," said Razi. "And they await your leadership."

The five men made their way past several mules which were feeding from a trough in Razi's courtyard, and went into the ancient prince's mud brick majlis. One of the mules had watched this procession with curiosity. Soon afterward, an old woman entered the majlis and served them green coffee and dates.

Joseph's Seed

Forty-Eight

Camels

"Come with me, Mr. Frank." Prince Momduh called from his car. The Governor of Jabalain showed up that morning at seven a.m. at the JADCO reservation, wearing his army uniform. He came alone, in Mustapha's Land Rover. He found Frank already at work in Mr. Ashamary's office.

"We will have a party at my palace today. You are invited–and by the way–you will meet the king. He is arriving by jet from Riyadh this afternoon.

"Will Mr. Ashamary be coming?" inquired Frank.

"I do not think so. My father does not like him. He thinks he is a pest. Besides, someone must stay here to mind the store–no?"

As they drove off, Mr. Ashamary watched through the window of his office. Then he picked up his bugged phone and called the palace in Jabalain.

"Yes, Sayed the provisions officer please. Yes this is Sheikh Ashamary. Yes I understand that the king does not wish to see me. Anyway, the provisions you ordered? I wish to contribute them to his majesty's pleasure. Yes free of charge. Yes, my driver Abu Diab will deliver them in three hours, no later. Fresh produce and fruit from our greenhouses, and watermelons–the king loves watermelons–and a young freshly killed lamb. If there is anything else, please do not hesitate to call. *Takht Amrak* ya Sayed, at your command."

Hijazi Ashamary hung up the phone slowly and smiled; a deep and satisfied smile.

"You will meet a great man today," said Momduh. In fact, that makes you famous in some way. You are almost related to my father now, you know," the young prince laughed a hearty laugh. Frank couldn't bring himself to smile–even in pretense.

"Anyway, he wanted me to bring you today, so I did." Momduh sobered up. He did not like his companion's lack of enthusiasm when he himself felt exhilarated.

They were passing through the Military City now. It was a common route for Momduh, who was its commander. He swung now into the headquarters building, got out, and said to Frank: "Come."

Inside, he spoke rapidly to some officers in Arabic, confident that Frank could not comprehend–but Frank understood verbatim–for Mr. Ashamary had tutored him well this past year.

"Have the king's chambers prepared," Momduh was saying. "–and the control room–No, no women will accompany him. Whether this is the day I can not tell, but all systems must be in readiness as if it were! All cities are on standby for mobilization. Perhaps Muhammad Ali will issue the order before the day is out. "Mobilization must be complete in two days–therefore the third day is it. The Lord of the Hawks will welcome us from within the Zionist Entity. No, it is not official, you know I do not have the authority, But I am quite sure that Muhammad Ali will issue the order today."

"*Yalla*, I am in a hurry," he said then in English. "You remember Mr. Frank," he was talking to the officer who had arrested Frank that day on the road to Al Kharge.

Joseph's Seed

"*Kaif el Hal?*" said the officer, patting him on the back. "How are you?"

"Kwayss," said Frank. Everyone laughed. To their minds, Frank was a fool. But Frank was becoming less of a fool all the time.

At the palace later that day Frank recognized many of the dignitaries he had seen at the Sheikh's party, also several he had seen on the evening news but never before in person. Again there were many beautiful bejeweled Arab women accompanying their husbands, the most important sheikhs and princes in the land. There seemed to be two distinct groups now: The older, more traditional Arabs in their flowing robes, and the "young Turks" in their army uniforms. Momduh seemed to be the leader of the latter group. Muhammad Ali the Yemeni was clearly the leader of the former.

But the party was conspicuous for its absences too. For one, the ridiculous old billionaire Sheikh Tawali was not there. Frank wondered if he was still alive. For another the singsong voice of Ustez Doudeen was missing, as was the sarcastic Shareef. Frank felt a pang–for Debbie was missing also.

Also the king was not yet there, but Momduh had informed him that he had arrived at the palace and would soon make his entrance. Presently, a white bearded Arab announced: "His Majesty, Bandar Jibreen Ibn Abdul Lateef, King of Arabia, King of the Holy places, King of Mecca, King of Medina, King of *Al Kuds*." Frank knew the meaning of "*Al Kuds.*"

The tall slim, regal king of Arabia in his white silk thobe with his sky blue gutra entered slowly. His subjects kissed his beard as he passed. He smiled and waved graciously to others. When he got to Frank, Momduh said, "Your Majesty, Mr. Frank Costello."

"Your Majesty," Frank submitted.

"Ah, yes, Mr. Costello," said the king as he passed by, and the powers that be celebrated their imminent victory.

Not long afterward Momduh approached Frank.

"That nuisance of a sponsor of yours, Ashamary—I wonder if you could help me a moment. He was supposed to deliver the food for this party, but it seems that he forgot the watermelons. Don't worry, they have arrived now, but there is some question—it seems—about how many go here and how many go to the market. Please straighten out your foolish driver before I throw him in jail. Anyway, he is asking for you, and I do not want any commotion. Do you understand, Frank?"

"Don't worry," said Frank. "I'll take care of it."

"Good, hurry because my father wants you to accompany us soon to the City."

Frank went down to the kitchen and immediately jumped into the truck helping the driver to unload watermelons. They selected twenty big ones and Frank said: "That's enough uh, what's your name? I haven't seen you before."

"*Shukron, Shukron, ya mohandes*, I mean boss. I am Abu Diab. Allah will save you."

"Thanks," said Frank. "Uh, these watermelons are a mess in here," he pointed inside the truck. "I'll help you fix them. Otherwise we'll lose money." Inside the truck, Frank told the Egyptian a tale.

"*Shukron, shukron*," said the driver. And he was gone.

"You think we are savages," said King Bandar. He walked down the corridor now with Frank, holding his hand. It was the evening of First Day.

"No, sir, I don't," said Frank.

Behind them walked Muhammad Ali the Yemeni, Prince Rasheed, the Minister of Defense, and other ministers and princes who were followers of the king. Behind them were Momduh and several other young officers.

Joseph's Seed

"I would have allowed you to divorce your wife honorably, you know. We have very specific laws concerning that subject–very civilized; but never mind that now. It is past. She was kidnapped by the bedouin, I think. It is they who are still savages."

Frank recognized the big steel door at the end of the corridor. It was the Control Room. They entered.

In the cavernous room was a computer network with twenty or so terminals around the periphery of the room. On one wall was a large screen, and on another, a trajectory grid. Technicians were at work at several of the terminals. On the trajectory grid a projectile was moving from square to square in a large arc. At the foot of the arc was a computer enhanced rendition of a city: a city with skyscrapers. Flashing in sequence on the large screen were various missile silos and strategic locations on the surface at which mobilization was under way. There was a master control console–and a throne-like seat in the center of the room.

"My technicians are running what they call a mock up, a test run, you would say. This is not the real thing. Not yet."

"But why," asked Frank. He no longer felt afraid, for there was nothing left to lose.

"You ask why? But it is simple. I must fulfill my destiny."

"Why do you want me to see?"

"Who knows?" said the king who was staring intently at the grid. "You may be the one to tell the story to the world. Do you know the one place in the world where the most Zionists are concentrated in one place?"

"Why, Israel, I guess," said Frank.

"You are wrong," said the king. "It is. . ."

Just then there was a commotion at one of the consoles. Several of the technicians converged on one of the terminals and were looking at the screen, making adjustments.

"What is it?" said the Yemeni, who also moved in to look at the screen. Then he whispered something to the king.

"Yes, put it on the big screen," ordered Bandar.

A security camera from one of the guard posts outside of the fenced periphery of the city was trained on–camels. Men riding camels. At first there were just a few. Then gradually, thousands came into view.

"Tsk, tsk," snorted the king in disdain. He waved his hand as if to dismiss them from the screen. "It is the bedouin I see. Find out what they want Muhammad, a handout no doubt."

During the next hour they watched the scenes on the screen with interest. At first soldiers tried to bully the tribesmen. Then when that didn't work, they walked with them holding hands or sat and drank tea with them. All the while they discussed matters. The senior officers were reluctant to take a strong hand for although their troops were loyal, foreign Muslims, most of the officers were of bedouin stock. These tribesmen were their kin. It was a conflict of military duty versus family and tribal loyalty. Not easy to resolve, so they dealt with it in the manner of the desert.

By and by, Momduh and some of the senior officers had located and negotiated with the tribal leaders. Finally, they reported to the king, who was waiting below in the Control Room.

"Their leaders are Prince Razi Al Atebi, and Sheikh Moneef Mulafic," reported Momduh. "They demand a majlis with the king. If the Zionists are to be attacked, they say, they should be leading the battle as they have always done. They insist."

The king snickered. He turned to the Yemeni. "Do they expect to lead our tanks and missiles and jets with their camels?" But into the console he said: "Tell the honored Sheikhs that I will consider their proposal. However, I need some time. Tell them to make camp where they sit, and we will discuss matters further in the morning."

Momduh conversed with the leaders for a few more moments and then returned to the screen. "Prince

Razi says that your offer is acceptable. He says to tell you that there are two thousand stars in the sky, and that you should come up and join him by the campfire."

"Tomorrow, *Inshalla*," said the king smiling wistfully. "Now return to your duties my son. You have much work to do."

Momduh returned as ordered, but all through the night, campfires flickered in the desert. bedouin from the outside had much to say to the bedouin within.

Neil DeRosa

Forty-Nine

Sweet Revenge

A few hundred miles to the north, a shy dark haired girl with horn rimmed glasses sat at a desk typing. She was a receptionist at the technical information center at the Nuclear Research Institute in Damona. A delegation of scientists from the Technion in Haifa was in the process of installing certain state of the art modifications to the institute's mainframe computer. She was to be their guide and liaison. The former guide had become ill.

The delegation's lead scientist, Avigdor Gurshon, had telephoned to say he would be in to arrange the following week's itinerary. There was still much work to be done.

He stood before her now, signing the register.

"Are you new here *motek*?" he inquired with a condescending smile. "I haven't seen you here before." His Hebrew was impeccable, like a scientist's; he even had a Haifa accent. It was wasted on the girl though; she could barely understand him. She did however, recognize his voice–and the way he moved.

"*Ktzat*," said the girl, looking up from big horn rimmed glasses. "I immigrated only last year, I am American."

"Oh really!" exclaimed the scientist. "Then I'll speak

English." His English, she thought, although not quite impeccable, still sounded sexy, just as she remembered it.

"Have you gathered the necessary passes and clearances? You know, this has been quite a nuisance. We have been working here for a week now and you would think they would know us by now. I've never been in a place which is so paranoid."

"Yes," said the girl. "One never knows who to trust. Take you, for example. You appear to be perfectly normal. All of your credentials are in order. Your reputation is known to us. But Maybe–just maybe, you're not who you seem to be. Who knows? You could be a famous terrorist preparing to blow this place up. After all, no one here actually knows you personally. You could have had plastic surgery."

The scientist laughed easily. "You are too much," he said. "I can see that you like a good mystery. You know, I have the strange feeling that I've 'seen you somewhere before. ' I think that is an old line, no? Are you married? Perhaps we can have lunch later."

"A mystery? Yes I like mysteries, except this one is solved." Then she pulled out a gun and stood up from behind her desk.

"You're through, Ahmad. You don't look like Ahmad, but I'd bet my life on it. In fact, I have.

"You're under arrest Ahmad Daweesh, alias Dowi Al Harbi, alias Baal Bazz, although I'm not as sure of the last as I once was. Well, it doesn't matter. Whoever you are, you deserve to die for what you've done. And I'm going to kill you."

"You're crazy, *gveret*," he said, reverting back to Hebrew. "This must be some kind of joke." Then like lightning, he lunged at her across the desk. She fired hitting his shoulder, but he kept coming.

Then the two doors to the reception room burst open. Several agents rushed in, guns drawn. In a moment he was subdued.

Sadya walked in behind the agents.

"Are you alright Dvora? He asked.

"A bit shaken," she said. "But okay."

"So," he said, now turning to Ahmad. "You have finally returned to your homeland. The Lord of the Hawks? Or at least his lieutenant, so it now seems. You have one consolation, I would say. You will at least be allowed to die at home. It may seem strange to you, but I feel your pain. Because of it, I do not hate, but only pity you."

"It does not matter," said Dowi Al Harbi, now speaking Arabic. "Soon you will all die. Nothing you do can stop it. Baal Bazz can not be stopped by ones like you." He lunged again, bleeding, this time for Sadya. The agents dragged him from the room.

After he was gone, she said to Sadya: "How can he have gotten so far; a few more modifications, and there would have been a catastrophe. They only discovered the irregularities yesterday. How could it have happened?"

"There are traitors among us, like any other people," said Sadya. "But be assured that they did not will the destruction of their own people. It was gain they were after. They stood to make millions for allowing a few mere "secrets" to be stolen–by the Russians, they thought. It is sad. It is always sad.

"I only wish, my dear, that we could rest now that we have found Ahmad. But alas, we must still capture Baal Bazz before it is too late. But where would he strike if not here?"

Fifty

A Bedouin Solution

The Kingdom of Arabia occupies the major portion of the land mass known to the Arabs as *Al Jazira*, "The Island," and known to the rest of the world as the Arabian Peninsula. The Land of Israel was placed by Allah in the tiny Northwestern tip of that great land mass, perhaps as a thorn in the side of the Arabs , perhaps to keep them keen in their service and devotion to Allah. It was there briefly in ancient times–and now it was back. But this time, a Leader had been called upon by Him to remove the thorn once and for all. It wasn't enough to simply remove it however, he had also to remove the source of revenue for that thorn–namely the Hub of World Jewry's finance–New York City.

Truly then, Bandar Jibreen Ibn Abdul Lateef, King of Arabia felt called on by Allah to do just that. Now he had the means and the deed was imminent. But he knew that if he acted against the Will of the people–especially as that Will expressed itself in the minds of the leaders of the original people of the land, the bedouin–he would never be honored as a true Arab king. Bandar remembered not long ago when one of their leaders, Moneef Mulafic, had been here in the Control Room. He was a businessman whose company had worked on the project, but he was also a bedouin. He was looking at the computer enhanced trajectory grid pointing to that city.

"What will keep the Americans from destroying you–destroying all of us–after you do this?" Mulafic had asked.

"Three reasons." The king replied, for he had long studied the American mind. "First, they need our oil, desperately. They fear nothing more than hard times. Second, the Left in that country, which is half of them, will pay any price for peace. It is a question of the 'haves' against the 'have nots. ' They will do anything to keep their Right from getting too much power–even sacrifice this." He turned and pointed to the skyscrapers. "And third, they hate the Jews–have always hated them. They will blame them and leave us alone–at the worst, they'll try to sue us."

Mulafic said nothing.

🐪 🐪 🐪

On the morning of the Second Day therefore, after consultation with his trusted aid Muhammad Ali the Yemeni, Bandar called the tribal leaders to join him in the Control Room to lead the Great Jihad against the hated Zionists. Thus it happened that the ancient bedouin chief Razi Al Atebi, and the sheikh Moneef Mulafic had come below with a few other chiefs and their "sons," among whom was a huge man known only as Abdullah.

"You will help me fight the battle in the only way it can be fought in these times," the king explained to them now, "by the aid of the weapons of modern science. These too are tools of Allah." Moneef Mulafic, who was not yet old, had no trouble accepting the concept. But Prince Razi balked.

"In all of the wars I fought at your father's side," he complained. "We fought as men should fight, on the backs of camels. If we are intended to defeat the Zionist, Allah will not let us fail–even as he did not let us fail in those days."

"Your words are true," agreed the king. "But did not even my father use English guns? Did not even you make use of the tools of science when you installed the great watering machines on your farms? And do you not have televisions now in your town? Do not forget that we Arabs have often been leaders in science– as for example in the days of our great Empire. Trust me oh sheikh, Allah approves of these new methods."

But the old man only said, "I don't know. I don't know," after that he watched the big screen as if it were a television and said very little.

Just then an aid who was watching the technician at the fax machine cried out: "Your Majesty! They have captured Dowi Al Harbi! The coded message has just come through from our friends within the Zionist Entity!"

For some moments the king said nothing but only sat in his chair as in a trance. Then the Yemeni whispered something in the king's ear. Frank, who had been made to sit at the king's feet, was the only other to hear. He understood.

Then the king's face brightened. "It does not matter in the slightest," he announced. "It would have been a mere diversion anyway. You see my aid, who was really not so trustworthy as I once believed, had planned to set off some explosions to create confusion among the Zionists. So he failed. *Ma'alaish*, it changes nothing. My plan can not fail.

"Order the Movement to begin, now!" he told the Yemeni.

Throughout the day and the evening of the Second Day, millions of Islamic troops marched. They moved on the highways of the kingdom in endless caravans of vehicles–military and civilian–heading inexorably north-west. They moved from the kingdom's client states of Iraq, and Syria, and Jordan. They moved in ships up the Red sea, and down the coast of the Mediterranean from Syria. They did not however move from the land of Egypt or from the tiny sheikhdom of Kuwait. By the end of the Second Day, they were in position and waiting–on three boarders of Israel–for the command of the king.

Meanwhile, a few thousand bedouin with their camels now grazing lazily in the desert above watched and waited also. While the mobilization from King Waleed City was underway, the king's troops in their armored vehicles were pelted with stones and rotten fruit by the bedouin. At the request of the king, their leaders tried, but not very enthusiastically, to illicit the cooperation of the tribesman through the guards with radios above. But they were an undisciplined mob.

"You see," said the king to his newfound confidant at his feet. "They are nothing but savages." He said this to Frank in English. Mulafic, who understood, glanced over but said nothing.

Finally when the bulk of the troops led by commander Momduh, were gone from the City and nothing remained but a minimal "defense force," the bedouin above began taking down the fence.

This activity, of course was monitored from the Control Room. After being briefed by the officer in charge, the king ordered, "Make them stop! Shoot them if they do not obey."

"*La, la, la,*" countered Razi Al Atebi. "Don't shoot. I will go up and make them stop."

Then Frank asked, "Can I go too?" The king denied his request out of hand, but Frank persisted. "If you want me to tell the world what happened, I'll have to see it. Besides we won't be gone long, anyway, where would I go?"

The king smiled as if at a child. "I suppose it can not hurt," he said. "Go! But return soon. You have much to see here." So Frank and the ancient sheikh

Joseph's Seed

with a few of his sons thus ascended the shaft.

It took Razi some time to quiet these troublesome bedouin. But after much confusion, he succeeded and was ready to return below with his sons. Frank was with him when he returned. He sat again at the king's feet. Above, unseen by the cameras, a handful of bedouin rode away on their camels. If they were noticed, nobody paid attention, for it was known that the bedouin are fickle.

When these riders arrived at the JADCO reservation nearby they exchanged their camels for two fueled up Toyota Land Rovers provided by Mr. Ashamary, and headed Northeast at breakneck speed. As soon as they arrived in Kuwait a few short hours later, Fahad's men made arrangements for their quick transfer by air to Egypt and from there to Israel. They had received vital information from Frank and had to move fast.

Back in the Control Room, men slept on the floor as nomads do, or took refreshment, or just sat in circles on cushions on the floor. Technicians changed shifts, and activity was monitored throughout the night. The king left the room and returned after a few short hours, for he could not sleep. During the night also, two of the old sheikh's sons went above for provisions from their camp, and returned shortly. This was allowed, for they were seen as no possible threat. Thus passed the night of the Second Day.

On the morning of the Third Day, one of the sons of the old sheikh stood and spoke thus to the king:

"Do you think our people will love you for this, or hate you? Will the Americans lie back and do nothing fearing their enemies, or strike back and destroy you? Will our neighbors the Egyptians serve you, or stab you in the back? Will you be able to overcome the Zionists by force of sheer numbers–without the help of your best warriors, the bedouin, or will their nuclear might and their air power destroy you?

"It is hard to know oh, brother. Is it not? Truly your

fate is in the hands of Allah."

Bandar was thunderstruck. How had his hated rival gotten in here? But he could not speak.

"Kill him!" ordered a voice from behind the king. It was the Yemeni. But before that voice could be obeyed, the head from which it came rolled on the floor, cut off by one swish of Abdullah's blade.

Then, for one brief moment, Bandar became King. "No!" He shouted. "You will not stop me now." He grabbed a gun which was in a compartment of his console. "Seize them!" he ordered the armed guard present in the room. But no one moved.

"I said seize them!" the king ordered. "If it is him you are afraid of I will kill him myself." He turned quickly and shot Abdullah through his left eye. The giant died instantly. Then he swung around quickly and shot at his brother. But he did not hit his brother, he hit instead the Arab who dove into Mustapha's path and took the bullet into his own chest. As he dove, the man's *gutra* fell off. He had a white beard and pale sun burnt skin. It was Rex Lawton.

Just then the lash of old Razi's whip pulled the gun from Bandar's hand. But the king stood up and drew his dagger.

"You will not stop me," he screamed. "I am king! Push the buttons! Push the buttons!" When no one moved, he lunged at Mustapha with his dagger. The brother moved easily to one side and struck Bandar on the back of the neck as he passed. The king stumbled, and then lunged again. Mustapha drew his own dagger, the one he had once held to his brother's throat. But this time Bandar showed no fear.

Then the two brothers were locked in mortal combat, the world stood still as fate made its decision. Bandar fought valiantly, for evil is not impotent when it is fighting for survival–when its dream of power is in the balance. But it was no use. The king was finished–for his brother's knife sunk deep into his heart.

As he slipped from Mustapha's arms and out of this

life, he said: "I only wanted our people to have pride. What was so wrong with that?"

"No," said the victor. "Not pride, but power." And he let him slide. He went then to his dying friend.

"How're you doing old buddy," he said, kneeling. "Hold on. We'll get you fixed right up."

"Nah," said the Texan. "I always wanted to go home to die. Guess I did." And he did.

Mustapha lay the American's head down. Then he looked to his trusted friend Abdullah and said: "Allah will save him." Next he turned and said to Frank: "We're getting you out of here right now. There is someone who needs your help."

Neil DeRosa

Fifty-One

The Hawk's Prey

With the entire nation of Israel mobilized and standing ready to launch a preemptive strike against the combined forces of Islam lined up at its borders, Baal Bazz went to pray. It had long been the fervent vow of Arab kings never again to pray at the holy Dome of the Rock–the very spot where the Prophet Muhammad had ascended into heaven–until Jerusalem was again in Arab hands. The Lord of the Hawks now felt justified in that very act for the deed was done. It was only a question of time–less than an hour.

He went in to pray. He was descended from the great Arab family from which the leaders of Jerusalem had come. Hence in Palestine he would be king. He would be the first–and last great Arab to pray here. Nothing else would matter after that.

He lay out prone in supplication to the just God who was about to return to him what was his. It was inevitable now. The people were afraid; few had come to pray, but he was not–for he had made this happen.

It was he who had spread the seed. The seed of hate. The seed of hope. The seed of Arab intelligence and power. The seed made possible by tapping the fabulous wealth of Joseph Tawali, the richest Muslim in the world.

He had made possible the rise of king Bandar. He had convinced Tawali of the necessity of financing the military armament of Arabia. He had created the legend of Baal Bazz, the Lord of the Hawks, and let the world believe that he was Dowi Al Harbi, the Arab historian.

Now they had captured Al Harbi–but it mattered not in the least for the world was about to begin anew.

He bowed again in prayer. "Yes I certify that there is no God but Allah–but even if there is no God at all, it matters not because fate is stronger than all things. It was meant to be."

A few more came in to pray; still there were very few in prayer. They were afraid, but soon they would have nothing to fear. Soon he would deliver them. He looked at his Rolex: "Fifteen minutes now, we shall hear the first explosion. It is such a shame–to destroy these beautiful mosques: Al Aqsa, and after it, the Dome of the Rock. When they hear of it–when my people see it–for the border is very near–they will go insane with rage. Only victory will satisfy them after that. There will never again be a Jihad such as this.

"We will say that the Zionists destroyed the great mosques and that will be reason enough to destroy the Jews once and for all. Later I will build a more beautiful mosque on this very site and it shall be ours forever.

"Very few ever knew who I was. Only Al Harbi, who would never tell for fear of losing face, the Yemeni, and a few trusted loyal servants.

"A yes, my trusted servant Shareef," he said aloud. "But what are you doing here? Ah yes, the Yemeni has sent you to tell me of Al Harbi's failure; but don't trouble yourself. I already know; I know all. Never mind, all is well. Come to my side and join me in prayer–a prayer of victory."

"Shalom, boss," said Shareef, adjusting his scull cap for he was not used to praying. "Everything ready?"

"Shhh, yes everything is ready. Why do you use their ugly words? Yes, the first will go in ten minutes; we must make haste the moment we hear it. There will only be five minutes after that before the next one goes–fine?"

They prayed.

"One minute now–Allah is Great!"

"Ten seconds–Muhammad is his prophet!"

"One–*Ashadwan*..." The sound was familiar in the world of Baal Bazz; from the first explosion of the Hebron Holocaust to many others after that, to the Ambassador Hotel in Tunis, to this. It was a deafening sound designed to remove half of the Al Aqsa Mosque, to scatter the debris in such a way as to allow his escape. The rest would go up minutes later.

"Come," he said to Shareef. "We must move quickly. Even now, our people will be accusing the Jews." They donned their *gutras* and slipped into their sandals and headed for the back alleyways of Jerusalem.

Flash! Flash! Flash!

"What is it, Shareef? Hurry! What is that light?

"Just a minute, boss. I think some tourists want to take your picture."

"This is no time to joke."

"It's no joke, boss."

"Mr. Doudeen, I presume," said a man with a camera in his hand.

"What! –is it–Frank? Mr.Costello? –But one such as you can not capture one such as me." He pushed Frank aside and began to run–straight for the narrow streets and hidden alleys where he would find refuge and escape as he had found so many times in his youth.

"Maybe," said another voice. "But I can." And Clement Schmidt made a flying tackle and caught the great Baal Bazz before he could disappear into the darkness.

"It's him," said Clement to Sadya Bar Kama who was now approaching with Debbie and Mr. Snead. "We both witnessed and filmed the act of sabotage. Are the other bombs diffused?"

"It is being done at this moment," said Sadya. "It is a pity that the Mosque had to be partially destroyed. It is a beautiful structure. But it was probably necessary for his people see something like this done by one of their own."

"I suggest," said Mr. Snead. "That you make haste to get on the wire with Mustapha. He's got some fast talking to do or you're going to have a big war on your hands."

"Negotiations have already begun," said Sadya. "God willing there will be no war."

""You're beginning to sound like an Arab," said Shareef. The old man smiled.

# Fifty-Two

Choices

Weeks later, at the Marriott Hotel in Riyadh, Clement Schmidt explained: "It wasn't easy to cool the fires, but if anyone had the ability it was Mustapha. He had two things going for him: First, the bedouin loved him. Most of the Rasheedi officers were bedouin, and as soon as they heard of the coup, the majority swore allegiance to him immediately. Of course, a few were hardened in their opposition and they had to be delt with.

"Second, his own organization was already in place. At every point on the front and in the kingdom itself, Mustapha's men were ready to take over. It didn't take much force, mostly reason. Most saw the folly of war the minute the prime mover for war was out of the picture.

"So he's in the saddle now. What he'll do with the power remains to be seen. It's too bad he couldn't be here with us today, but as you can imagine, he is a very busy man these days. Fahad might be able to shed light on that subject though. He'll be here shortly. Shareef went to pick him up at the Airport. You might say that I'm very optimistic, though."

"I still don't understand," said Debbie. "If Shareef

knew Baal Bazz was Doudeen, why did he wait till the last minute to tell us? Why not sooner?"

"Why don't you ask him yourself," said Snead. "Here he comes with Fahad now."

When Debbie repeated her question to Shareef, he said, "Professor Doudeen told me next to nothing. When I overheard him speaking with the Yemeni, I completely misread the signs. I thought that Doudeen was embezzling Al Tawalli's funds, and that the Yemeni knew about it and was bribing him."

Present at the Marriot now were Snead, Fahad, Clement, Debbie, Shareef and Frank. They had met for a last Friday brunch before going their separate ways. This time, however, they were seated in the family section. One early change to be noted was that the family section was now more "integrated" than it had previously been. There were people in Muslim and Western attire commingling peacefully.

"It was Frank," continued Shareef, "who figured out what was really going on. Why don't you tell them, boss?"

"No." said Frank. "You're doing fine."

"Don't forget," continued Shareef, "that Frank was never let in on the real nature of Debbie's mission. He knew she was spying for Snead, but not that she was after Al Harbi, who she believed to be Baal Bazz. So I guess it never occurred to him to tell me his theory sooner–not until he found out what she was up to and perceived the obvious danger of her chasing the wrong man."

"Not Baal Bazz, but not the wrong man either," said Debbie.

"How did you know then?" Debbie asked, turning to Frank.

"I didn't. But putting two and two together, I was pretty sure. It was the subterfuge. Doudeen reeked of it. Doudeen the dapper, high powered businessman and Doudeen the Arab dignitary almost seemed to be two different people. More than a few times, he was in the news in Riyadh and either in Jabalain or out of the country at the same time. At first I thought that they showed old footage as current news, but Mr. Ashamary assured me that wasn't the case. There were other things also, like hearing of Baal Bazz's terrorist act on the news more than once when Doudeen was out of the country, but never when he was present. Of course each thing by itself isn't convincing, but put them together, and add to the mix the mysterious secret between Doudeen and the Yemeni which Shareef overheard, and I was pretty sure–almost sure–what it meant. When Shareef mentioned that the Yemeni's brother, a security officer, had negotiated with Doudeen on some matter, I remembered something I had read... Of course, my suspicions were confirmed when I heard the Yemeni tell Bandar that Doudeen was about to blow up the Dome of the Rock and the Al Aqsa Mosque in Jerusalem."

"The most important piece of information, Mustapha received," said Fahad." It prevented a war."

"Stopping Al Harbi was no small feat either," said Frank, looking at Debbie. "The carnage caused would have been terrible"

Debbie looked at Frank for a moment and smiled.

"Sadya was sure," she said, "or thought he was, that Ahmad Daweesh alias Dowi Al Harbi, the man he had hunted for years, was the great Baal Bazz. He convinced me–and Mr. Snead of it. But in the end he was proved wrong.

"He had made his judgment on psychological grounds, for he saw in Ahmad, a man of boundless hate. Aside from that, he never had any real evidence. That was why the authorities never took Sadya's theory seriously. In hindsight we know that he lacked evidence because Ahmad did not in fact mastermind the Hebron Holocaust. Doudeen, who was the leader of an underground organization from Jerusalem, did. He had recruited Ahmad's brother to do the dirty work, and then swore him to secrecy.

"Ahmad had unusual looks and charisma. When Bandar first guessed that he was the mastermind of Hebron, Al Harbi found it to his advantage to let him believe it. This stroke of luck fit in perfectly with Doudeen's diabolical plans. When the legend of Baal Bazz began, Al Harbi provided just one more layer of subterfuge. Of course, he soon became a terrorist in his own right, but not Baal Bazz."

Then Clement turned to Fahad. "We were wondering about the kind of regime Mustapha will set up. Will he abolish the monarchy?" "It is too early to tell," said Fahad. "That decision and many others will be announced in the coming months. But you can be sure there will be changes. The most difficult change, that of educating the people, will take time."

After awhile Frank said, "I'm going to miss Rex."

"We all are," said Clement. "But think of it this way. He gave his life for a cause he believed in. He died for people he loved. None of us understood–and therefore loved–the Arabs as Rex did."

When they finished brunch and were leaving, Clement said to Debbie: "Now can we talk?" Debbie glanced toward Frank, but he wasn't paying attention.

"Okay," she said. "Let's go." They walked into the lobby and from there out into the hot Riyadh Sunshine.

"I was trying to tell you in Cairo," he began. "But then decided it had to wait–that you were wrong about what I felt about you–your people–your religion."

"How so? I want to hear now."

"Back in Jabalain, I put on an act. I pretended to be a Nazi. I didn't think I would be quite so successful. But I'm glad I was. You see–you were becoming too happy. I knew what you were getting into, even if you didn't. I didn't think you could survive it, unless you could learn to hate. So I helped you by making you hate me. My being German, I guess it was easy for you–to go from love to hate, I mean."

"Do you think I love you?"

"Do you?"

"Yes. But would you believe that I love him too? I mean Frank."

Clement said nothing.

"I'll have to go back with him–to see if I can get back what once was. I don't know if this was real life or if that was. I know I keep saying it to you, but I still need time to think. Maybe we're through, but maybe we're not. I want to spend a year writing about what happened here, then we'll see. Time will tell." She took him by the arm, and they headed back to the Marriott. "What about your wife in Wichita? Will you go back to her?"

"It's possible."

Frank was waiting in the lobby. He was putting film in his camera when she came up to him. He looked up briefly, then went back to what he was doing.

"Are you ready to go home now?" she asked.

"Just a minute," he said. "I'm almost finished."

The End

Joseph's Seed

Neil DeRosa